monsoonbooks

A CHINA DOLL IN KL

Ewe Paik Leong is a Chinese-Malaysian writer and the author of bestselling *Kuala Lumpur Undercover*. He earned his online BSBA from Southwest University, Kenner, LA, USA. Ewe lives in suburban Kuala Lumpur with his family. *A China Doll in KL* is his seventh book and his second work of fiction.

Also by Ewe Paik Leong,
published by Monsoon Books

Kuala Lumpur Undercover

A China Doll in KL

Ewe Paik Leong

monsoonbooks

Published in 2014
by Monsoon Books Pte Ltd
71 Ayer Rajah Crescent #01-01, Singapore 139951
www.monsoonbooks.com.sg

First edition.

ISBN (paperback): 978-981-4423-84-7
ISBN (ebook): 978-981-4423-85-4

Copyright©Ewe Paik Leong, 2014
The moral right of the author has been asserted.

All rights reserved. No part of this publication may be reproduced, stored in a retrieval system, or transmitted, in any form or by any means without the prior written permission of the publisher, nor be otherwise circulated in any form of binding or cover other than that in which it is published and without a similar condition being imposed on the subsequent purchaser.

Cover design by Cover Kitchen.

This is a work of fiction. Names, characters, businesses, places, events and incidents are either the products of the author's imagination or used in a fictitious manner. Any resemblance to actual persons, living or dead, or actual events is purely coincidental.

National Library Board, Singapore Cataloguing-in-Publication Data
Ewe, Paik Leong.
A china doll in KL / Ewe Paik Leong. – First edition. – Singapore : Monsoon Books Pte Ltd, 2014.
pages cm
ISBN : 978-981-4423-84-7 (paperback)

1. Prostitutes – Malaysia – Kuala Lumpur – Fiction. 2. Serial murders – Malaysia – Kuala Lumpur – Fiction. I. Title.

PR9530.9
M823 -- dc23   OCN868256637

Printed in Singapore
16 15 14   1 2 3 4 5

This novel is dedicated to
Jacqueline Woo-Ewe
Eveline Ewe
Lee Chang Hong
Maria Stephanie Ewe
who give my life so much meaning and
brighten my every day.

Prologue

Nguyen opened his eyes. His jaw ached, and his temples throbbed. He rolled over sideways on the mouldy mattress, groaning, and peered at the made-in-China alarm clock beside him: its glow-in-the-dark hands showed 2:11 a.m. Nguyen decided to get himself some Panadol from the twenty-four-hour 7-Eleven down the road.

Last evening he had worked long and hard at the chicken-rice restaurant. Not only had he washed three hundred plates and six hundred forks and spoons, but he had peeled one kilogram of chicken-feet skin using his bare teeth. These would be drenched with oyster sauce, he thought hungrily, and garnished with fresh parsley to be served to the customers. At the end of the month, he would be paid extra wages for these services. His wife lived in Ho Chi Minh City and was pregnant; he needed the extra cash.

Nguyen got up, slipped on his Japanese slippers and left the small flat he lived in on the sixth floor of Agate Apartments, the garbage bin of affordable accommodation on Changkat Thambi Dollah Road. He trudged down the corridor and waited in the lobby. The lift dinged, and when its doors opened, his next-door neighbour Xiaoqian stepped out of it, dressed in a tight and strappy leopard-print blouse.

Nguyen saw that a guy was clinging to her; he was scraggy and tall, very pale, with unkempt hair that almost covered his forehead. He looked like he was in his late twenties or early thirties. A cigarette dangled from his mouth, and the man stopped to light a match, the yellow flame illuminating his face, making his big dark eyes shine like black onyx stones. He had a brown bag slung over one shoulder.

As they stepped out of the lift and passed him, the fragrance of ylang-ylang wafted from Xiaoqian.

Turning to her, Nguyen smiled and said in Mandarin, 'Oh, you must attract customers like ants to sugar. Can I buy you coffee tomorrow morning?'

'You should be drinking coffee with your wife,' Xiaoqian said jokingly, 'not me. And I wouldn't eat your restaurant's chicken-feet skin even if you gave them to me free.'

Half an hour later, Nguyen returned to his room, swallowed two painkillers and tried to sleep. He heard the squealing of bed springs in the next apartment – it sounded as if a cat was being skinned alive. This was nothing unusual for him though; he heard these sounds whenever Xiaoqian brought home her customers.

He started to doze off, but then jerked awake when he heard a muffled scream. Then, a loud thud on the wall. He sat up on his mattress. There was another thunderous thump on the wall. *What is going on in there?* Had someone thrown a piece of furniture against the wall? Nguyen stood up, hammered his fist against the wall.

'Xiaoqian, are you OK?' She did not respond. 'Xiaoqian, please answer me.' Silence. He knew something was wrong.

He ran over to Xiaoqian's apartment and turned the doorknob.

It was locked. Nguyen kicked at the plywood door until his Japanese slipper flew off. He then took a step backward, crouched into a sprint-start position and lurched forward, ramming into the door with his shoulder. The door creaked at the hinges but didn't give way. Nguyen rammed into it again. The screws at the doorjamb holding the hinges came off this time, breaking away pieces of wood. He flung open the door and rushed inside, scuttling past the living room and into the bedroom.

Xiaoqian lay naked in bed, her body covered in blood. Nguyen saw that the man he had seen with her in the lift earlier was at the flat's casement window, about to climb out and onto the fire escape ladder. He rushed to the window and grabbed the man's shirt by the collar. The killer turned to face him, and their eyes met momentarily. The man's face was splattered with drops of blood. He swung his right hand at Nguyen's face, and it flashed with the glint of metal. Nguyen saw the knife coming and released the man, then instinctively jerked his head backward and let the blade swish past him. The killer scrambled down the fire-escape ladder, and his figure soon faded into the darkness.

Nguyen turned around to look at Xiaoqian's body. He could feel his eyes bulge with shock as he took in the scene of her murder, and for several seconds he couldn't blink. He heard the sound of his heartbeat crashing in his ears. The prostitute's breasts had been sliced away. Where her bosom had once been, there remained only two bloody masses of white tissue. The bed sheet beneath her was soaked with her blood. Her eyes remained open, staring up at the ceiling.

Nguyen scampered back to his flat. He used his mobile phone to call the police.

Monday 5 April

Dusk had fallen over Kuala Lumpur. The driver pulled up the taxi in front of the New Peng Hwa Food Court. In the backseat, Meisu opened her purse, paid the meter fare and stepped out onto Pudu Road; Ace Electronics Building stood on her right, and the Golden Dragon Hotel in front of her. She squared her shoulders as she entered the food court, dressed in a tight tank top and miniskirt.

Inside, she paused for a breath and, like a circling vulture seeking its carrion, surveyed the scene around her. She took in the bustling hawker stalls, the ladles moving inside metal pans, the swirling steam and smell of stir-fried spices rising from pots, the blue-and-red neon lights and pirouetting fans above the rows of white plastic tables. Only a few of the tables were occupied that night, most probably by diners, johns-to-be and hooker-watchers. Meisu was not disappointed though – the night was still young. Besides it was the beginning of the month, and this meant that the men's wallets would be bulging with their salaries.

As she walked past the first row of tables, her eyes scanned the occupants: a couple of men were engrossed in animated and loud chatter with their female companions. There were bursts of laughter, a muffled giggle and a gasp of disbelief. No possibility of a sale here.

She sashayed ahead. A man with a huge and round belly sat alone on the second row, pulling at long strands of noodles with a pair of chopsticks and then dropping them into his mouth. He wore a loose long-sleeved shirt and thick spectacles that were nearly slipping off his nose. *He looks stupid. Easy meat.*

A sweet smile plastered on her face, Meisu approached him.

'*Qing ai de*, why are you alone? Let me make you happy, OK?' She spoke to him in a mixture of English and Mandarin. She pulled out a plastic chair and sat beside him, crossing her bare legs.

The fat man, startled by her sudden appearance at his table, stared at Meisu's deep cleavage for a few moments. 'What's your price like?' he asked in English

'One hundred and eighty, inclusive of the motel room. Time limit's one hour.'

He put down his chopsticks and sipped at his glass of iced Chinese tea, staring into Meisu's face, admiring her. 'Where's the motel?'

'It's called Loveboat, and is only ten minutes away. Near the Pudu post office. A nice place and worth the walk. You'll be my first customer for tonight. See how lucky you are?' The man put down his glass and gave her an excited grin.

Meisu smirked to herself. *Aww, so young. Doesn't even know to hide his feelings.*

He wiped his mouth with his sleeve. 'One hundred and twenty is the market rate here,' he said. 'How much lower can you go?'

Meisu shook her head and smiled. 'You get what you pay for. If you buy cheap, you only get a quickie.'

Fifteen minutes later, the john was on top of Meisu in one of the rent-by-the hour rooms at Loveboat Motel. His lard splashed down onto her belly like a mass of quivering jelly.

'Oh my goodness! You're going to give me a bellyache later,' she grimaced. 'Get up, get up. We'll do it standing.'

She stood with her face pressed against the faded floral wallpaper, her back arched. After one, two and three thrusts, the fat man ejaculated.

Ich ... What a wimp. Such quick gravy, Meisu thought as the man paid her. *He's not going to have many kids.*

Meisu walked back to New Peng Hwa, settled down and ordered a soft drink. She scanned the other women weaving around the tables. She knew that they were not as pretty as her, that they could not beat her killer curves. That's why she could command a premium price of one hundred and eighty, while they had to charge much less for their services.

When she had almost finished her drink, her cell phone rang.

Meisu took it out from her leather purse. '*Wei,*' she said.

A man replied in English: 'Is that Meisu?'

She answered in English as well: 'Yes, I am. May I know who this is?'

'My name's Lawrence. Where're you?'

'In the food court.'

'Which part of it?'

'I'm sitting near the pork-noodle stall, at the left.'

'Hold on. I'm coming over.'

She emptied her glass and sucked on a small piece of ice. Within moments, a man in his early thirties stood by her table.

'Hello, I'm Lawrence. I called you just now. Can I sit down?' He had on a button-down Caribbean-blue shirt with a yellow necktie that almost reached his crotch, and sported a slick comb-over hairstyle.

Meisu gestured with an open palm to a chair beside her. 'How did you get my phone number, Lawrence?'

He sat down beside her and his small eyes flickered toward hers. 'From a friend. He booked you last week.'

'So, you also want to hire me?'

'Not me. My boss wants to book you for his client. It's for an overnight session.'

Meisu tucked strands of stray hair behind her ear. 'Who's he?'

'Who's who?'

'Your boss's client.'

'An important man. He's with my boss now at a Bukit Bintang hotel. They're discussing business. If you agree, I could send you there immediately.'

'Why did you choose me?'

'My friend has been coming here regularly. He says you're the best in New Peng Hwa. According to him, you also speak excellent English.' Lawrence smiled, revealing crooked teeth. 'Where did you learn it?'

Why is this jerk trying to be so chummy with me? Why should I tell him that I graduated from Guilin Tourism School or that I learnt English there?

'Can I have the name and cell phone number of the friend who recommended me?' she said simply.

'I'm not sure what name he's given you, but he's Soo Songchai to me.' He fished out his cell phone from the case pouch hooked to his belt, flipped open the cover and pressed a few buttons. He read the number aloud from the screen.

Meisu took out her phone and checked if the number matched the one in her address book. It did. She looked up and asked, 'Give me your name card, please.'

Lawrence pulled out a leather wallet and extracted a glossy name card, handed it to her.

She held the name card in one hand and squinted at it. The photo of the man who sat in front of her was printed on it. The text beside it said, 'Everlasting Industrial Supplies Berhad. Lawrence Leow, Business Development Manager.'

Satisfied with Lawrence's name card, she asked him about what she would be required to do for the customer. They agreed on a price of one thousand ringgit for an overnight booking.

'This way, please. My car is parked in the back,' Lawrence said, rising to his feet. He strode to the entrance with Meisu in tow. They stepped out of the food court and onto an access road; the business development manager turned right and walked down an alley that led to an open car park at the back of New Peng Hwa.

After a forty-minute-long drive on Sultan Ismail Road to Lexington Hotel, Meisu found herself and Lawrence taking the lift, then walking onto a carpeted corridor, towards a suite. He knocked on the hardwood door, opened it and ushered Meisu inside with an open palm. They entered and he closed the door behind him.

A stout, almost bald Chinese man wearing gold-rimmed glasses was sitting in a living room filled with expensive furniture and lit by soft yellow lights. Beside him sat another man, an Arab, tall and sporting a trimmed beard. He had a long face and a longer nose. Both men were dressed in neckties and business jackets.

The thick and soft carpet sank under Meisu's stilettos as she walked towards the men.

'Sorry to interrupt you both, sir. I've brought Miss Meisu with me,' Lawrence said to the bespectacled Chinese man. The latter beamed at Meisu.

'Welcome to Kuala Lumpur, Miss Meisu. Come on … Please have a seat while I discuss some business with my friend here.'

Meisu proceeded to seat herself at the chocolate-coloured club chair opposite the Arab. The woody notes of patchouli and musk hung in the air around him. She crossed her legs at the ankles and placed her purse on her lap, making sure its Gucci tag was faced towards him. *Well, how's he to know it's an imitation?* She rested both hands on the arms of the chair. The fabric was made of hemp, she recognised, and the cushioning felt like natural latex foam rubber. As the two men continued to talk, her fingers went to the steel locket hanging from her neck; she played with it while she watched the men.

The bespectacled Chinese man turned to the Arab and said, 'As I was explaining, Mr. Yasser, we've a service centre in Dubai that gives full technical support. And it is staffed with Arab technicians and engineers.'

Mr. Yasser picked up a comb-bound sheaf of papers lying on the coffee table, studied them for a moment and looked up. 'But your price is expensive. There's another supplier from Taiwan – Chiang Kai Shook Engineering Works – who's much cheaper. It's hard to justify your price to my board of directors.'

'The Taiwanese are not stupid. They'll sell the machinery for a cheap rate but charge you exorbitant prices for the replacement parts. You can't use parts from other companies as this will invalidate their warranty. So, that's how they get their customers by the balls, if you'll pardon my French, Mr. Yasser.' The bespectacled Chinese man leaned forward, a stony expression on his face, and continued in a lowered voice. 'The price includes a ten percent commission for you. We're also offering Miss Meisu and this executive suite to you … *Free* of cost for tonight.' He reached inside his jacket and pulled out a shiny, black-nibbed pen. 'So, can we close the deal now?' He placed it on the coffee table.

Mr. Yasser put down the documents and stared at Meisu as a snake would at a rabbit. There was silence for a few moments.

The bespectacled Chinese man added, 'Miss Meisu was booked from Singapore, especially for you. She's an international social escort and flew in this afternoon. This sex goddess serves only exclusive clients like you.'

Mr. Yasser ran a hand through a head of thick dark hair and looked down at his shoes. 'I don't know. If you were me, how would you justify this purchase?'

'Tell your board of directors that our company competes on quality not on price. Initial investment is high but low maintenance and voluminous productivity assures quick ROI.' He turned to Meisu, who caught his beady eyes, which shone like the black pearls made in the Zhejiang province of China. 'Miss Meisu, would like to show Mr. Yasser your undergarments?'

'With pleasure.'

Mr. Yasser suddenly sat upright, his eyes growing big with desire. She rose to her feet and slowly slipped the spaghetti straps of her top off her shoulders, then pulled the pink spandex over her head. Her 36D bosom poured out of her silky black Chantilly-lace bra. Mr.

Yasser's jaw dropped. Beads of sweat sprang onto his forehead.

The bespectacled Chinese man smiled at Meisu, then ran his fingers down her hour-glass figure and gave it a thumbs-up. Meisu gave Mr. Yasser a coy smile then unzipped her chestnut miniskirt, slid it slowly down her 38-inch bottom and to her hips. She let it fall to her ankles, revealing a pair of nougat-coloured lace panties that barely concealed what lay beneath them. By now, Mr. Yasser's crotch had turned into a big bulge. *It looks like a bag of French fries*, Meisu chuckled to herself. She saw that a little thread of silver drool was hanging from the corner of his mouth.

Mr. Yasser shot a glance at the bespectacled Chinese man. 'Yes, you're right. Perhaps I can explain to my directors about the quick ROI.' The Arab leaned towards the coffee table, grabbed the fountain pen and signed the sales agreement. He then lifted a black briefcase that lay by his feet, placed it upon his lap and opened it. From inside, he took out a rubber stamp and an ink pad. Mr. Yasser stamped all the copies of the documents and handed them to the bespectacled Chinese man.

'Signed, sealed and delivered!' Mr. Yasser announced breathlessly.

The bespectacled Chinese man grinned and shook hands with the Arab. 'You've made a wise investment. Now, let us leave you and Meisu alone here for some private time.' He rose to his feet and then winked at Meisu. 'Please give her a big tip if she renders you good service, Mr. Yasser.'

Tuesday 6 April

Detective Inspector Daniel Chu arrived at Agate Apartments at 3:40 a.m. Accompanying him were a uniformed policeman and a forensics technician, who brought along a camera and an attaché case. The inspector was not in uniform; he wore dark slacks, a casual short-sleeved shirt and a faded denim jacket.

When he reached Xiaoqian's flat, Inspector Chu noticed that a group of foreign workers had gathered outside the doorway, gossiping and gesticulating amongst themselves.

'Who discovered the body?' Chu asked them as he walked in.

'I did, sir,' said a Vietnamese man, stepping out, his pants rolled up at the ankles. 'My name's Nguyen.' He led Chu and the forensics man into the bedroom, while the uniformed policeman stretched a yellow tape across the flat's doorway to keep out curious bystanders. 'I also saw the killer briefly. He tried to attack me.'

Chu eyed the mutilated corpse lying on the bed and felt the skin on his back crawl. The eyelids weren't fully closed. He could see the milky white of the irises, the thin crescents visible beneath the curly eyelashes. The forensics technician began to photograph the corpse from different angles.

Chu turned to the Vietnamese man, 'Please wait outside. You've to come to the station to help us in the investigation.'

He pulled out a notebook from his pocket. He scrutinised the crime scene before him. On either side of the queen-sized bed were small square tables. He opened the drawer of one of the tables and found a blister pack of aspirins, a bottle of Eye Mo, three packets of Durex condoms and a few boxes of Chi Kee Teck Aun pills, used for treating diarrhoea.

A metal ash tray sat on the other side table. Chu went over and sat on his haunches to examine its contents closely, without touching them. Three cigarette butts lay on a thick layer of ash. Two had red lipstick stains on them, and printed on both of them, just before their filters, was the word 'Salem'. The third cigarette butt had 'Kent' printed on it.

'Bag these butts, please,' he called to the forensics technician, who was now looking for hair on the bed sheet with a magnifying glass.

Beside the ashtray lay a black matchbook: 'Crazy Legs Club' was embossed in gold on its front. The inspector flipped the cover open and found the club's address on the inside. He jotted down the particulars into his notebook. He then yanked open the drawer of this side table as well. Inside, he found a tourist map of Kuala Lumpur, the April 2010 edition of *Feminine*, a Mandarin magazine and a People's Republic of China passport. He opened the passport, confirmed that it belonged to the victim, and then scribbled down her particulars.

Next to the bed was a waste bin, and it contained four condom wrappers. But there was no sign of the used condoms anywhere in the bedroom. They had probably been flushed down the toilet.

Chu got up and opened the twin drawers of the wooden dressing table that faced the bed: he found bras, stockings, panties, a box of sanitary pads and a few make-up products. A portable wardrobe made of blue-coloured fabric stood at one corner of the room. Chu crossed the room and unzipped its front cover to reveal skirts and skimpy dresses hanging from a rod. On the wall next to the wardrobe, a pair of bra and panties, a leopard-print blouse and a pair of denim shorts dangled from iron clothes hooks. In the pockets of the shorts, Chu found a packet of Salem cigarettes and a wallet that contained some coins. He handed them to the forensics technician.

Chu then entered the attached bathroom. It was fitted with a toilet, a sink and a shower. He looked behind the rotting wooden door and found cotton towels hanging there from hooks.

He went back to the living room. The only furniture there was a three-level wooden shoe rack placed near the door. A pair of slippers and a pair of flat pumps sat on its top shelf.

A smell permeated from the small kitchen-cum-dining area, and he traced it to the leftovers he saw in the trash can. On a badly scratched wooden dining table sat a butane-gas camp stove, a thermos flask, two porcelain cups and a plastic jar containing several sachets of Ipoh White Coffee. Satisfied that there were no clues to be found in the living room or the kitchen of the victim's house, Chu closed his notepad. He left the crime scene with Nguyen in his car.

* * *

Meisu was taking a taxi from the Lexington Hotel to her condominium in Cheras. The clock on the dashboard showed 9:15 a.m. Leaning back on the mesh-fabric seat, she stifled a yawn and switched on her mobile phone. A prompt appeared on the screen: 'You have six unread messages.'

The first SMS was from an unknown number: 'Can I come tomorrow at 11?'

Meisu typed in a reply: 'Sure, I'll be working as usual tonight. From 8.'

The second message was from Yehua: 'Want to eat lunch tomorrow? I know a great spot for delicious barbecued pork in Ampang. We can meet at Ampang Point Shopping Centre. It's only half an hour from your condo. Also quite near to my place. '

Meisu remembered the first time she had met Yehua. On this April's Fool Day, only a day after her arrival in KL. That evening, a cab had dropped Meisu outside a twenty-four-hour fast food restaurant at the tourist strip of Bukit Bintang Road. She had stood on the sidewalk, scanning the palm-lined stretch that ran past a five-star hotel. Most of the stores had been closed, except for a few reflexology centres. At a taxi rank, three drivers were seated on the kerb, chit-chatting. Up ahead, four or five girls were just hanging around on the road. Pedestrian traffic was still brisk, with men spilling forth from the adjoining Alor Road and Bukit Bintang Hill, walking out of the bistros, restaurants and sidewalk stalls. Twenty minutes rolled by, and Meisu had just stood there. 'Hey, that's my spot!' A loud voice had shouted at her suddenly in Mandarin. Meisu felt a flush creep into her cheeks, and she turned to see a woman striding towards her. The woman looked like she was in her early thirties, and wore an aquamarine polka-dot shirtdress with a sash tied at her waist.

Nervously, Meisu replied in Mandarin as well, 'Oh, sister, I'm sorry. I didn't know. This is my first time here.'

'Why don't you find and claim your own spot on Bintang Walk?' The woman wore her hair in a side-swept fringe over her oval face, with bangs that reached her eyebrows.

'Bintang Walk? Where's that?'

'You don't know?'

'I'm new to Kuala Lumpur. I only arrived yesterday.'

'Oh. I'm sorry that I yelled at you. I didn't mean to be nasty. My mood's not good – I just had a lousy time with two horrid clients. My name's Yehua. Can we be friends? We're far from home, and we can help each other.'

After a short chat, Yehua had suggested New Peng Hwa to Meisu. 'A cab can take you there easily,' she had said. Meisu had worked at the food court ever since.

Meisu sent her friend a reply: '*Hao*. We can meet today at 2:30 p.m. I'll wait at the main entrance of Ampang Point.'

The third message was from another unknown number: 'I'm Weilai. Your customer Robert gave me your number. Can I come over to view the apartment on Thursday at 5 p.m.?'

Meisu's belly fluttered in anticipation. She hoped that this girl would replace Rongrong, her former flatmate and Meisu's high-school friend. Rongrong had arrived in KL a month earlier, and she had soon run into some hard luck. Three days after Meisu had moved in, immigration authorities had raided the spa where Rongrong worked. Rongrong and fifteen other girls had been arrested. Now, they were all in a temporary detention centre, held there along with illegal Bangladeshis, Vietnamese, Cambodians and Indonesians, all of them waiting to be deported.

Meisu had no choice but to take over Rongrong's condominium. She called her prospective flatmate and spoke to her: 'Weilai? I'm Meisu.' A pause. 'Yes, Thursday will be fine with me. Bye.'

The fourth message read, 'Where are you? I want to come over at 2 tonight?' It was from another stranger.

'Darling, you can meet me at any time tonight after 8. New Peng Hwa. Please call when you arrive,' Meisu typed.

As Meisu was about to send the message, a motorcycle zipped into the lane of the taxi, and the driver braked, jerking Meisu forward. She gazed out the window for a moment, taking in the traffic coming against her: trucks with coughing klaxons rumbled, motorcycle horns screamed angrily at cars, buses careened in and out of their designated yellow lanes. Such a vibrant city, this *Jilongpo*. Especially when compared to Guilin, her hometown. Would she be able to find her fortune here, like she dreamed she would? She had moonlighted as a hooker in Guilin for more than six months. But the need to be discreet had made it difficult for her to earn much there.

She looked down at her cell phone again and opened the fifth message. It was from Frankie: 'Why is your hp off? R u working tonight?'

Meisu gave a whimper of mirth as she recalled this thirty-something client who had hired her only three days earlier. He had a bad stutter and a fetish for toes. She gave him a reply that she knew would stir up his feelings. 'I miss you, dear. I'll be waiting for you tonight.'

The sixth message made her breath catch in her throat. It was from her cousin in Guilin. 'My father is scheduled to get a heart bypass operation done on April 26. The Guilin Huashan Hospital needs a deposit of 15,000 yuan. The balance amount of 20,000 yuan can be paid after the operation but before my father's discharge. My mother and I don't have sufficient money. I beg you to help save your uncle's life. Please send me the deposit as soon as possible. I'll slowly repay you.'

She switched off her mobile phone and leaned back on the seat. Her eyes felt moist as she closed them.

* * *

The taxi passed Leisure Mall, turned left and entered a cul-de-sac behind the shopping mall. Its brakes squealing like a pig in a slaughterhouse, the vehicle stopped outside Opal Condominium. Meisu got out and strode past the guardhouse, and a sole Nepalese guard raised a hand to the side of his head on seeing her. Meisu ignored the mock salute. She headed to the self-service cafeteria in the first block and ordered an egg sandwich and a cup of Horlicks.

She sat beside an open side-swing window that offered the view of a children's playground, partially shaded by jacaranda trees. As she sipped the steaming Horlicks from a paper cup, she observed a man sitting on a wooden bench in one corner of the playground; on his lap sat a little girl of about four years. The man bounced the child from his one knee onto another, singing to her. 'Rickety, rickety, rocking horse, over the fields we go ...' The girl giggled. The man then began bouncing both his knees. 'Rickety, rickety rocking horse, giddyup, giddyup. Whoa!' With both hands, he hugged the girl and lifted her up, above him.

Meisu remembered the first time her stepfather had asked her to sit on his lap. It was a Sunday, and her mother had gone out to shop for groceries. She had been seven years old then, dressed in a frock, her hair tied into a meatball at the top of her head. Slapping his knee, Uncle Dejiang had said to her, 'Little darling, come here and watch television with me.' He had switched to a channel screening cartoons. A smiling Meisu had climbed onto his lap, turned towards the television and leaned back against him, comfortably snuggled in his arms.

While she had watched television, his hand had begun to slowly stroke her face, then her right leg. After a while, it had travelled down to her inner thigh. This had caused her skin to tingle. Uncle Dejiang repeated the slow stroking motion with his fingers for several seconds. Meisu had felt strange; she had wanted to come out of his grasp. Suddenly, his hand had slipped beneath her panties, his fingers wriggling between her thighs. Meisu had tried to pull herself away from him but Uncle Dejiang's other hand had wrapped itself tightly around her waist, like a python trapping its prey.

He had then shoved a finger inside her. Pain had stabbed through Meisu, and she had writhed. She wanted to yell but Uncle Dejiang's had cupped his hand over her mouth. His finger had slid in and out of her. When he finally pulled his hand away, Meisu's eyes were covered in a film of tears, her mind racing for answers. Uncle Dejiang had pressed his bristly chin against her cheek and said, 'Was that pleasurable? Now, don't cry. Let this be our little secret. Don't you dare tell anyone about this, understand? Mama will beat you if she finds out.'

Meisu could not remember the number of times Uncle Dejiang

had done that to her. When Meisu was around twelve or thirteen years old, Uncle Dejiang had entered her room in the middle of the night and raped her. He threatened her with severe beatings if she told anyone. The violations had been repeated almost weekly for a year after that, until he had died of a heart attack.

Two years later, her Mama succumbed to breast cancer, and Meisu had to move in with her aunt, her Mama's younger sister.

Meisu took a bite at the sandwich. *Yuk! The cook's hopeless. Can't even fry an egg properly.*

She watched as a man dressed in a track suit entered the cafeteria with a little girl, her hair tied in two braids. The man swung the girl up on his arm, and they moved to the counter. 'What do you want to eat, dearie?' The man pointed to the wall menu behind the counter and began to read aloud the items. 'There's egg sandwich, tuna sandwich, chicken salad sandwich, curry puff, hot dog with bun, French onion soup and muffins. You can also get some coffee, tea, Milo, Horlicks, hot chocolate.' Pointing to the wall menu, the child murmured something, and a nerdy-looking server immediately started preparing the orders. When the food was ready, the man set the girl down, and then carried away from the counter a tray holding a bowl of soup, a plate of sandwiches and two paper cups. He and the little girl settled down at a nearby table. The man inserted a spoon into the soup, filling it up, and then blew at it before he fed it to the girl.

Meisu remembered how good her aunt had been to her. When she had been down with measles, she had cooked chicken broth and spoon-fed Meisu as she had lain in bed, burning with a fever.

The man went back to the counter and borrowed a knife. He cut the sandwich vertically to make three finger-shaped pieces. Holding a piece with a serviette, he passed it to the girl's dainty fingers.

When Meisu had turned twenty-one, her aunt's husband, Uncle Qibao, had organised a simple birthday party for her. They had given her a steel locket on a chain. Meisu remembered how she had opened the locket and had become breathless with joy. A cute picture of a rat, her Chinese Zodiac sign, had stared back at her. The pinyin words '*Xin xiang shi cheng*' – 'Succeed in your heart's desires' – were etched beside the critter.

For a few moments, Meisu gazed down at the empty cup in her hands. Then she typed a reply to her cousin: 'Yes, I will send the deposit as soon as I can.'

She finished her food and left the cafeteria. She took the lift up to her apartment, which was located in a separate block on the seventh floor.

* * *

The harsh afternoon sun struck Detective Inspector Chu between the eyes, making him squint as he walked out of his car. He was in the parking area of Kuala Lumpur General Hospital. The inspector paced to the mortuary block. He was still dressed in last night's clothes. The muscles of his arms and legs felt knotted, and bristles stuck out from his unshaven chin. He had not slept a wink since checking out the China-doll's flat.

The smell of disinfectant assailed his nostrils when he entered the morgue, and he headed quickly to the office of Dr. Latifah Yusof, the pathologist. Through the glass panel on the door, he saw her sitting at a desk cluttered with files, scribbling on a pad furiously. She was wearing her doctor's coat, and had her head covered in a green *tudong*.

He knocked at the door, and then entered with a smile. 'Good afternoon, doctor. How're your kids doing?'

Dr. Latifah's brown lips turned up into a smile, and she put down her pen. She peered at him through a pair of thick-framed horn-rimmed spectacles. 'Naughty like before. But thankfully, the eldest is going to attend school next year.' She rose to her feet and stepped away from her desk. 'Come on in ... I just finished writing the autopsy report. You can get it from my secretary. You're busy as usual? I read in the newspapers that the city's crime rate has gone down?'

'Telling the press that the crime rate has dropped was just PR crap. My plate's full actually. From arson to murder to gangland slayings.' Chu and the doctor exited the room and walked down a short corridor that led to the autopsy suite. In the centre of the room stood a steel table about nine feet long and two-and-a-half feet wide. On an instrument trolley beside the table were scattered Dr. Latifah's sinister-looking tools of trade: an enterotome, a Hagedorn needle, a scalpel, a pair of toothed forceps, a bone saw, a vibrating saw and a pair of rib-cutters that resembled pruning shears. Chu and the doctor entered another door to the death's filing cabinet. Inside the cool room, the skin on Chu's arms broke into goose bumps. Dr. Latifah moved to a wall that had more than thirty metallic drawers set into it. They resembled the safe deposit boxes of a bank. Each drawer was about two feet in breath and width.

After scanning the drawers, she bent down and pulled at one: it slid out with a slight creak. The naked body of the China-doll hooker was lying in it, her eyes with its curled lashes half-closed, her big toe tagged. Her skin looked like that of a steamed Hainanese chicken. A Y-shaped incision on her torso had been sewn up with twine using a baseball stitch. From his trouser pocket, Chu took out a digital camera and clicked a few shots of her face. These photos would be more useful than those in her passport; those photos were several years old.

Dr. Latifah looked down and pointed to the neck of the corpse. 'See the ligature marks here? The cause of death was strangulation. The murder weapon was probably a thick cord. There's petechial hemorrhaging around the pupils of her eyes. The Hyoid bone was also broken.'

Chu placed the camera back into his pocket. 'Hyoid bone?'

'That's the horseshoe-shaped bone located under the chin.'

'Any seminal stains in any of the orifices?'

'No, but there were scrapings beneath the victim's fingernails. While she struggled, she must have scratched her assailant. I've sent these for DNA testing. There's no trace of alcohol or illegal drugs in her bloodstream. And her lungs did not contain any water or liquid. Stomach contents were normal, just some partially digested food.' Dr. Latifah gazed at the mass of exposed adipose tissue on the chest. 'Her breasts were sliced off using a sharp instrument. The cuts were clean. Based on the angle, I can say that the killer was most probably right-handed.' The doctor sighed. 'Poor girl. Were her breasts found?'

'We searched the back alley where the killer took off. But there's no trace of them.'

Dr. Latifah nodded pensively. 'Well, I'm afraid, Detective, that you're dealing with a psychopathic killer. And I strongly suspect that he will kill again.'

* * *

The pale man entered his study and drew the curtains to keep out the afternoon sun. He moved to his battered desk, sat down and switched on the computer. He took out the memory card from his camera and inserted it into the system unit. He double-clicked the mouse: the image of a woman with her upper torso mutilated appeared on screen.

Yesterday's whore put up a tough fight. She thrashed about wildly in bed and kicked the wall a few times too. Even scratched my back. Too bad that didn't work, you whore. He chuckled. *What a euphoric high I felt when I wrapped the cord around her throat and pulled the ends with all my might. Good always triumphs over evil, you bitch. Ah, how amazing it felt when I was slicing away her big, fat breasts. That moment was more pleasurable than an orgasm.*

The pale man clicked 'print' on the screen and waited. The printer let out a soft whirring sound then produced a colour printout, sliding it out onto its output tray. He grabbed the paper, held it up, and then cut the image out of the A4-size paper with a pair of scissors. He put the image face-down on the desk and rubbed a glue stick all over the paper's edges.

From a drawer, he pulled out a hardcover scrapbook and flipped to a blank page. He picked up a felt pen, scrawled 'Third Victim – After' at the top of the page and pasted the printed image below the heading. Leaning back against the chair, he let out a sigh of deep satisfaction. He turned to an earlier page in the scrapbook, to the page that had the heading 'Third Victim – Before'. The image on that page showed the same hooker standing there, wearing a miniskirt, leaning on a concrete pillar in a sheltered sidewalk.

The pale man slowly flipped through the scrapbook, running his fingers over all the 'Before' and 'After' images he saw stuck there, admiring his handiwork, relishing his success.

These prostitutes seduce innocent men when they're alive. But with their tits slashed away, they can do no harm. Hah! They can't even seduce male ghosts anymore. He burst out laughing. *These bitches need me to teach them a lesson, to send them back to hell where they come from. These pictures will document my success in this war against evil women. Soon I'll be a cultural icon among men with a strong moral compass. And this scrapbook will show them what I have achieved.*

He opened the drawer and put the scrapbook back inside it, smiling gleefully.

* * *

After taking a cold shower to shake off the sleep from her eyes, Meisu pattered out of the bathroom. It was 1:30 p.m. She had been awakened by the bedside alarm clock. From a closet, she took out a white bra, a pair of matching panties and a short sleeveless dress. She adjusted the bra as she wore it, bending over at the waist until her breasts had settled comfortably into its large cups. Then she rose and hooked the clasps at the back, put the straps over her shoulders. She slipped her legs into the white panties and wriggled herself into the dress. Posing before the mirror in the closet, she turned about this way and that, admiring her curvy figure and the snug fit of the dress. *How lucky that I was born with these killer curves.* She knew she had to capitalise on her assets while they were still supple and firm.

Meisu walked over to the dressing table with its triple mirrors and sat on the stool before it. She thrust her face towards the middle mirror and examined herself. She knew that her soft alabaster skin was her most outstanding feature. So were her double-lidded eyes, turned upwards like a cat's, lending Meisu a wild, feline look. Despite the late hours she worked every night, the broken snatches of sleep she managed to get in the afternoons always refreshed her and made sure she didn't look tired or get dark patches of fatigue under her eyes. Her long and silky hair, pulled back in a bun by a barrette at the back of her head, revealed a high forehead. Her slender eyebrows arched over her eyes gracefully.

She looked into the side mirrors, which gave her a profile view of her face. A flaw in her rather round face was that her cheekbones were not prominent enough. Aware of this imperfection, she took out a highlighter from the dresser's central drawer and used a brush to accent the upper part of her cheekbones. Meisu was aware that as a total package, she was attractive, was a blend of sophistication and sensuality.

She sat upright and raised one arm behind her head, examining her armpit in the mirror on her left. Then she repeated the procedure with the other arm. Satisfied that her armpits were still smooth after her last shave a week ago, she took out a Shanghai-Vive-brand deodorant from the dresser and sprayed it copiously under her arms. She reached for the handbag she had used last night and took out a lipstick and compact to round off her grooming. Finally, she released her dark tresses from the barrette and parted it down the middle.

A thirty-minute taxi ride brought Meisu to Ampang Point. She entered the main entrance and scanned the crush of shoppers. Yehua was waiting for her at the information counter, a shopping bag dangling from her arm. After exchanging greetings, they walked out of the mall and crossed the road to Soong Kee Restaurant. The lunch crowd had melted, and they were among the five or six customers sitting in the eating-house. One stall sold rice and an assortment of dishes contained in aluminium trays. Another stall displayed several types of roast meat dangling from iron hooks inside a glass case. Yehua ordered them plates of barbecued pork, barbecued chicken, roasted pork and a pot of Tit Koon Yam tea.

When the plastic platter of meats was brought to their table, Meisu speared a morsel of barbecued pork and dropped it into her mouth. The caramelised sweet glaze on the meat made her nod her head in approval. 'The meat's delicious. How did you know this place?' she asked, spearing a piece of chicken.

'My client brought me here once.' A grin crossed her friend's face. 'He's married with six kids. Poor man. His wife's as fat as a pig,' Yehua said, chewing into a piece of pork. 'He showed me her photograph.'

'Mmmm … The chicken's also outstanding. Crispy skin, soft succulent meat … How's business in Bukit Bintang?'

'The usual. An African tried to pick me one night though. That fellow stood seven feet tall. He asked me for my price for an hour. I told him I'd charge him one hundred ringgit per inch.' Yehua guffawed, the skin at the corner of her eyes wrinkling into crow's feet. 'The man curled his lips and walked away.' She scooped a spoonful of rice into her mouth. 'How're things going for you?'

'Not bad. A big-spender booked me overnight for his foreign client. His manager even drove me to the hotel. The suite had a living room, a bedroom and a kitchenette, all beautifully furnished.'

'If I were you, I wouldn't accompany a stranger in his car. Always go by taxi – it's safer. Last month, one of our China sisters was found dead in a motel. I read about it in a newspaper. Two months earlier, there was another case. The victim also came from China.'

'There's crime in every city of the world, not just here.' Something soft touched Meisu's left ankle, and she looked down, startled. A skinny orange cat with a bobtail was rubbing itself against her ankle.

'Oh, such a darling cat. But it's so pitiful.' Meisu put down her fork and spoon, then rose and went to the rice stall. She came back with a fried fish and coaxed the cat outside to the pedestrian walkway. 'Come here ... Meow ... Meow ...' She put the fish on the sidewalk for the cat and returned to her table.

'At the end of the month, I'm going to Bangkok to renew my visa,' Yehua informed her. 'You want to join me? Air tickets are cheap if we purchase them early. Approval will require two or three days. We can stay in a budget hotel, split the cost. I've planned to come back through Penang. It's less suspicious with immigration than if you had entered through KLIA.'

Meisu thought about it for a moment. 'OK, I'll come along with you.'

'That will be wonderful! I'm also hoping we can work together to find more business?'

'How?' She sipped a mouthful of Chinese tea.

'Can we swap our clients' contact numbers? We can then send

them text messages offering our services. Many men like to try out new girls.'

'Sure. When I've collected more contacts, we can meet again,' said Meisu. She wiped some sauce off the corner of her mouth and smiled at Yehua.

* * *

Alvin Au was in his studio at Central Market Annexe. He stared at the cotton canvas propped on a wooden easel before him. It showed a charcoal sketch of a portrait with shadow lines. It had been commissioned to him more than a week ago by a walk-in customer. His right hand trembled as he dipped a flat brush in ochre and began to block in the backdrop. He worked on it, his muscles straining, his mind churning like a typhoon. He had been off alcohol on Saturday and Sunday, and he knew that if his will power continued to hold out, he could grow stronger in his battle to stop drinking. But right now, he found that his strength was draining out of him, his will to stay sober evaporating slowly from his innards.

Alvin heard the sound of someone approaching and turned to the door. A balding European man wearing a batik-print shirt walked in. Along with him was his fat blonde wife, who had on a t-shirt that said 'I Love Kuala Lumpur'.

Alvin was in no mood to prattle on about the tone and character of his works. He looked away before the couple could speak to him.

The couple walked around the studio, moving from one painting to another. Alvin's self-portrait caught their eyes: in the painting, they saw a man who looked to be in his early thirties, his soft and dark eyes set in a face that was wide at the temples but narrowed down to become a small chin. The subject had a head of thick hair that was parted and combed to the sides, and a nose that was broad and with large nostrils. They studied the painting for a few moments, before moving on to another one.

The couple didn't buy anything from him. When they left, Alvin shot a glance at the wall clock. It showed 12:30 p.m. *Surely, one small bottle of beer would not hurt. Hell, it might even sharpen my sensitivity to colours, steady my hands and help me churn out a better painting.* Alvin took a long breath, making up his mind, then washed his brushes in turpentine and arranged them into their proper holes on the easel. After locking the studio's shutter door, he sauntered past the Central Market and into Hang Kasturi Road. No shop or eatery in Central Market sold alcohol, so the nearest place he could find some was Zhing Khoong Coffee Shop at the end of the road.

A ten-minute walk brought him to the fan-ventilated old-style shop, and he ordered a plate of steamed chicken-drumstick with rice. The Myanmar waiter asked if he wanted something to drink, and Alvin immediately asked for a big bottle of Anchor beer. He wolfed down the chicken rice and poured the refrigerated beer into a glass filled with ice cubes. He purposely paused for several seconds and looked out at the passing cars and motorbikes, watched them belch out grey fumes into the road. The holding-back was to test his own resistance. *See? I still have self-control. I can stop anytime I want.* He then raised the glass to his lips and took a big gulp – so big that his cheeks swelled like a puffer fish's. His insides sucked in the beer, as if it were the elixir of life. By the time he had emptied the bottle, he felt better. He was tempted to go for another but decided against it as he had a work appointment in the afternoon. He walked back to the studio with a spring in his step.

A few hours later, after doing a little more work on the portrait, he decided that he was done for the day. He took out five canvases, still mounted on their frames, from under his desk and wrapped them in sheets of old newspapers. He locked up the studio and carried over the paintings to his blue Myvi sitting in the car park.

In Bangsar, the city's outskirts, he drove past chic condominiums and their wide garages with gleaming expensive cars, admiring them, wishing he owned a house like that. He drove on until he had reached a double-storey bungalow, and then entered its driveway. 'Ken Stellar Gallery' was printed with metal letters on a wooden panel beside the building's front door. The door was open, and a security guard wearing a peaked cap at a rakish angle sat outside it.

Alvin got out of the car and took out his wrapped paintings from the back. He entered the gallery and ambled down a corridor, glancing at the paintings that were hung on its walls. Some of the works done in a German Expressionism style grabbed his attention, and he stopped briefly to study them. Further down the corridor hung silk-screen paintings, painted by the city's blue-chip artists.

Turning left, he sauntered down another corridor. The walls here were filled with more paintings, done in various styles, ranging from abstract to wildlife, from landscape to realist, from paintings of flowers to portraits of nudes. The last corridor led to an open space about the size of an outdoor pavilion.

At one corner of this space was a man, dressed in a long-sleeved beige shirt and a blue Pierre Cardin necktie; he had a receding hairline and his nose was shaped like the bill of parrot. He sat at a huge teak desk, in front of two large filing cabinets.

The man looked up when Alvin walked in. 'Yes ...What can I do for you, Mr. Alvin Au?' He did not bother to stand up. 'Please take a seat.'

Alvin sat down on the cushioned chair the man pointed to and placed the package of paintings beside him. 'Mr. Koh, can you help me out, please,' he said. 'Please buy five more of my paintings. I need money urgently.'

Ken Koh leaned back in his armchair, sighing. 'Ten of your paintings are still unsold.' His high forehead was mottled, looking like a sheet of brown paper on which water has been dropped and dried. 'I'm stocking too many of your paintings already.'

Alvin shifted uneasily in his chair. 'Sales in my studio have been poor. This is the off-peak season. My studio rental's overdue.' He placed his package on his lap then started to unwrap it. 'Please have a look at my latest works. They—'

Ken dismissed Alvin with a quick wave of his hand. 'No, there's no need for me to see them. But perhaps I can help you in another way.'

Alvin's thoughts froze for a moment. 'How?'

The gallery owner leaned forward and rested his arms on the desk. 'There's an alternative,' he said in a low voice. 'Why not sell your paintings under another artist's name?'

'What do you mean?' Alvin leaned forward too, his belly knotted.

'What I say remains in this room, understand?' When Alvin nodded, Ken continued. 'There's this old famous artist, a client of ours – arthritis has almost crippled his hands, and his eyesight's failing. I can ask him to sign his name on your paintings. For a fee, of course. His name guarantees quick sales. The foreign tourists who come here like his paintings. They won't know the difference. Your signature style is similar to his.'

'Who's he? How long has he been doing this?' Alvin sputtered.

'That's none of your concern,' Ken snapped. His posture was relaxed, his eyes nonchalant.

'That's cheating! Cheating the buyer and cheating myself. We'll be committing fraud. It's wrong.'

'Wrong?' Ken snorted. 'This is business, and in business, nothing short of murder is wrong. Look at things this way – no one gets harmed by this. The tourists hang the paintings in their living room, you get your money, the ageing artist is happy. Everyone wins.'

Alvin shook his head. 'No, no, I won't do it. This is deceitful, and also very insulting to me. I'm among the best artists in the city, in the same league as George Gong. I've just not been discovered yet. Do you know that when Huntington Hotel opened in Stesen Sentral, they had bought two hundred of Gong's paintings? One painting for each suite. He's now a rich man.'

'Why are you talking about George Gong? He's not relevant to this issue. Anyway, I know about his windfall.' Ken leered, his top lip drawn above his teeth like a cunning hyena. 'But do you know how much corruption was involved? Right from the interior decorator to the hotel's general manager. In the end George did not make that much. Alvin, let's get back to the matter at hand. You say you need money, so I'm opening a door for you to make some money. Just do this for five or six of your paintings, get through this difficult period. I'll buy them from you.' He inhaled deeply and tilted his chin upward. 'So ... What's it going to be? Do you agree to these terms?'

Alvin remained silent, considering, wondering what he should do; Ken was watching him, waiting for an answer. Alvin mentally added up his ex-wife's overdue alimony, the cost of next month's art supplies and his monthly living expenditure. A lump rose in his throat. Finally, he threw up his hands in exasperation. 'Alright, alright, I agree.'

Ken slid forward on his seat. 'Now, Alvin, show me what you've brought with you this time ...'

Alvin stepped out of the art gallery with a cheque in hand. He drove back to his studio, fished out one of his bank statements and wrote down his account number on the back of the cheque. He then kept the cheque in his wallet. *This will get me through the month.* He heaved a sigh of great relief.

* * *

After her lunch with Yehua, Meisu had collected her ironed clothes from a launderette in Leisure Mall and had returned to her condominium for a restful nap. Now, wearing a slim-fit strapped mini dress, she walked amidst the tables in New Peng Hwa. As she passed each table, the men turned their heads to ogle at the plunging neckline of her dress, while the women, the other hookers, flared their nostrils in apparent envy.

Suddenly, a peroxide blond man in his early twenties walked up to her. 'Miss, my boss wants to talk with you. Now,' he said. 'He's waiting in his massage centre. He has something to discuss with you. Can you follow me?' A walkie-talkie was hooked to his belt, and he wore a single earring.

Meisu's skin tingled. 'What do you mean by boss? And who are you?'

'I'm called Big Dog. My boss is the head of the Red Centipede Society. His name is Ouyang Lifu.' He lifted his heels and rose slightly for a moment, hooking both thumbs in his belt hoop. 'We control business activities in New Peng Hwa. Please don't make my job any more difficult than it has to be. His place is at Gajah Road, only ten-minutes away.'

'Where is Gajah Road?'

'Further down this way, under the flyover. Can we go now?'

Meisu clutched at the handbag slung over her shoulder, suddenly anxious. 'How do I know you're telling the truth?'

Big Dog threw a glance at a nearby table; seated there were three giggling bimbos dressed in skimpy tube tops and miniskirts. 'You can check with those girls there. Ask them if I'm Big Dog and if they've heard of Ouyang Lifu. You'll know I'm telling the truth.' There was frost in his voice.

'Alright. I'll go meet your boss.'

'This way, please.' The frost melted. He smiled at her.

Meisu's chest tightened as she followed the ruffian out of the food court. It was pitch dark outside, the night sky overcast with clouds. Under the glowing street lamps, they walked down the kerb of the drag, reaching a flyover that bustled with passing vehicles. They walked on until they had come to a block of shophouses. Meisu saw the sign 'Ouyang Traditional Massage' on top of its entrance.

Big Dog entered the red-carpeted staircase at one side of the building, and she followed suit. They reached a thick five-panel wooden door. He pressed the doorbell button on the wall, and the door opened with a loud *clack*.

Big Dog led Meisu into a rectangular room lit by three brass lanterns that hung down from the ceiling. For a moment, she gawked at the furniture designed in a classic Chinese style, inlaid with mother-of-pearl and jade. Flush against one wall stood tall huanghuali cabinets with dragon-carvings on its door panels; they contained huge long-necked jars decorated with painted peonies and cranes. Upon the floor lay a tiger-skin rug, the animal's head still fully intact. On a mantelshelf sat the fierce-looking Taoist God of War, one hand carrying a Phoenix-beaked sabre. Four rosewood chairs and a mahjong table with scattered tiles stood near a corner.

A forty-something man with protruding cheek bones sat at the other end of the room. He occupied a wooden chair, its palmette carved into the head of a kylin, its legs shaped into claws. A slender neck supported his bullet-shaped head. The man was poring over a spread of cards on the wooden writing table in front of him.

When Meisu had reached him, he rose to his feet and extended his hand across the table. 'Welcome to the headquarters of the Red Centipede Society,' he said in Mandarin. 'My name's Ouyang Lifu. May I know yours?'

Meisu held his hand and shook it, noticing that he had a tattoo of a centipede on his slim forearm. 'Please call me Meisu.' She sat down, facing the triad godfather.

'What a nice name.' His small, slanted eyes smiled at Meisu. 'I'll come straight to the point, Miss Meisu. My men informed me that you've been working at New Peng Hwa for several days.'

'What's that to you anyway?' Her pounding heart beat grew louder in her ears.

The mobile phone on his desk rang, and Lifu picked it up. 'Ouyang Traditional Massage. Uh-huh …Yes, we've girls from Vietnam, Cambodia and Thailand,' he said in English. 'Outcall is two hundred and thirty. You must pay thirty for transport if you reject the girl. Hmm, yes. Of course, it's a full package.' He paused. 'Which hotel are you staying in?' He grabbed a pen and scribbled in a spiral-bound notepad. 'OK, she'll be there in around forty minutes.' He put the cell phone aside, jabbed a button on an intercom and spoke into the receiver. 'Ah-Meng, drop a Vietnamese girl at Lakeview Hotel. Room 2164. Full-service.' The triad godfather turned to face Meisu and continued in Mandarin. 'New Peng Hwa is our territory, Miss Meisu. On behalf of the Red Centipede Society, I'd like to offer you protection.' He blinked a few times. 'But, in this world, nothing is free. Protection fee is three thousand per month, payable on the first day of every month. In return, some privileges will be accorded to you.'

He paused and raised his right thumb. 'First, you'll be allotted a room as a work station in Ace Electronics Building – I'm sure you've seen my girls bringing their customers there? You'll have unlimited use of the room.' He extended his index finger. 'Second, if the cops are coming, you'll be notified through a phone call. So, you can carry on your business without worrying about getting arrested. However, if despite being warned, you still get arrested – maybe because you were engaged with a client – we can still get you out. We'll stuff cigarette-money worth one thousand eight hundred into their assholes and you'll be released within twenty-four hours. Which means you can continue your work immediately. You'll have to repay us this bail-out money, of course.' He straightened his middle finger. 'Third, if any customer of yours gets unruly or gives any trouble, just phone any of our duty supervisors, and he'll deal with the rascal accordingly. That, Miss Meisu, sums up my proposal.' He closed his fingers and sat back in his chair, waiting for her to speak.

'I'm using budget hotels so I don't need any room. And my clients have been nice to me so far,' Meisu said simply.

'In that case, protection fee will be one thousand and five hundred.'

'What will I get in return?'

'Only two roads lead to New Peng Hwa, and we've eyes on them both. We also feed little devils who act as our informers. You'll be informed of impending raids.'

'I get only that for thousand five? That's pure extortion! I would like some time to consider.'

'Consider? Tsk-tsk.' Lifu's upper lip curled over his teeth. 'Allow me to borrow a saying from Confucius: there are three ways we can learn wisdom. First, by reflection, and that is the noblest. Second, by imitation and that is the easiest. Third, by experience, and that is the most bitter.'

'Is that a threat?'

'I'll give you forty-eight hours to consider.' He gestured with a sweep of his hand. 'Now, Big Dog will escort you back to New Peng Hwa for your safety.'

* * *

Alvin sauntered over to Sultan Road in Chinatown. His familiar seat at a corner table in Seahorse Chinatown Restaurant was waiting for him, sheltered by a colourful rectangular umbrella and draped with a yellow cloth that flowed to the kerb. A Vietnamese waiter brought him a bucket filled with ice and a big bottle of imported Japanese beer. He set down the bucket with a soft thud and handed Alvin a laminated menu. *It is good to be in a familiar place, where they know what drink I would order.* Alvin crossed an ankle on one knee and started to shake his foot excitedly. His spirits were high now. After giving a cursory glance to the menu, he ordered a plate of chicken chow mein.

While he ate, Alvin wondered about where he could go for some after-dinner drinks. He knew all the drinking places in Chinatown. He knew that the Pink Panda Pub, located next to Gospel Hall on Hang Jebat Road, and only ten minutes away from here, and it would be open by now. The bartender there was very friendly, and the place sold all kinds of hard liquor, cocktails and wines. Kai Kow Liquor Store, nice and comfortable, furnished with wooden tables, was also within walking distance. *But, hell, it is a Chinaman's spot, frequented by Chinese butchers from the Petaling Street Wet Market, and by menial Indian workers and ugly transsexuals*, he thought with disgust. Alvin was an artist. He would not lower his dignity by patronising such a spot. Alvin ate his chow mein, quickly downed his beer and looked toward the direction of the Pink Panda Pub while he waited for the waiter to bring the bill. Ten agonizing minutes passed, and then he paid the bill and left quickly.

Like a shark drawn to the smell of blood, he walked into the Pink Panda Pub, pushing open its solid wooden door. Along one wall of the pub ran a long chrome-trimmed bar complete with a brass rail. Alvin saw that a row of men with big bellies and bald heads already sat atop the bar stools. He picked a corner spot and settled on a leather divan. When a waitress brought him a plate of salted nuts, he ordered a Bloody Mary.

By the time Alvin had finished five more cocktails, the place was jammed to the rafter, and he couldn't even hear himself think. He asked for the bill and flicked his wrist to look at his watch. It was 11:30 p.m. When the tab arrived, he fished out his wallet, spread the notes and counted them. He realised that he'd have only a few ringgit left after paying the bill. *Oh God! Not enough money to take a cab home.*

He tried to think of a way to fix this. *Wait, there's no need to panic yet.* His bank had a branch with an attached twenty-four-hour ATM in Kotaraya Complex. He also had to drop in his cheque anyway.

A twenty-minute hike brought him there, and he deposited Ken Koh's cheque into a machine. Alvin then moved to an ATM and slid his card into it. He pushed the necessary buttons and waited in anticipation for the much-needed cash. 'Wrong PIN entered' appeared on the machine's display. *What's my PIN?* He searched his foggy memory, as if rummaging through a pile of dirty clothes in a laundry basket. *Is it my date of birth? Is it my identity card number?* He inputted another six digits. 'Wrong PIN entered' flashed at him again. *Shit. If only I had saved the PIN in my hand phone.* He cancelled the transaction and retrieved his plastic card.

He stumbled onto Hang Lekir Road, now crowded with tourists and shoppers, and carefully moved through the surging crowd, frequently turning about to avoid being pushed or bumped into. He manoeuvred himself past a pimply Chinese boy wearing braces and munching on a waffle; a braless blonde backpacker with bobbing breasts; a lanky African dressed like a pimp from Harlem; a turbaned Sikh with a long beard; a massive mass of a body covered in a black burqa and an accompanying obese man dressed in a ratty t-shirt; a pretty teenage girl with her hobo bag slung over her shoulder; a geezer hunched over his wooden walking stick, barely able to move; a white man holding a camcorder to his eye and recording everything he saw.

By the time, he got back to Central Market Annexe, his legs were trembling like a rattlesnake's tail. He could hardly stand. *Geez, they feel practically boneless.* He knew it was impossible for him to drive now, so he went back to his studio, unlocked it and collapsed onto its tiled floor. A security guard brandishing a billy club came to investigate the noise, and Alvin, barely in his senses now, managed to lift his head and croak, 'Friend, pull the door down, please.' He turned to lie on his back and within a few minutes, he was fast asleep.

Wednesday 7 April

'I brought you some coffee.' Her voice sounded like it was coming from a scratched LP gramophone.

Detective Inspector Daniel Chu glanced up from the report he was typing. His partner, Detective Sergeant June Qwong, stood in front of his desk, holding a paper cup in each of her hands.

'Thanks,' Chu said, 'but I don't remember asking you to bring me this. Did you get anything from the databases?' He studied her face for a moment. *Shit, she is as ugly as sin. And to make things worse, she is taking a romantic interest in me.*

'I just thought you might like to drink some coffee. The caffeine will keep you alert.' She paused to take a sip from her cup. 'Yes, I have found something in the victim's marriage records. She had a marriage of convenience. I'll give you the details during the meeting. In fact, Superintendent Sofian just punched in. Give him a couple of minutes to settle down, and we'll go in.' Tied tightly into a bun, her hair only accentuated her hook nose and protruding chin, giving her a granny-like appearance.

Why couldn't my assigned partner be like those hot female police officers in Hawaii Five-O? Chu sulked while he drank his coffee.

In between sips from her cup, June said, 'Two other call girls have been reported murdered the same way, and I've collected their files as well. I want to bring to your attention that I noticed something similar among all three victims – their hair was parted down the middle. Perhaps you should include this observation in your report.'

Chu set down his paper cup on the table and sighed, 'Come on, that's just a minor detail. It could be just a coincidence.'

June smiled and said, 'See how helpful and sweet I am to you?'

Chu did not respond.

When they had emptied their cups, Chu and June got up and strode down a corridor to Sofian's office. The door was open, and Chu could see the bulky brown-skinned superintendent sitting inside, hunched over a sheaf of papers. When Chu knocked on the door, he looked up. 'Come in,' he grunted. 'Close the door and sit down.' Heaps of files cluttered the small room, and an anti-corruption poster was pasted on one wall.

Chu and June sat down facing Superintendant Sofian.

Sofian pushed aside the papers on his desk and leaned back on his chair. 'OK, Inspector and Sergeant, brief me on the details about Tuesday's murder.'

Chu looked down at his report. 'The victim was a prostitute from China, twenty-eight years old,' he spoke in a voice devoid of emotion. 'Working name was Xiaoqian but her real name, as given in her passport, was Xiong Caiqin.' He turned to glance briefly at his partner. 'Sergeant June has notified the China Embassy about this case.' He paused. 'I collected the autopsy report yesterday. The victim was strangled, and then both her breasts were cut off. Two other victims – both of them also call girls and Chinese – were murdered and mutilated in the same manner. In San Peng Apartments and in Chinatown Paradise Inn respectively. I believe the same man committed all three murders. Although Xiong Caiqin's valuables were missing, I don't think robbery was the motive for her murder. I believe that the theft of the victim's cash was incidental. I'll be pursuing this case from all angles.'

The superintendent did not say anything in return. Chu inhaled deeply as he continued. 'The killer could hate China prostitutes; he could have possibly contracted HIV or STD from a hooker and wants to take revenge – that's why Jack the Ripper did his killings in London in the late eighteen eighties, by the way. Our guy probably picked the prostitutes at random.'

From the corner of his eye, Chu glimpsed Sergeant June nodding her head in apparent admiration of him. She suddenly cut in, 'There's a second theory as well – the killer could be a hatchet man for a syndicate's pimp. The pimp might have had a grudge against the three women. Maybe they walked out of their contracts and left behind huge debts. Or they might have had disputes about clients and money with the disgruntled pimp.'

'And the third theory is that,' Chu finished, 'this man had been abused by a mother, stepmother or female guardian during his childhood. And also possibly scorned or rejected by beautiful, heavy bosomed women. The trauma has caused him to become an extreme misogynist. Therefore he kills to feel superior.'

'What is a misogynist?' the superintendent asked.

'A misogynist is a woman-hater.'

'I see. Any leads?'

'The victim's fingerprints were found on a few condom wrappers.

The killer's prints were not found at the scene of the crime. But the victim's neighbour saw him, the killer. Our artist has produced a photofit from his description.' From the case file, Chu pulled out a sketch made on an A5-size paper and held it in front of Sofian.

'Get our public-affairs people to release this picture to the press. That will make the bastard sweat a bit.'

Chu put the picture back in the case file. 'I'd rather not, sir. All that publicity in the press will only cause him to hide.'

Sofian scowled. 'I think that will be good, don't you agree? The killer will be scared and will be unlikely to attack again.'

'I don't want him to run away from KL. I've found some interesting leads that I'd like to pursue. We found a nightclub's matchbook at the scene. It belonged to the Crazy Legs Club. It's very likely that the killer was a customer there. I'll be asking questions at Crazy Legs. As for the next lead, Sergeant June will take us through it.'

The sergeant cleared her throat before she began. 'I've checked with the national marriage database. The victim got married to one Anthony Tee seven months ago. Of course, it's a fake marriage. I went to Anthony's residence, as provided in the marriage records. He wasn't in, but I found out from his neighbours that he works as a masseur in the Total Male Executive Spa on Imbi Road. Anthony Tee doesn't have any criminal record. I've also ran a check with City Hall. The spa is licensed.'

'I'll be interviewing this Anthony Tee in the afternoon. Sergeant June will be collecting the DNA reports from the forensics people and from the hospital pathologist in a few days' time. I am hoping to find some DNA evidence on the cigarette butts we found at the victim's apartment, as well the scrapings we got off her fingernails.'

'In that case, if you catch the suspect who fits the description, and if his DNA matches with the one found at the scene, the case is solved.'

Chu nodded. 'Yes. And when we find the killer, we'll know his motive.'

* * *

Alvin tapped the turn-signal bar and manoeuvred his car into the driveway of the old double-storey bungalow on Utara Road that housed the Vanity club. A parking attendant waved his torchlight's beam to guide Alvin into an empty parking space. The bungalow's surroundings had once functioned as a residential area for the old money crowd but soaring commercial prices had lured its property owners to sell out. He got out of his car and strode towards the club's entrance. Earlier, he had partaken a hearty dinner of Chinese hotpot at Chinatown, along with two bottles of Danish imported beer. This had lifted his mood, and he had decided to spend the rest of his night at the club.

Wednesday isn't a bad time to chill out at Vanity Club, he thought with a hopeful smile. Wednesday night was Ladies' Night, after all. *Perhaps I'll meet a woman who'll help me forget my pain for a while.*

He paid the cover charge at the door, to a dark-skinned man with a handle-bar moustache who looked like a villain from a Bollywood movie. As he entered the club, Acid Trance music spilled over him, vibrated in the laminate flooring under his feet. Along one wall ran a row of plush-lined seats, filled with men and women. Many others were dancing on the club's LED dance floor while overhead strobe lights flashed on them. The place was exactly what its young and flashy clientele expected it to be.

Alvin skirted the dance floor and shouldered his way through the crowd, making his way up a flight of stairs. He came to a bright rectangular room with a row of booths on its either side and with several tables running down its middle. At the end of the room was a bar. Alvin liked it up here; it wasn't as noisy. He moved to the bar, leaned over and called for the barmaid. The marble bar felt cold against his skin. When she came over, Alvin ordered a Salty Dog. The barmaid looked ugly, like she was trying to grow a moustache but wasn't quite successful at doing so. While the cocktail was getting ready, he sat on a swivel bar stool and fished a crumpled packet of cigarettes from his shirt pocket.

'Hi! Can I bum a light?'

Alvin's eyebrows shot up, and his breath hitched for a moment. He turned to face a woman standing beside him. She was baby-faced with a fleshy nose, full red lips and stringy hair. She had on a floral swing dress with plaited shoulder straps and a scoop neckline. For a moment, her resemblance to his ex-wife rendered him breathless.

The young woman smiled and raised her voice so she could be heard over the music. 'Can I borrow a light?' Her eyelashes waved a flirtatious hello to him.

Alvin then saw that she was holding an unlit cigarette between two fingers, was waiting for him to light it. He fumbled in his pocket for his lighter. He snapped open the lighter when he found it and held it up. As she leaned forward to light the cigarette, he cupped his hand over the flame to shield it.

She took a deep drag from the butt and exhaled a stream of smoke. 'Thanks.'

'You're welcome. Did you forget to bring your lighter?' He smiled at the woman.

'My girlfriend took it. She's dancing now.' The woman gestured to the dance floor downstairs.

When his drink was served to him, Alvin fished out his wallet from his pocket and paid for it. He then turned to the young woman beside him, 'Can I buy you a drink?' *Christ, it had been years since I have spoken this line.* It felt nice to be wooing a woman again.

'That's sweet of you. Thanks.' She asked the barmaid for a Classic Shirley Temple and sat down beside Alvin.

The woman's name was Susan Tang, and she was an A&P executive at Curvey Fitness, the city's popular women-only fitness club. Her girlfriends had brought her here to cheer her up; Susan had just broken up with her boyfriend. Her friends had hooked up with two handsome guys though and had headed to the dance floor with them.

'Your pals shouldn't have abandoned you,' Alvin said.

Susan shrugged. 'I'm glad they're enjoying themselves.'

The barmaid served the mocktail to Susan, and Alvin paid for her drink. 'Keep the change,' he said to the barmaid.

Alvin and Susan continued to talk as they sipped their drinks. They discussed work, their favourite TV shows, their hobbies and their love for travelling to new places. Alvin wasn't sure how long they had been speaking to each other but it seemed like hours. Susan was giggly and energetic, and Alvin was beginning to like her. It had been a while since he had a nice chat with a woman he liked.

Drinks were ordered and were finished quickly. Susan waggled a shoulder at him coyly and adjusted a bra strap. 'Are you married?' she asked, smiling.

'I'm divorced. No kids, thankfully. So, there're no complications.'

'A nice man like you divorced? With all due respect to your ex, how did she let you go?' She laughed. 'Well, don't give up on women yet. There're still a lot of wonderful women out there.'

Alvin tapped one foot against the bar, moving it to the beat of the music. 'Do you like art?'

'Well, yes. But I like artists more. Especially artists like you.' She giggled.

'Like me? What do you mean?' Alvin probed, grinning.

'Artists are sensitive – they're sensitive to the environment and to other people's moods. But in your case, you retain your masculinity as well. I like sensitive men with a healthy amount of testosterone,' she said, sipping her drink, staring into his eyes.

Alvin returned her gaze. 'So, are you looking to start a relationship with a sensitive and masculine man any time soon?'

'Yes. I want to. I would like to settle down soon with such a man, and start a family with him,' she grinned. 'I love children. They're so cute.'

Alvin frowned. 'Would you marry but not have children?' Alvin asked, his voice suddenly growing unsteady.

'Nah, what's the purpose of marrying if you don't want children? I want to experience giving birth, no matter how painful some people say it is. Motherhood is a wonderful experience. Imagine being able to create a new life!'

Alvin's thoughts froze. His shoulders sagged. His eyes blurred over as he recalled his visit to the fertility clinic.

He and Karen had gone there together. That had been two years ago. Butterflies had fluttered in his chest, and he had held onto his wife's hand with his own clammy hand.

'Next please,' the receptionist had called as a pregnant woman walked out of the doctor's room. It was their turn to go in.

A bespectacled doctor in a white coat asked them to take seat, had then offered them a warm smile. Once they had settled down in the chairs, the doctor flipped opened a file on his desk and scanned the contents, slowly turning the pages as he spoke. 'Mrs. Au, the pelvic ultrasound did not show any cyst, fibroid, polycystic ovarian syndrome or polyp. Also, the hysterosalpingogram doesn't show any blockage of the fallopian tubes or any abnormality of the womb. In other words, your tests are normal.'

The doctor had then turned to Alvin. 'Now, Mr. Au, I'm afraid I've some unpleasant news for you. The urine test produced normal results but the sperm analysis shows sterility.' He paused. 'Your sperm are produced in normal quantities but they've abnormal morphology. In layman terms, it means they lack the normal structure needed to penetrate and fertilise eggs.'

Alvin's cheeks felt hot. His pulse raced. 'Why? I mean, what could have caused this?'

'It's hard to pinpoint a specific cause. Possibilities include exposure to radiation or chemicals in the workplace, mumps or groin injury after puberty, family genetic disorders and even drug abuse.'

'Is my condition treatable?' Alvin had asked, gripping the arms of the chair.

The doctor had only given a slight shake of his head, confirming

Alvin's worst fears.

During the drive back home, Karen had not spoken a word. She had simply stared out of the window. Her silence had hit Alvin's chest like a cold rock.

'Thinking of something?' Susan's voice broke into his memory.

Alvin blinked. 'Oh? Sorry. I was wondering if I'd forgotten to switch off my car lights.'

'Are you usually free on weekends?'

Alvin sighed. *Let's just get this done with. What's the use of starting a relationship with this chick when I can't pursue it to its logical conclusion?*

'Sorry, I give art lesson on Saturdays and Sundays. Why?'

Susan reached out to touch his hand. 'I thought we could do lunch.'

'It'll be my pleasure. I'll call you when I can find time.' He pulled away from her and jerked a thumb towards the exit. 'I'm afraid I got to go. It was nice meeting you,' he said, feigning a smile.

Alvin rushed out of the club. *This has turned into such a crappy evening.* He stopped at Genting Kelang Road and popped into a pub next to a Kenny Rogers outlet. He bought himself a one-litre bottle of Thai whisky. Beer wouldn't be enough for tonight. Only strong alcohol could kill the gremlin of depression growing quickly inside him.

When he entered his condominium, he kicked off his shoes and placed the whisky bottle on the living-room table. He then had a cold shower, towelled himself dry and put on clean pyjamas. Then he emptied the ice cubes from the fridge into a lidded plastic ice bucket. Holding the ice bucket with one hand and a glass in the other, he plodded to his armchair. He used a pair of tongs to drop a few ice cubes into the glass, then filled the glass with whisky.

He took a big gulp of the drink. The alcohol, hot and cutting, almost made him gag as it went down his throat. He stared at the framed photo of his ex-wife he still kept on the mantelpiece, and his eyes turned moist. He put the glass down and leaned back. His chest jerked as his sobs racked his body. He thought about the fateful day he had lost Karen, the memory of it piercing him like a splinter of broken glass.

A few weeks after the medical test, he had suggested that he and Karen adopt a child. But his in-laws had not agreed. *If only that bloody crone and that wily geezer hadn't interfered in his personal problem.* Later, he had suggested artificial insemination but Karen had said that she needed some time to consider. For several months, she had continued to be the epitome of a model housewife: she had cooked, had done the laundry, had cleaned the house and had waited for him to come back from work every evening.

One morning, however, Alvin had realised that he had forgotten to take his pen drive to work. At that time, he had worked as an illustrator in a publishing house. The pen drive had contained two important illustrations that were due for submission that day. He had decided to go back home during the lunch break to get it.

Four hours later, he had returned to his condominium, had unlocked its door and entered it. He had heard soft, romantic jazz playing on the living room's CD player. His eyes had moved to the shoe rack beside the doorjamb. A pair of men's Bata shoes lay on top of it; the shoes did not belong to him. As he walked in, confused, the ceiling fan had caught his attention. His eyes had widened with shock. A black brassiere was dangling from one of its blades. On one arm of the couch lay a pair of black panties; on the floor lay a man's short-sleeved shirt, a pair of rumpled jeans and a pair of John Master briefs. His saliva had turned bitter in his mouth. Alvin had rushed into his bedroom.

'Oh, dear god! Yes, yes, yeeeeeees!' Karen's screams came from the ensuite bathroom.

A man's voice grunted after her, 'Hallelujah! I'm coming!'

They had left the door open. Alvin stepped into the bathroom. The plastic curtain of the long bathtub was drawn, and the shower was running. With a flourish of his arm, he swept aside the curtain. Jesus Christ! Alvin reeled back in shock. It was Pastor Patrick Poh in the shower with his wife. Alvin and Karen attended Mass at his church on Tun Sambanthan Road. Karen and the scrawny pastor were standing in the bathtub, the shower's water falling over their naked bodies, their lips locked. *This bastard always preaches morals and fidelity during his services. Yet here he is, fucking my wife.*

Startled, they pulled away from each other. Karen glared at him. She stood defiantly before him, with her legs spread wide apart, her arms akimbo. Alvin's face grew hot, as if it were a kettle about to explode.

'You bitch!' He raised an open palm to slap her, but the pastor caught his wrist and pushed it away.

'Don't you dare hit me, you stupid man!' Karen yelled. 'Man?' she then snorted. 'I can't call you that now, can I? You're no better than a eunuch!'

'You're the one I just caught cheating, and you have the nerve to call me names?' Alvin bit into his lower lip angrily and tasted blood, warm and metallic.

'No need to get upset, brother,' the pastor said, stepping between Alvin and his wife. 'Karen and I will be getting married after she finalises her divorce with you.' The pastor then turned off the shower. 'Come darling.' He took Karen by her hand as they both gingerly stepped out of the bathtub. 'Let's dry up, get dressed and scram. It's best you spend the night in my place. This blank-firing guy can stay here and cool himself down.' He steered her out of the bathroom, brushing past Alvin.

Alvin's legs had turned to rubber, and he had crumbled to the floor. He felt as though a swarm of bees were buzzing about his face. They had entered his ears and flew out his nose. He had opened his mouth to call out to Karen, to scream at her, but words had failed to come out.

He had started drinking that day to forget what had happened. He had never stopped drinking after that day.

Alvin picked up his drink now and swirled around the ice cubes in the glass. He choked for air as he remembered it all again. He finished off the whisky in one gulp then poured some more from the bottle and downed it as well. After the tenth glass, he finally couldn't remember Karen and her betrayal. His brain felt like it was stuffed with cotton. He slouched in the armchair, his hand holding the empty glass, dangling over the chair's arm. His eyelids became heavy, and he let go of the glass. As it fell to the floor, shattering, he fell, too, into a sudden sleep.

* * *

The Total Male Executive Spa, located next to a Chinese shark-fin restaurant, looked like any other decent spa from the outside. Posters of men getting facial treatments and of sweaty men sitting in sauna booths ornamented its glass walls. Chu pushed open the front door and entered the reception. He was immediately greeted by loud jazz music – it was a funky track, with a throaty sax carrying the melody. He headed straight to the curved wooden counter, decorated with a small bronze fountain on one side and a potted kentia palm on the other.

A twenty-something man wearing a pink sleeveless singlet smiled and said, 'Good afternoon, sir. Can I help you?' His shrill voice could shatter glass.

'I'm looking for Anthony Tee.'

'Right now, he's working. He has another client after the present one. Would you like to pick someone else? Please look at the monitor, sir.' Before Chu could reply, the male receptionist tapped at a switch beneath the counter and a wall-mounted monitor behind his head sprung to life. The image on the screen showed a bright room filled with six or seven young men, all of them dressed in tight t-shirts. They were sitting on a long purple divan. 'You can pick anyone you like, sir.'

Chu dipped into his trouser pocket and pulled out his yellow police card. 'I'm Detective Inspector Daniel Chu, C.I.D. I'm on official business here, not seeking a massage. I want to ask Anthony some questions.'

'Oh, sorry, I didn't know.' The man shrugged his shoulders and forced a smile. 'I'll inform him after he has finished with the present client. Please sit down.' He gestured with a limp wrist to the sitting area. It was furnished with a glass-topped rattan table and with several cushioned chairs arranged around it.

Chu saw that a man was already slouched in one of the chairs, fiddling with his mobile phone. He settled into the chair furthest away from the waiting customer, the rattan creaking slightly under his weight. A couple of magazines were lying on a rack beside the table. He picked one up and started to flip through its pages impatiently. When he was finished with it, he tossed the magazine aside and let out a sigh. *This is taking too long! Has Anthony got scared and run away?*

Before he could go back to the reception to check, the frosted glass door at the end of the room slid open with a rattle. A young man clad in a pair of blue Lycra bike shorts and a sleeveless t-shirt that displayed his broad shoulders entered the reception. He closed the door behind him, walked up to the waiting customer and said, 'I'll be with you in a minute, sir. Sorry.'

The young man then turned to Chu. 'I'm Anthony Tee.' His face was knitted in a frown. 'Can I see your I.D., Inspector?' He ran his fingers through his spiky hair, obviously nervous.

Chu rose to his feet and flashed his police card. 'Is it alright if we talk in here?

Anthony plopped down on a cushioned chair opposite Chu. 'Sure, no problem. Fire away, Inspector.'

'Is Xiong Caiqin your wife?'

'Yes, she is. Has she been busted for something or what?'

'No, she has been murdered.'

Anthony's big eyes got bigger. 'Holy shit! When? Where?' He blinked rapidly a few times.

'On Tuesday, in her working apartment. You should know where the place is?'

The masseur flinched a little too dramatically, and then jerked back. 'Her working apartment? What's all this rubbish, Inspector?' His voice turned hard. 'She's been living with me ever since I married her. Two days ago, she left town, went to Port Dickson. Caiqin loves to swim.'

Chu raised his voice. 'Cut the crap, Anthony!' He turned to look at the waiting customer about six or seven feet away, but he seemed to be engrossed in playing a game on his cell phone. The inspector locked his eyes onto Anthony's again. 'I know your marriage to Caiqin was only on paper. Prostitution's none of my business – that's something our anti-vice department should worry about. However, murder is my business. And it's a murder I'm investigating now. So, please give me your co-operation.'

Anthony's voice thickened. 'How did you know I work here?' His eyes turned to flint.

'We have our sources. Now, tell me … How did you get to know her?'

The masseur remained silent, his face still unyielding. But then he hunched over after a moment, giving in, resting his arms on his hairy knees. 'My client was also her client,' he said in a low voice. 'He told me Caiqin was looking for a husband because she wanted to get a long-term visa. A lunch meeting was arranged, and we made a deal. She agreed to pay me five hundred every month. After some initial paperwork, we went to the National Registration Department in Putrajaya and got our marriage registered. Then we had some photographs taken together at a studio. Those photos were to be used as our cover, just in case she got into trouble. After that, I applied for a spouse visa for her. Those immigration suckers gave her one year. Then I started meeting her once every month to collect my payment. We'd meet for lunch at a coffee shop on Changkat Thambi Dollah Road, close to where she stayed. She was a good paymaster, very prompt.'

'Where were you between 11 p.m. on Monday night and 2:30 a.m. on Tuesday morning?'

'I was here. Working. We close at 3 a.m. If I don't have a client, I'll be in the glass room. My fellow masseurs can vouch for me. So can my boss who's here every night. I went straight home after the spa closed.'

'Was Caiqin a freelancer or was she tied to a syndicate?'

Anthony rested his fist on the chair's arm, propped his head up as he spoke to Chu. 'She started out in a syndicate-operated karaoke bar in Kepong. One day, its head honcho forgot to send his candy to the gutter rats – pardon my expression.' He gave Chu a snide smile. Chu ignored it. 'And the KTV got busted. Caiqin escaped by crawling down a drainpipe. She was in her underwear. She got shit scared after that incident and moved to a food court in a bad part of the city. I'm not sure which one. But she worked the graveyard shift.'

'Was she having any problems at work that you are aware of? Any pimp, any boyfriend or any loan-shark bothering her? Either at the food court or her former KTV.'

'Not that I know of. She seldom discussed her personal life with me.'

'Her mobile was missing. What's her contact number?'

Anthony stood up. 'Let me check my moby. I'll get it from my locker.' He walked off and returned a few moments later. He read her contact number aloud from his cell phone. Chu opened his notepad and scribbled it down.

'I need your contact information as well,' Chu informed Anthony as he left the spa. 'Don't leave town for a few days. I may need to talk to you again.'

* * *

'Hello, darling, can I be your girlfriend?' Meisu purred. She draped her arm over the shoulder of the lean man. His face was pitted and scarred and he looked to be in his late twenties.

The lean man, dressed in a grey t-shirt with a 'Liverpool' iron-on, tilted his head back and drained a glass of beer in a few gulps. He pulled Meisu to the chair beside him and said, 'Becoming my girlfriend's not good enough. Can you be my lover for an hour?'

Meisu smiled at him. Last night, Ouyang Lifu had given her forty-eight hours to make her decision. *To hell with him. Every hour in New Peng Hwa counted. The place is crawling with horny men.*

'Sure, and it will cost you only one hundred and eighty. A nice room is included in the price.' She batted her long, mascara-curled eyelashes at him.

'Wow, that's too much. What will I get for my money?'

'A full strip and sex with a high-level GFE, darling, and I'm sure you'll come back for some more. Come on, let's go. We can get a room at Loveboat Motel.'

The customer finished the rest of his drink and stood up. Meisu walked out of the food court with the lean man in tow. When they had reached the sidewalk of Pudu Road, they held each other's hands and strolled to the motel. The walk took about fifteen minutes.

As they approached the entrance of the motel, Meisu noticed that a young man stood under its lighted front porch. Stout and bull-necked, he had a corpselike complexion. Meisu's chest tingled. *Who is this guy? Only a gangster would idle around here at this hour.* Meisu grasped her customer's hand nervously, wondering if Lifu had sent forth this man to threaten her.

As she and her customer neared the entranceway of the motel, the thug smiled at Meisu. Then he put both hands to his mouth and shouted, 'Prostitute! Prostitute and her client!'

Meisu's john flinched. 'What? What's happening? What's going on?' He turned to Meisu, his face pallid.

The thug shouted again, 'Prostitute's client!'

Before Meisu could say anything, her customer let go of her hand and ran away.

Meisu strode up to the thug angrily and glared at him. 'Damn you! Why did you frighten away my client?'

The thug tilted his chin, rolled his eyes and looked away. *Bloody hell! This has to be the work of Ouyang Lifu.* She knew for sure now. The bastard was harassing her. Firing a barrage of nasty words at his hatchet-man wouldn't achieve anything. To snuff out the extortion threat, she would have to deal with the chief hoodlum. *But how?*

Meisu decided to check out the Springtime Inn, which was also within walking distance from New Peng Hwa. As she had expected, there were two thugs stationed outside the inn's entrance as well. There was no other convenient motel left for her to conduct business any more.

As Meisu trudged back to New Peng Hwa, she remembered something she had once read: according to Sun Tzu, if you know the enemy and know yourself, you need not fear the result of a hundred battles.

At the food court, she threaded between the tables to search for Big Dog but she couldn't find him. She headed to Ace Electronics Building, walking past a small lift lobby packed with hookers and their johns. She had heard that the building had once been a small, thriving mall specialising in electronic goods. It had now morphed into the city's cheaper version of Singapore's Orchard Towers. A 'Not Working' sign greeted her at the lift, scrawled with felt pen and stuck onto the closed doors with scotch tape. She walked up to the first floor, cursing her high heels. When she reached the Kim Wah Café, she saw that it was filled with prospective customers, tootsies, drinkers and johns, its tables and chairs overflowing to the corridors outside. Curious people milled around the place, ogling at the skimpily dressed women. Meisu spotted Big Dog seated on a plastic chair by the fire-escape staircase.

She approached the bouncer. 'Big Dog, I need to talk to you.'

'Talk about what?'

'About Lifu. Can you help me, please?'

'Even if I wanted to, I can't. Just pay the protection money.'

'I just need ten or fifteen minutes of your time. Please. I need to talk to you. I just want to know as much as possible about Lifu. I'll pay you fifty ringgit.' She opened her purse.

'No, Miss Meisu. Not here.' He glanced around him and rose to his feet. 'Come, we'll go somewhere else. Follow me. But from a distance.'

Big Dog tramped down the fire escape staircase and reached the ground floor, then proceeded to the front entrance of the building, which faced the Pudu wet market. The market was covered in darkness, its stalls closed and silent. The stench of rotting vegetables and chicken faeces occasionally wafted in with the wind. The bouncer strode a few paces to the front sidewalk and buried himself in the shadows, waiting for Meisu to move closer.

When Meisu approached him, she opened her purse and handed him a fifty ringgit note.

'What do you want to know about Ouyang Lifu?' he asked, folding the note and slipping it into his jeans' back pocket.

'For starters, how old is he? What does he like?'

'Why you want to know this?' A puzzled frown creased Big Dog's forehead.

'I just want to get to know him, how his mind works. If I know that, I could possibly negotiate with him or work out a deal regarding the protection money. So, please tell me everything you know about him. His character, his strengths, his weaknesses, his likes and dislikes.'

'Miss Meisu, when I joined the Red Centipede Society, I went through an initiation ceremony. I drank chicken blood mixed with wine and took thirty-six oaths before a deity. I cannot break them.'

Meisu half-whispered, 'Big Dog, darling, no one will know. Trust me, please. I won't tell anyone.' She stepped closer to him, edging him against the wall, and gently fondled his crotch. 'Let me reward you in another way then, OK?' She started to unzip his pants.

Big Dog's jaw dropped open. 'Miss Meisu, what're you doing? My first oath is to be loyal to my master.'

Meisu drew down his pants to his knees, and then pulled open his briefs.

'My ... My second oath is to maintain secrecy.'

When Meisu lowered her head to Big Dog's crotch and started to suck on him, he let out a moan. 'My third oath is to ... Oh, that's nice ... Ah ... That feels so good.'

Within a few minutes, Big Dog's resistance melted away. Meisu stood upright, spat on the sidewalk and wiped her lips with a tissue.

'So, Big Dog, darling,' she smiled. 'Will you help me now?'

Big Dog nodded, pulling up his briefs and pants. 'Hmm, well, let me see. He's turning forty-three this year – a Monkey according to Chinese calendar. Has two young mistresses but is still crazy for young girls.' He gave a slight shake of his head and smirked. 'I heard his sex appetite is voracious – he can do it five times a night. He's also into gambling – especially card games. Blackjack and gin rummy are his favourites. He likes challenges so he plays for high stakes. His ego is big, and he wants to be perceived as a trustworthy gentleman. But what he really is differs from the public image he wants to give himself. He will keep his word if he says it in front of other people. However, it's different story if he promises something to you in private. He can be very devious.' A pause. 'That's all I know about him.'

'OK. Thank you, Big Dog.'

* * *

The pale man with long hair raised a half-empty beer can to his lips and tilted his head back, letting the cold and crisp brew flow down his throat. He felt so alone. He really missed his Mama, wished she was here with him. As he drank, his mind flew back to the past, to the day when everything had gone wrong for him. To the day his family had been broken up by that bitch.

He had been sixteen or seventeen then. He had been staying with his parents in a flat in a seedy part of Kuala Lumpur.

That day, Mama had looked very worried. Seated in the kitchen, they had been eating dinner. She had to leave for work after dinner; she worked the night shifts as a dispenser in a twenty-four-hour clinic. Her brow was knitted in a frown as she lifted a spoonful of rice to her mouth.

'Son, can I talk to you about something? I need your help,' she suddenly said. 'These few months, your papa's been behaving strangely. He's been very cold toward me.' Her eyes filled with tears. 'Every morning, when I get home, I've been checking his wallet. On one occasion, I found a motel parking receipt, and another time, there was a cabaret bill. On several occasions, the cash in his wallet was even missing. I suspect he sneaks out of the house when I'm at work. Son, I need your help. Tonight, try to stay up, and then go to our room late at night to check if Papa is still there.'

'OK, Mama.' His insides had twisted in worry. He had never seen his mother looking so weak. He had to help her. He grimaced, knowing that he would probably doze off in class the next day, and that his teacher would twist his ear to wake him. But he was ready to pay that price for his mother.

Papa had returned home as usual that evening. He remembered his father now, remembered how he had looked – a man of average built, with a beaked nose, and sunken temples that looked as if a hammer had struck them. After eating his dinner, Papa had sat in the armchair, alternating between reading his newspaper and watching TV. When the clock in the living room had struck twelve, he had switched off the TV and gone to bed.

In his room, the pale boy finished up his homework. He then lay down in bed, under the groans of a slow-moving ceiling fan, reading a comic. He was already yawning, but he fought away the sleep. He waited for his father to fall asleep, so he could go and check on him like Mama had asked.

A noise suddenly alerted him. It sounded like the soft clang of a padlock against the metal of a grille door. He slowly got out of bed, sneaked out of his room and tiptoed to his parents' room. Slowly, he turned the door knob and stuck in his head. Under the muted yellow light of the bedside lamp, the figure of his Papa could be seen in bed, covered in a blanket.

He returned to his own room, relieved. He could finally get some sleep.

'This morning, I found a new motel parking receipt in your Papa's wallet. And there was only twenty-two ringgit left in his wallet,' his mother said to him at dinner the next evening. 'Son, are you sure that Papa stayed home last night?'

'Yes, Mama, I saw him sleeping. I checked on him at around one-thirty.'

'That's odd,' Mama said, looking unconvinced. 'Would you do me another favour? Will you check on him again tonight, please?'

The night was sweltering hot, and the boy lay in bed, sweating, dressed in a short-sleeved singlet and shorts. He was bored but wide-awake, staring at the pirouetting ceiling fan above him. At around

1:30 a.m., he thought he heard the same noise again – the *clang* of padlock against the door. He tiptoed out of the room, opened the door to the master bedroom and poked in his head to see.

Papa was in bed, a blanket drawn over him. Just like last night. His gut however told him that something was not right. *Why is Papa covering himself with a blanket on such a sultry night?* He entered the room, moved to the bed and, plucking up his courage, pulled the cotton blanket away. His jaw dropped. What lay in Papa's bed was not his father. It was an effigy that had been made to look like him. What had seemed like Papa's head was actually a basketball. His legs were two hockey sticks wrapped with t-shirts. His torso was two bolsters tied with raffia strings.

He rushed to the living room and phoned Mama.

'Come to the clinic now! Ride your motorcycle here and take me to the Daisy Motel & Cabaret on Alor Road. That's where he goes. I want to catch that bloody cheat with his hands in the cookie jar!'

The wind flew in their faces as the boy zipped through the deserted streets, his Mama riding pillion behind him. They stopped outside the notorious rent-by-the-hour motel. He parked his Honda Cub on the kerb, and then he and his mother stood outside the motel's entrance, waiting. The Sikh watchman had abandoned his chair on the sidewalk and was sitting on the platform, smoking a smelly cigar, watching them quietly.

A little while later, the glass door swung open and the boy's father strode out with a woman, his hand wrapped around her slender waist. The woman had on a low-cut blouse, and her large breasts, the size of ripened winter melons, popped out of it, quivering like jelly as she stepped onto the pavement.

Mama rushed towards them. '*Lou kung* [Husband]!' She had hollered, her voice suddenly turning guttural. 'Who's that vixen? She's a prostitute, isn't she?'

Papa was startled by her outburst. 'You bitch!' he had screamed back at Mama. 'How dare you follow me here?' He snarled, his lips curling over his teeth. 'And don't you dare call my girlfriend names!' He placed a protective arm over his companion's shoulder.

The pale boy had just stood there, shocked, unable to speak.

His mother had moved closer to Papa and glared at him.

'Girlfriend? Choose between her and me! Who do you want?'

The prostitute had tipped her face to one side and sneered at Mama. Her fingers wrapped around Papa's arm and gripped him tightly.

'You sure that's what you want?' his father asked.

'Yes! Let's get it done and over with now!'

'I want my girlfriend!' his father said simply. 'I am not coming back to you anymore. I'll return to pack my clothes in a few days' time. Then it's sayonara between us.'

Papa had then sidestepped them, and walked away with the prostitute in tow. The prostitute had turned around to look at them, flashing them a mocking smirk before she had disappeared into the shadows of the car park across the road.

A few moments later, two headlights burst into life, and a Proton Waja growled up the street, rushing past them, leaving the boy and her Mama standing in a cloud of dust. Mama had turned towards the car and spat vehemently on the road. Then she had hugged the pale boy tightly, her body racking with sobs. 'He's gone, my son. He has left us for that whore.'

As the pale man opened another can of beer, the hooker's smirking face came back to him. His throat constricted, and his tongue felt swollen. The bitch had broken up his family. She had ruined Mama's life.

He thought again of her big bosom, bouncing up and down as she walked away with Papa. He wanted to cut them off.

* * *

After taking a shower, Meisu lay on her bed, wide awake, with the ceiling light switched on. Her muscles felt tense, her eyes wide open. How could she deal with Ouyang Lifu? Meisu now knew that Lifu had a weakness for gambling, for playing card games and for betting high on them. She also knew that she was great at gambling herself, that she could beat him if luck was on her side. She wondered if she should take the risk. She remembered how she had gambled her way out of great trouble once. Meisu had been sixteen then. She remembered it like it was only yesterday.

Dressed in jeans and a floral top, she had walked up to the front porch of the tea house. Her heart was beating fast. *Bah, the cup of rice wine I had earlier has not calmed my nerves. And I hope Auntie doesn't notice there's a little less wine in the bottle.*

The previous night, her boyfriend had given his father's car keys to Meisu, at her request. She had driven the car to a birthday party. On the way, while trying to avoid an oncoming truck, she had scraped it against a tree. *I never expected his father to be so ruthless. He is giving me just two days to come up with the one thousand yuan needed for the car's repair.* Her boyfriend's father had threatened to approach her uncle for compensation if Meisu could not come up with the money. Meisu did not want her uncle and auntie to know about this. Especially because she did not have a driving licence yet and was not allowed to drive.

This is my way out. I will win the money here. She made her way past a row of overhead red lanterns and walked through the open doors of the tea house. Earlier that afternoon, Meisu had found out that the place doubled as an illegal gambling parlour. She was certain that she could make the thousand yuan she needed here. Located on the bank of the scenic Ronghu Lake, the tea house was housed in a single storey terracotta-tiled building decorated with square pots of bamboo. Several motorbikes and scooters were parked at the side of it.

As she walked into the hall, she saw five or six dark wooden tables arranged there with benches. All of them were occupied. The men and women looked like farmers and factory workers. *Hmm, looks like a lower-class establishment.* Set against one wall was a half-moon display cupboard, its shelves arranged neatly with rows of clay teapots. A sweet and earthy aroma hung in the air.

Meisu treaded between the tables, moved to the end of the hall and squeezed past a three-fold wooden partition. She saw an open door to the left, possibly leading to the place's kitchen, and a closed wooden door on the right. She stepped up to the closed door and knocked.

A small window, about three inches square, opened to reveal a man's eye. 'What do you want?' The voice was cold and crisp.

'I want to gamble.'

'There's no gambling here. Go away.'

'Wait. My father used to come here. He would leave me outside to drink tea and eat snacks while he gambled inside. That's how I know this place.'

The eye looked to the right and to the left, checking, and then Meisu heard the sound of a latch being unbolted. The door swung open. She stepped into a brightly lit room filled with cigarette smoke. *Aha! I've got over the first obstacle. The deities indicated I'm lucky today when I cast the divining blocks this morning. I hope they're right.*

The bouncer closed the door behind her and bolted the latch. The clatter of mahjong tiles came from one corner of the room, where several matronly women and paunchy men sat at a table. A wizened old man at another table was vigorously shaking a porcelain soup bowl with both his hands, while holding a plate over the bowl as lid.

'Place your bets! Place your bets!' he hollered. As if in a finale to his performance, he lifted the bowl above his head, shook it a few more times then gently put the bowl on the table. He lifted up the plate to reveal three dices. 'Seventeen!' he announced. Three men at the table groaned while a third fellow, his face creased in a smile, pumped his fist into the air.

A girl of about eleven moved about the room with a porcelain teapot in her hand, filling up the gamblers' empty cups. A few men sat alone on wooden chairs, sipping tea and observing the goings-on. A semi-circular wooden table stood in another corner. A man with a bulbous nose was stationed at the table and was toying with a deck of cards in his hands.

Meisu moved to the table and asked, 'What card game is played here?'

'Blackjack.'

'I don't have money,' Meisu said, 'but can I bet my scooter?'

The dealer laughed, showing her a missing front tooth.

'I'm serious.'

'Please talk to the boss over there.' He jerked his chin at a fat man wearing a Mao cap; the man's boss, upon noticing Meisu, rose from his chair and walked over.

'*Lao ban*, this girl wants to wager her scooter,' the dealer informed.

The fatso turned to look at Meisu. 'Oh? You want to stake your scooter? Why?' he asked in a plummy voice.

'My father has met with an accident, and I need money urgently for his surgery. I don't have the time to find a buyer for my scooter.'

'What model is it?'

'It's manufactured by Riya, fifty c.c. Only a year old. Worth about four thousand yuan.'

'Where is it?'

'Parked outside. Number plate is 41409. Red. Road tax is still valid for eight months.'

'Let me look at it.' The fatso left the room and returned in a few minutes. Meisu was getting anxious.

'Fine. I'll wager you two thousand yuan against your scooter.'

'But, that's way below its market value.'

The fatso knitted his brows. 'Take it or leave it.'

From her handbag, Meisu took out a key attached to a Riya keychain and slammed it on the gaming table. 'OK, fine! This is my scooter key. Only one hand.' She pulled out a wooden stool from under the table and sat down.

The fat man nodded to the card dealer. 'Please proceed.' A few people made their way to the table to watch the game.

The dealer shuffled the cards and slammed the deck on the table. 'Cut.'

Meisu took about one half of the cards and placed them on the table, and the dealer completed the cut by taking the remaining cards and placing them on top of those that had been cut off.

The dealer took a card with one hand. 'Your turn,' he said.

Meisu gingerly picked a card and held it in her palm, then pressed it to her bosom. She threw a wary glance at the fatso boss, who stood a couple of feet away from her. *I don't think he can see my card.* Beads of sweat appeared on her forehead.

The dealer drew a second card, and was followed by Meisu.

'Do you want another card?' the dealer asked.

'No.' Meisu felt her stomach twist inside her.

'Open!'

Both players laid their cards face up on the table. Meisu's total was nineteen, and the dealer's was seventeen.

The fatso grabbed the Mao cap off his head and threw it angrily to the floor. '*Ta ma te*! Pay her!' he barked at the dealer and strode away.

I won! Meisu wanted to jump with glee as the card dealer reached into his waist pouch, took out a wad of notes held together by a rubber band and threw it on the table. *Wow! This is such easy money! I should learn more about gambling!* Meisu stuffed the stack of notes into her handbag. *The deities were right. Today is my lucky day! Now I can pay one thousand for the car's repair, and keep the other thousand for myself.*

As she got up and started to walk towards the door, the dealer called out to her: 'Miss, you left your scooter key on the table.'

Meisu returned to the table to collect the key. She thanked the dealer and walked out of the room. *I don't own a scooter.* She chuckled to herself. *I just looked at the number plate and road tax disc of one of the scooters parked outside. And this is just a fake scooter key I carry around.*

From that day onward, Meisu was gradually sucked into the dicey world of gambling. And she found that she seldom lost. On most days, the deities and their luck seemed to be on her side.

Meisu's mind was like a grasshopper now, leaping about, wondering if she should try her luck and gamble against Lifu. *First, let me find out if luck is indeed on my side.* She rolled to the side of the bed and grabbed her mobile phone from the side table. She sat on the mattress with her legs crossed at the knees and searched the phone book. She finally found the number she was looking for.

'Hello? Is that Frankie?' A pause. 'Hi. How are you? I'm Meisu. And darling, I wish to thank you for the business you've given me so far.' A pause. 'Sure, sure … Yes. Now, I want to ask you something. Do you know any good tarot card reader? Price is not an issue. What's important is that he or she must be accurate.' Another pause. 'Yeah, I've got a personal problem.' She waved away a mosquito whining about her face. 'Master Ong in Central Market? Where's this place? Oh, I see … So, the train stops outside, just across the road. But I've to change trains? OK, thank you so much, darling. Bye-bye. Yes, see you soon.'

Thursday 8 April

Holding open a red parasol, Meisu walked the hundred yards from her condominium to the bus stop, and then got into a waiting taxi, closed her parasol and dropped it in her handbag. As the vehicle sped into the city, she looked out the window. Two towers shaped like cobs of corn reached into the sky, and further in the distance, a tower with a diamond-shaped peak shimmered in the scorching sun. The taxi entered an old quarter of the city. The meter ticked fourteen ringgit. Her stomach fluttered in anticipation of reaching her journey's end. Meisu realised that the architecture of the buildings outside her window had changed from the modern to the historical. Arches that looked like keyholes and shaped like basket-handles sat on top of some buildings. Others were mounted with elaborate domes.

After zigzagging through the narrow streets, the taxi deposited Meisu on the road outside the Central Market. As she walked into the crisp and cool air of the building, she found herself feeling suddenly refreshed.

'Where can I find Master Ong, the fortune teller?' she asked at the information counter. Many colourful brochures were arranged in plastic racks over the counter's desk.

A petite brown-skinned girl smiled back at her. 'Upstairs. His shop faces the Thai restaurant.'

Meisu walked up a staircase and past a line of stores selling pareos, kaftans and blouses in batik motifs before stopping outside Master Ong's. The soothsayer sat at a huge, antique desk, reading a Chinese newspaper. Behind him, a poster-sized physiognomy chart hung from a tack. On one side of the shop's wall hung a traditional calendar, consisting of a picture of a tiger and a stack of tear-away sheets for dates. The top sheet said 'Thursday, April 8'. The smoke from a piece of sandalwood incense stuck into a copper pot drifted into the fortune-teller's face.

He looked up. 'Come in, please,' he said, putting aside the newspaper. Master Ong looked like he was in his fifties, His hair was cropped short and had a few streaks of white, and his ear lobes were long. He wore a cherry-red long-sleeved kung fu shirt with a Mandarin collar and frog-closure buttons. His appearance inspired confidence in Meisu.

Meisu sat on a wooden chair placed across the soothsayer's desk. She scanned the contents of the desk and saw a copy of the *Chinese Almanac 2010*. Above the tome, on a mantelpiece, sat a golden statue of a deity, about six inches tall, and next to it was a small copper urn holding a lighted joss stick.

'What type of consultation do you want?' Master Ong asked. 'Tarot card? Palm reading? Face reading?' His voice sounded deep, like the strains of a tuba.

'How much for a tarot-card reading?'

'Thirty ringgit only. You can only ask one question. For the second question, I charge another thirty. Understand?'

'Yes.'

'So, what's your problem?'

She put her bag on her lap and placed her elbows on the desk. 'I would like to challenge a man to a card game. The stakes are high. Will I win?'

The soothsayer pushed a note pad and a ball pen across the desk to her. 'Write down your name and date of birth. Along with the details of the man you would like to challenge.'

'According to the Western or the Chinese lunar calendar?'

'Western date of birth.'

Meisu wrote her name both in English and in Chinese characters and then the details about her birth. She also wrote down Ouyang Lifu's year of birth.

Master Ong scrutinised the information provided by Meisu. 'You don't know Ouyang Lifu's date of birth?'

She shook her head.

'If I have his birth date, the readings can be more accurate.' From his desk drawer, the fortune teller took out a package; it was wrapped in cloth and was about half the size of a book. Meisu saw that it was a plastic cylinder containing wet tissues. He pried open the lid of the cylinder with his thumb. 'Please wipe your hands,' he instructed.

Meisu tugged out a piece of wet tissue from the cylinder and used it to wipe both her hands. She threw the crumpled tissue into a trashcan beside the desk.

Master Ong unwrapped a white towel to reveal a stack of laminated tarot cards. He held the deck facedown over the glowing joss stick and uttered what sounded like a question. He placed the cards on the table. 'Shuffle the cards with your left hand. At the same time, concentrate on your gambling opponent. Picture him in your mind.'

Meisu scrambled the cards on the desk, moving her palms in a clockwise and then an anti-clockwise direction. She then closed her eyes. The image of Ouyang Lifu's face, as gaunt as an opium addict's, appeared in her mind's eyes. 'OK, done,' she said.

The fortune-teller gathered the cards. 'Divide the cards into three piles. Use your right hand.'

Meisu cut the deck into three smaller piles.

'Which stack appeals to you the most?'

She pointed to the middle stack. 'This one.'

'Put that stack on top of the other two.'

Meisu obeyed him.

Master Ong picked up the deck and spread out seven cards in the shape of an ellipse. He leaned forward and gave the cards an once-over, then looked at Meisu.

'The first card shows your past. You've picked the World card, but it's reversed.' He placed his finger on an inverted card with a picture of a globe. 'You've taken a big step in changing your life. This could be either a change in location or a change in your work. You're now in a new phase. However, something or someone from the past is still affecting you in some way. Perhaps an ex-boyfriend? Or a family member? Or even a past experience. You understand?'

Meisu nodded. She had started to finger the locket around her neck nervously.

'Right now, you're determined to achieve your goals. Actually, there're plenty of opportunities for you to do so, but you've to create them. They won't fall onto your lap. Your energy level is also high, and you're optimistic. You might be a fighter, but that doesn't mean you should make enemies for yourself.' A pause. 'Now, a big project may be coming your way. Should anyone offer you a business partnership, consider it seriously. If you were to play a lottery, you've a good chance of winning.

'Here's the Devil card,' he said, pointing to a card. It had the picture of a man with a goat's head. 'I'm afraid this is not a positive card. Your gambling opponent may resort to cheating to win. He's very cunning and proud. He's a control freak. To him, losing face is like losing an arm. I'd advise you to be prepared for his dirty tricks.'

He frowned at Meisu as he moved on to the next card. 'I'm a bit concerned about this card.' He tapped at a Hanged Man card. The card showed a young man hanging upside down from a tree branch with a rope tied to his one leg. It was in an inverted position. 'Something unpleasant may happen within this period if you're not careful. Maybe you'll lose your handbag to a thief. Or you might be involved in a vehicle accident. Or your house might catch fire. Just be careful. Avoid travelling alone and going to the ATM at night. If possible, go pray at a temple. Ask for protection from the deities or from your ancestors. Understand?'

Meisu nodded glumly. Her skin tingled on hearing the soothsayer's warning.

Master Ong moved on to another card. He gave her a small smile. 'A man may come into your life pretty soon. See this? The Lover card,' he said, pointing to a card that showed a naked couple in embrace. 'There may be a romantic involvement but the relationship won't be easy. Both of you need to adjust to each other. He'll draw a lot of strength and support from you. I'd advise that you place your own needs first, but do take every chance you possibly can. This relationship could lead to a new and happy life for you. Do you understand?'

Meisu heard the shuffling of feet behind her, and turned to see a European couple standing at the entranceway of the shop.

Master Ong greeted them, 'Sit down, please. Just give me a minute.' His gaze then returned to the spread of cards before him. 'The last card is a Chariot,' he said. 'This is a good card. From its position, I believe it means victory.' The card showed a horse-drawn chariot driven by a man in battle armour.

'The victory will give you peace of mind and freedom in whatever you're doing. As long as you give the gamble your best shot and guard yourself against possible deceits, I expect that you will win.' A pause. 'That's all I have to say.'

Meisu opened her purse, fished out three ten-ringgit notes and placed them on the soothsayer's desk.

'Good luck to you,' Master Ong said to her. He gathered the spread of cards that had told him of Meisu's future and returned them to the deck.

Meisu thanked him, and then started down the corridor to browse the stores. She made a short stop at a shop selling handicrafts carved out of wood, seashell, coconut shell and cinnamon stick, but didn't find anything she wanted to buy. She proceeded to the food court and had a lunch of sizzling noodles and a glass of guava juice. Then she left for the ground floor and started to wander down the corridors, looking at more stores.

A clown in a polka-dot jumpsuit was standing outside one of the stores, handing out leaflets and balloon animals to passersby. As

Meisu walked past him, the clown – his eyes and muzzle painted in white to produce a wide-eyed expression, his mouth in a bright red smile – stepped towards her and stared at her bosom. He said something to her in Cantonese.

Meisu did not understand him. 'What did you say?' she demanded in English.

The clown repeated what he had said in English. 'Is that fashion? Wearing your grandma's push-up bra is obscene!'

'You shithead! Do you want me to call the security guard?' Meisu screamed at him. She then ran her hands down the skin-tight, pink sheath dress she was wearing and flaunted her curves to the clown. 'I'm not wearing a push-up. My tits are all natural. Your *mother* probably wears a ratty push-up bra.' Meisu stormed away before the clown could react to her outburst.

What would I do if I lost the gamble? Meisu wondered on the taxi-ride home. The answer was simple. She would simply scram from New Peng Hwa and street-walk in another part of the city. Maybe move to that island called Penang, where Lifu's tentacles could not reach her. Yehua and her friendly client, Frankie, could advise her of other options.

About midway through the ride, her cell phone rang.

'It's me – Weilai,' the voice said from the other end. 'I'm in a cab now, heading to your apartment. You're in, right?'

'Oh, I'm sorry. I forgot our appointment. But I'm on my way home now. Will get there in about forty minutes.'

When Meisu got back to her apartment, she found Weilai waiting downstairs in the lift foyer. The girl had a heavy-jowled face and wore a collared t-shirt and denim shorts. They exchanged pleasantries, and then took the lift to Meisu's apartment.

'The place is partially furnished,' Meisu said as she removed her shoes and placed them on a rack near the door. 'Where do you work?'

'A karaoke centre on Ipoh Road.'

They were standing in the living room. A plastic folding table and two chairs stood in the middle of the room. A fixed-line phone and two jars containing sachets of beverages sat on one corner of the table.

'I bought this stuff,' Meisu said, gesturing to the furniture.

Meisu and her visitor walked to the small kitchen. 'You can do simple cooking here, if you want to,' Meisu pointed to a butane camp stove next to the aluminium sink. She turned the stove on and then off to show Weilai that it worked.

'What happened to your apartment?' Meisu asked.

'The friend I was sharing it with got a lucky break. She is getting married. Her future husband's a Malaysian. She will move out by the end of the month, but I don't want to take over the tenancy. I'm not sure how long I'll be here.'

Meisu opened the fridge. 'There, plenty of space to store your food.' A bottle of cordial, an opened can of Ma Ling brand luncheon meat, a bottle of mineral water and three bottles of China-made Yue Sai skincare products were arranged on the fridge's top shelf.

'How did your friend meet her future husband?' Meisu asked as they entered the spare bedroom next to the kitchen.

'He was her regular client,' Weilai replied, looking around.

Meisu walked up to the window and opened the curtains. Beams of sunlight slanted onto the floor. 'This is the room I would like to sublet. My asking rent is eight hundred.' The room was fitted with a split air-conditioner, a wooden bed, a mattress with a sunken centre, a closet and a dresser with a chair.

'Can I bring clients back here once in a while?'

Meisu smiled. 'Sorry, that's not possible. If any resident notices this and complains, I'll get evicted.'

Weilai's face looked as though someone had told her that her credit card had been rejected. 'I'll consider the offer and get back to you.' She started to walk away from the bedroom. 'Thank you for showing me this nice place.'

When Weilai had left the apartment, Meisu changed into a loose-fitting and sleeveless cotton nightie. She lay on her bed, closed her eyes and tried to fall sleep. She couldn't. A word was buzzing inside her head, and would not let her sleep. *Marriage.* The word fluttered in her mind like a moth around the flame of a candle. Somewhere in this world, a man was waiting for her. *Where is he? How will I meet him?* It would be wonderful if he were a Chinese-Malaysian and if he were young, handsome and rich. *Would such a man disregard my past as a prostitute? Would such a man regard only my present as absolute?* The questions played over and over again in her head. As her mind became exhausted, the buzzing moths slowly flew away, and Meisu was finally able to doze off.

* * *

'Let me give it to you straight. A mainland-China girl had been murdered. Her mobile phone log shows that you called her on Monday. What was the purpose of your call?' Chu asked the plump man slouched in front of him.

Seated beside him, Sergeant June Qwong was typing in the man's name and other details from his identity card. Yesterday, after Chu had gotten hold of Caiqin's mobile number, he had instructed the sergeant to obtain an extract of the victim's call log from her telco. On the evening she had been murdered, Caiqin had received five phone calls – four before her death and one after. The owners of these mobile numbers had been called in to the station to give their official testimonies.

'Actually, I don't have much to tell you. She was just another hooker, one of many women I go to. I first met her at New Peng Hwa a couple of weeks back, and she took me to Springtime Inn. Her service was not bad so I asked for her contact number. On Monday, around nine or so, I called to ask whether she was working. She said yes, so I went up to her pad. That was at about 10:30 p.m. After we had sex, I left.'

June typed in the man's statement at a rapid-fire pace.

'Why did you go to her flat this time? Why not a motel?' Chu asked.

'I wanted to avoid paying for the room, and that was OK with her. So, she gave me her apartment's address.'

'When you arrived at her apartment, did you see anyone else in there with her?'

'No, sir.'

'Did you notice anyone hanging outside the building? Or in the lift foyer?'

'No, sir.'

'During the time you were with her, did you see her using her cell phone? Maybe she mentioned a name or some other detail while talking on the phone?'

'Yes, her mobile did ring while we were having sex. She answered the call. All she said was "OK, see you".'

Chu considered the man sitting before him for a moment, then dismissed him from the interrogation. *No point wasting more time with this tub of lard. He's useless.*

'Should you recall anything else, please contact me or the sergeant,' he said, as he handed back the identity card to the fat man.

June turned to the roly-poly. 'Mister, hold on for a second. You need to sign this statement.' The printer behind her spat out a sheet of paper, and June slid it across the table to the interviewee. The man scribbled on it, then left the room quickly.

The sergeant turned to Chu. 'The missed call the hooker received came from a public phone booth.'

'Where?'

'Bukit Bintang.'

'That might be the killer. How many people even use public phones nowadays? It seems like he's smart enough not to use his hand phone.'

'Well, if he's smart, tracking him down won't be too easy.'

A buck-toothed constable showed the second interviewee into the room. He was a skinny runt in his mid-twenties, with long and untidy hair that reached his collar and with a constant leer on his face. He wore a faded denim jacket, and a Bell helmet with a plastic visor dangled from his one arm.

'Can I have your I.C. please?' June asked.

The skinny man fished out his wallet, pulled out his identity card and tossed it to the sergeant.

'Mind your manners,' June snapped at him.

'Sit,' Chu instructed. He pointed to the empty chair in front of his desk.

The skinny man sat down, crossing his legs at his knees, and placed his helmet on the table. 'What's up, man?' he said, smacking a piece of gum between his teeth.

Chu caught a whiff of stale sweat from the man, mixed in with the scent of cheap cologne. He almost gagged. 'On Monday night, you visited a prostitute whose working name's Xiaoqian. Her mobile phone log has your number. Can you tell me what happened that night?'

The skinny man suddenly sat upright, clasped his hands together and rested them on his knee. 'Oh yeah, I read about that chick's murder in the paper. It was printed in a small column. It's really sad, man. This Xiaoqian performed very well. I've shagged her several times. On that night, I brought along my sex toys too. She was fantastic, responded well to the Rabbit Vibrator. That's a very noisy one.' He chuckled. 'After we were done, I left. Of course, I didn't kill her. In fact, we left the apartment together, walking hand in hand. My Harley Davison was parked downstairs. As I was riding out, I saw her walk towards Pudu Road.'

'How did you get her phone number?'

'I got it from a sex forum. A guy in a chat room gave it to me. Told me she was good.'

'How can I be sure you did not go back to her apartment?'

The skinny man scowled. 'What the hell are you getting at, man? You can check with my sugar mummy. She was waiting for me when I got back to the condo. We made whoopee and then stayed in all night.'

'Did you see anyone suspicious hanging around the hooker's place?' Chu pressed on.

The man thought about it, rolling his eyes upward, chewing into his gum. 'Um ... Let me see ... No. I don't think so.'

'Why do you need to think about this?'

'Hey, stop being a smart alec, man.' The skinny man's eyebrows shot up angrily. 'I wanted to be sure, OK? I did see a few foreign coolies in the lift lobby. On second thought, they were probably tenants – not suspicious characters, as you put it.'

'Sign your statement and get out!' Chu was running out of patience. *If the video camera was not on right now, I would have punched this bastard, made him choke on his own teeth.*

'Whatever, man.' The man scribbled his signature onto his statement and then tossed the pen to June.

Chu gritted his teeth. 'Who's next?'

'No need to get your knickers in a twist,' June advised with a smile. 'Anger's bad for your blood pressure.'

Chu sighed wearily.

A soft knock sounded at the door. A white-haired man wearing a knitted sweater crawled in, balancing himself on a walking stick.

Chu's mouth slackened and his eyes widened. 'Take a seat, Pops,' he mocked.

The old man sat with his hands clasped onto the handle of his walking stick. 'Good morning, gentleman and lady.' His voice crackled like an old rooster's. His white hair was combed straight back from the forehead. From his hip pocket, he pulled out his identity card and placed it in front of Chu. 'I'm Amos Ang, a pensioner. How can

I help you?'

Without looking at the identity card, Chu pushed it toward June. He stared at the geezer. 'A China-doll prostitute was found dead on Monday night. Her phone record shows that you made a call to her that evening.'

'Xiaoqian's dead? My goodness, the poor girl! She was like a granddaughter to me.'

'How do you know Xiaoqian?'

The old man put the stick across his knees and leaned back against the chair. 'I first met her a few weeks ago, when I was eating dinner at a hawker stall on Glutton Street. To be precise, the stall sold *bak kut teh* – the soup's extremely flavourful. Xiaoqian walked up to me as I was getting done and offered to sell sex, an offer I accepted. She then took me to her apartment.' He smiled at Chu. 'After the first fling, she gave me her contact number. Then, last Saturday, my daughter-in-law had made some double-boiled farm chicken spiced with old cucumber and ginseng for me. She said the soup promotes longevity.' The geezer flashed Chu a lecherous grin, revealing a set of teeth the colour of lemons. 'The soup also boosted my libido, so I decided to visit Xiaoqian again. I phoned to invite her to eat claypot chicken rice with me at Sayur Road, and she accepted. After a quick bite, we went to boom-boom in her apartment.'

'What time was that?'

The geezer's white eyebrows drew together as he made an effort to remember. 'I entered her apartment quite early, around eight. Eight something. I might have been her first customer that night.'

While June typed these details into the computer, the old man took out a handkerchief from his pocket and dabbed at his eyes. 'She was a sweet girl.' He blew his nose into it.

'Did you notice anyone near her place? Anyone suspicious?'

'No, I didn't see anyone there.' He paused and passed a hand over his face. 'I'm sorry I can't help you. Can I go now?' His voice was choked with emotion.

'Sure, Pops. Just sign the statement before you go.' The old man took out a pair of reading glasses from his shirt pocket to read the paper placed in front of him. He signed unsteadily with a shaking hand, and then rose to his feet. Sergeant June got up too, held the door open for the old man. As he started to waddle away on his walking stick, he turned around and said, 'If I recall anything that might help you nail the killer, I'll come in again.'

Chu waved his hand. 'Sure. We appreciate your co-operation.'

'We've a fourth interviewee,' June said after the geezer had shut the door behind him. 'He's a bartender. Called the victim at 3:15 a.m.'

The bartender, a handsome bachelor, worked at Bukit Bintang Road. He gave them a brief statement. A friend had given him Xiaoqian's contact number, said she gave great service. After he had cleaned up the bar for the night, he had called Xiaoqian but found that her phone was switched off. He didn't bother to leave her a message. He called it a night and went back to his apartment. 'The lift lobby at my place is fitted with CCTV cameras. You can view the recordings to verify my statement,' he said. 'I'm telling you the truth. I never met the dead girl.'

* * *

Big Dog escorted Meisu to the headquarters of the Red Centipede Society. She had accosted the bouncer at Ace Electronics Building and asked him to take her there. When Big Dog had checked with Lifu about this over the phone, the triad godfather had agreed to meet Meisu.

Meisu saw that a young woman was squeezing Lifu's feet, which he had rested on a rosewood stool. The woman sat on a small round ottoman, facing him. Beside Lifu was a tea table holding a dark clay teapot and three cups filled with tea. The fragrance of jasmine hung in the air.

As Meisu and Big Dog approached Lifu, the reflexologist turned to look at them for a moment. She was fair-skinned and pretty, and looked to be in her early twenties. 'Shall I continue, Mr. Ouyang?' she asked in Mandarin.

'Yes, please do.'

The young woman continued massaging the soles of his feet.

Lifu jerked his chin upward at Meisu. 'Yes, what can I do for you?'

'I would like to make a counter-proposal.' Meisu paused and threw an uncomfortable glance at the reflexologist.

'Yes, please speak up. We have no secrets here.'

'Instead of paying you a protection fee every month, I will make myself available to you sexually – at any time you might want my services – if you allow me to conduct business freely at New Peng Hwa.'

Lifu regarded her for a moment: Meisu had on a tight purple dress with a neckline that plunged down to her belt buckle. 'Listen, you slut, don't take me for a young fool!' He slapped one arm of his chair with an open palm. 'I've more supply of sex than I can handle.

What do you have that my girls don't?'

Meisu's heart started to pound. 'I'm sorry I underestimated the pretty flowers you already have in your possession. In that case, I would like to present my second proposal.' She took a deep breath. 'I understand you're a gambling man, and also a man of honour. Does that mean you'll not disgrace the Ouyang surname or the reputation of the Red Centipede by reneging on an agreement?'

'Naturally. Or I wouldn't be sitting here in this chair today, would I? Secret society dealings are based on trust and mutual respect.'

'Thank you for the reassurance, Mr. Ouyang Lifu. In that case, I would like to challenge you to a game of blackjack. If you win two out of three hands, I'll pay you the protection fee. But if you lose, I'll be free to work in New Peng Hwa without any interference from you. Would you like to accept my challenge?'

'I admire your boldness, Miss Meisu. But why should I accept your challenge? My men can continue to ... *persuade* you until you agree to pay.'

'But would that earn you respect from the other dragon heads? Let's fight fair, shall we?'

Lifu narrowed his eyes, considering her offer.

'Big Dog and this reflexologist are our witnesses,' Meisu continued. Lifu shot a glance at Big Dog, who was standing a few feet away from Meisu.

Meisu turned to look at the bouncer. She saw him run his hand through his hair, tensed, at a loss for words. 'How about 8 p.m. tomorrow? At New Peng Hwa. We'll play in front of your men and your night flowers.'

'What kind of game are you up to here?' Lifu demanded. 'This is such a trivial matter. Why do you want to make a public spectacle out of it?'

'Are you scared of losing?' Meisu smiled wryly. She decided to try another tack. 'The event will generate publicity for New Peng Hwa. When word gets around, more customers will come into the food court tomorrow. Just think about the popularity this win will bring you.'

Lifu took her bait this time. He thumped his hairy fists on the tea table. 'Fine, then. I'll call the Chinese newspapers and ask them to cover the event.'

'Thank you for accepting my offer, Mr. Ouyang. So let's lay the rules now?' She looked at Lifu in the eye, and he nodded his consent. 'The first rule – we'll play with a new deck of cards. The KK supermarket opposite the road sells playing cards. I've already checked with them. The second rule – neither you nor I will handle the cards. We'll pick a volunteer from New Peng Hwa to act as our dealer. This person must be approved by the both of us, and he or she will use a dealing shoe. This will make sure that the cards cannot be dealt from the bottom of the deck. The third rule – the cards will be opened only after the players have received them. After each hand, the drawn cards will be replaced and the deck reshuffled,' Meisu finished. 'Are you gentleman enough to agree to all these rules?'

'You've done your homework well, Miss Meisu.' Lifu grinned at her. 'These are fair rules, indeed. Yes, I agree to them. I'll meet you tomorrow at New Peng Hwa. I'll get one of my men to buy a dealing shoe.' He paused. 'If you would like to pray for some good luck, I'd recommend that you go to the Buddha Jayanti Temple.'

As Meisu turned to leave, Lifu let out a loud, mocking laugh.

Friday 9 April

Chu parked his car at Radius International Hotel and started to walk on the kerb, against the traffic. The evening crowd was beginning to gather at Bukit Bintang Hill. The music from the clubs was spilling onto the sidewalk. The dance bars along the drag had their doors open, ready to swallow the party animals that walked by. Friday nights were always good for such business. Ahead of Chu, lay the popular Crazy Legs Club. Within minutes, he had slipped through its doors.

Several of the tables around the dance floor were occupied. Chu sauntered to the bar. The bartender was tall and lean, and wore a navy-blue vest. His body looked like it could be bent into a knot. 'I'm looking for a man,' Chu said to him.

'Go to the Purple Boy pub then. That's a gay hangout. It's just down the road.'

'That's not what I meant.' Chu took out a folded piece of paper from his hip pocket. He flipped it open and pointed to the picture. 'Have you seen this man?'

'Who're you?' A wary look flashed in the bartender's eyes.

Chu pulled out his police card. 'I'm Inspector Daniel Chu from the C.I.D, and I am currently investigating a murder. Now, look at this picture and tell me if you know this man?'

The barman grimaced as he looked at the photofit. 'Nope. We get hundreds of customers every night. Impossible to remember all the faces.'

'Where's your manager?' Chu slipped the sketch back into his pocket. 'I want to talk to him.'

'He's not in yet.' A nervous tic tugged at the corner of the bartender's mouth.

'What about the *mamasan*?'

'She's in a meeting now.' He pulled out mugs from under the bar and arranged them in rows.

'Will she be long?'

'No idea.'

Chu took out a matchbook and waved it in the bartender's face. 'The man in the photofit was here a couple of nights ago. He left this behind at the scene of the crime.'

The barman pointed to a glass bowl full of matchbooks placed at the end of the bar. 'Any customer can grab one of those, if he wants to.' He shrugged. 'It can even get passed on from one person to another.' He waved to a chair. 'You can either wait for Mummy or you can come back another night.'

Chu looked at his watch. It was still early. He decided to wait. Half an hour rolled by.

Suddenly, a drum roll thundered on the small stage before him, and music blared into the hall. A coyote dancer, wrapped in a red pencil-skirt and illuminated by a spotlight, climbed onto the stage and started gyrating her pelvis to the quick staccato beats of the music. Her halter top was no bigger than a bandana.

A stout man, holding a fistful of money notes, climbed onto the stage. The dancer stopped dancing for a moment, letting him slip the notes into her cleavage. The stout man grinned then climbed off stage. The dancer started to move her hips again, in the shape of a figure eight. A man with blond hair and a black moustache strutted up to her and put a string of stapled cash notes around her neck. The dancer lifted his chin with her finger and drew him closer, like she was going to kiss him, but when the man pouted his lips, she pushed his face away. She then jiggled her breasts at him teasingly. Smiling, the blond man put two fingers to his lips and gently touched the dancer's forehead with them.

Chu looked away from the dancer's antics. He saw a woman approaching him, weaving her way between the tables. The woman, with her hooked nose and hollow cheeks, had the appearance of a wading bird.

'Good evening. I hear you're looking for me,' she said when she reached Chu. 'I'm Mummy Machiko. Can I get you a drink?'

'Sure.'

'What would you like?'

'A Pepsi, please.'

The bartender dropped a straw into the bottle and set it with a thud before Chu then walked away.

Machiko flashed the barman an angry glare. 'I'm sorry about James. He's an ex-jailbird and doesn't like cops.' She smiled apologetically at Chu. Her eyes were bright and lively. 'So, what brings you here, Inspector?'

Chu sucked at the straw. 'I'm looking for this man.' He showed her the suspect's photofit. 'We know he was here recently because he took back one of your matchbooks.'

'Oh, yes, I remember him. He came here on Sunday night. He booked Jessica, I think. Yes, it was Jess. He told me he wanted a GRO with big fun-bags,' she chuckled. 'Oh, his language was from the gutter.'

'Did he pay by cash or credit card?'

'Cash.'

'Can I talk to Jessica for a second?'

'Sure.' Machiko fished out her mobile and pressed a button on it, 'Jess, please come to the bar for a minute.'

Jessica appeared from the back of the club and walked towards the *mamasan*. Her dress was loose at the shoulders, tapering into a slim waist.

She looks like a goddess. Chu was unable to pull his eyes off her slender legs.

'Yes, Mummy?' Jessica's oval face was warped in a curious frown.

'This is Detective Inspector Daniel Chu. Could you tell him about the skinny client who booked you last week? The pale guy with long hair falling on his forehead, remember?'

'Yes, I remember, Mummy.' Jessica nodded.

Chu held the sketch up for her to see. 'Is this the same guy?'

'Yes, that's him.' Jessica leaned against the bar, resting her elbow on it. 'He wanted to book me out, but I wasn't interested. I didn't like that creep.' She took a deep breath to calm herself; Chu noticed her big breasts pressing against the folds of her dress as she did so.

'When he kissed me, he used his tongue to push a pill into my mouth. He said it was a vitamin. But I am not stupid. I spat the pill out when he wasn't looking. I knew it was Ecstasy.'

'Did he tell you anything about himself? Name? Occupation?' Chu put the sketch back in his pocket.

'He asked me to call him by some Christian name, obviously a fake one. He didn't talk much about himself.'

'Did he speak in English to you?'

'Well, a mix of English and Cantonese.'

'How long was he here?'

'About an hour or so. After some chit-chat, he asked how much it would cost to take me out after closing time. I told him I don't go out with clients. He was displeased, muttered some obscenities and left.' Jessica took another deep breath. 'I'm sorry I can't help you much.'

'Thanks, honey,' Chu said. He then turned to the *mamasan*, 'Is there a CCTV here?'

'Yes, we've one above the cashier's counter, so we can keep an eye on him. Another camera faces the entrance to the store. We keep quite a lot of expensive liquor there.'

'I see. Well, thank you for your help, ladies.' Chu got off the stool, ready to leave the club.

'Anything for you, Inspector. When you're off-duty, do pop in here sometime to chill out,' said the *mamasan*. 'We've many beautiful hostesses here to serve you.'

* * *

It was a little after eight when Meisu arrived at New Peng Hwa. Big Dog greeted her and showed her to a table that held a plastic dealing shoe and a 'Reserved' sign. Meisu took her seat at the table.

Like a champion boxer entering a ring, Ouyang Lifu strutted in a while later, dressed in a traditional tunic with the golden motif of a centipede woven onto its breast pocket. He was accompanied by two of his henchmen, their strong arms marked by centipede tattoos.

Both players consented to having a tootsie buy them a new deck of cards from KK Supermart. When the deck was brought to them, Meisu examined it carefully. She then selected a roast-duck hawker from one of the stalls to be their dealer. The hawker was a stout woman of about forty-five. She sat between the two gamblers.

'Do you know how to shuffle cards professionally?' Meisu asked.

With the deft movements of her fingers, the roast-duck hawker demonstrated the weave shuffle. Lifu nodded, indicating that he agreed for the woman to be their dealer. The hawker-dealer executed a table-riffle shuffle and plunked the deck on the dealing shoe.

'Shall we begin?' Meisu asked. Her face was fixed on Lifu's. *I'll win this, I'll win this, I'll win this.* She was wearing a red belted shirt-dress and matching watermelon-red pumps. Red was her lucky colour.

'Yes.' In one corner of Lifu's mouth was an ivory cigarette holder, from which protruded a clove butt, letting out its sweet-smelling smoke.

A crowd of people had gathered around the table by now: gambling aficionados, triad members, johns-to-be and floozies were watching them with eager eyes, some standing on their feet, others standing on chairs in the second and third rows. The spectators plied questions to each other in half-whispers about who were playing and about the purpose of their gamble.

'Head or tail?' Meisu spun a fifty-sen coin on the square table.

'Head,' Lifu barked.

The coin landed face down.

'First Hand! I'll deal to Miss Meisu first.' The dealer used two pudgy fingers to slide a card across the table to Meisu. Then she dispensed a second card to Lifu.

The players flipped open their cards. Meisu got a ten, Lifu a seven.

The hawker-dealer whipped out the second cards, let them skitter across the smooth table. Meisu got an eight, Lifu a six.

Lifu glanced at Meisu's cards. 'Hit!'

The hawker-dealer flicked another card to Lifu, who caught it with his palm. He opened it, and his eyes widened. The value was a nine. He was busted. The crowd murmured anxiously.

The dealer retrieved the dealt cards and reshuffled the deck for the second hand.

'Go, Meisu, go!' someone yelled from the crowd.

'Second Hand!' the hawker-dealer shouted. The first card that went to Meisu was a nine. Lifu got a five, and his jaw dropped.

Meisu's second card glided into her open palm. She slapped the card with her palm. '*Gong ka*!' She opened it to reveal an eight, and her throat felt tight and dry.

Lifu's second card was a three. The triad godfather grimaced and gave a slight shake of the head. 'Fire away!' he instructed the dealer. His third card was a ten. Lifu grinned, and a babble rose from the crowd.

The hawker-dealer reclaimed the cards and strip-shuffled them.

'Miss Meisu, I want to raise the stake for the final hand,' Lifu said.

'How?'

'Let us bet our last finger.' He raised his little pinkie in front of his face. 'The loser cuts it off. The original stakes also stand, of course.'

The crowd erupted in loud gasps and screams, horrified by Lifu's proposal. 'Oh Lord Buddha, blood's going to spill!' someone cried. 'Miss Meisu, don't do it!' a female voice shrieked. 'Keep playing. Let the game continue!' a deep voice yelled.

Meisu's stomach twisted into a tight knot. Unable to make up her mind, she opened her locket to glimpse at the inscription and the red rat engraved inside. If there ever was a time when her locket could bring her luck, it should be now. She closed the locket and gave Lifu a wary look. 'You're not serious, are you?'

'I'm dead serious.' Lifu's eyes shone like steel. He turned to a tall triad henchman next to him. 'Ah-Keong, please borrow a cleaver and a chopping block from one of the hawkers.'

The man returned with the equipment quickly. 'Here they are, Mr. Ouyang.' He placed the heavy wooden block and the gleaming cleaver in one corner of the table.

'Miss Meisu, you can still back out and concede defeat, if you want to.' Lifu flashed Meisu a mocking smile.

Her fingers still touched the locket around her neck. She recalled Master Ong's prediction. 'I accept your terms,' she said. Her will was growing stronger, numbing her fear.

'OK, good. Let's proceed with the game.'

'Final Hand!' announced the hawker-dealer. 'Loser chops off his or her last finger.'

Her announcement was followed by a pin-drop silence. The dealer whipped the first card to Lifu. With a stony face, he flipped it open to show a nine. The second card went to Meisu. It was a ten. The hawker-dealer, with sweat popping onto her head, slid a second card to Lifu. It was a seven. The dealer glanced at Meisu, wiping her sweat off her brows with her sleeves. She flicked Meisu's second card onto the table. '*Gong ka*!' Meisu yelled. The card was again a ten.

The hawker-dealer's eyes bore into Lifu. 'Mr. Ouyang, do you want a hit?'

The triad godfather took a deep breath and nodded. The dealer pushed the card, the most important one in this gamble, towards Lifu. He put his hand over the closed card, his thumb pressed against one corner.

Meisu stared at the card, her eyes refusing to blink. As Lifu slowly gazed down, she noticed that his face had turned ashen.

The triad master suddenly looked up and rubbed his eyes vigorously, as if something had fallen into them.

'Police! Police! A raid! Run!' a voice suddenly shouted.

The crowd scattered, and everyone ran helter-skelter. In the commotion, a thin beetle-browed man made his way to the gambling table and pushed the cards to the tiled floor, scattering them.

Lifu got up and started to walk away, his henchmen trailing behind him. Meisu sprang to her feet in a rush, causing her chair to topple over.

She darted ahead of Lifu, blocking his way out of the place. His henchmen glared at Meisu, but she ignored them. She wagged her finger at the triad godfather, 'Mr. Ouyang, you're a cheat! You took a look at your card and knew you were going to lose. So you signalled your men to create a diversion, didn't you? So you could escape.'

Lifu did not answer her. He sidestepped her, but Meisu cornered him again.

'What rubbish!' Lifu roared. 'I swear to the Sky God that I didn't open nor see the card. I didn't plan this diversion, Miss Meisu. But it does make the game a stalemate. You better go home, pretty flower. The cops will be here any minute.'

Meisu turned to the triad godfather's bodyguards. 'My brothers, you witnessed what happened. Did your master gamble fair?'

One thug looked from Meisu to Lifu, his lips pressed into a slight grimace. The second hooligan scratched his cheek and peered down at his sneakers, trying to be noncommittal. Lifu started walking away again.

'Mr. Ouyang, haven't you heard the Confucius saying, "forced with what is right, to leave it undone shows a lack of courage"?'

Lifu stopped and turned to face Meisu. He sighed, shoving his hands into the pockets of his tunic. 'Alright, alright … Out of magnanimity, I will allow you to solicit clients at New Peng Hwa without having to pay me a protection fee. However, keep your mouth shut about all this. Don't go round spreading rumours that I cheated. Or I'll have to withdraw this privilege.' He turned to his hoodlums. 'Please tell Big Dog and the others that I've exempted Miss Meisu from paying the protection fee.'

* * *

Alvin was seated at a hawker stall on Alor Road, watching the traffic pass by. Tourists strode on the sidewalk, weaving between countless tables, while cars and bikes crawled on the road's asphalt. He turned back to his dinner, catching a beef ball with his chopsticks and bringing it to his mouth. *Tonight is going to be great*! Fridays nights were usually great. The studio was closed on the weekends, and he could get as sloshed as he wanted. The painter sipped his mug of beer. It had been diluted by the melting ice cubes, and was a bit too subtle and weak for his taste. He liked the sting and instant warmth of neat liquor. *Well, the beer is good enough for now. The hard liquor can wait. The night is still young after all.*

A man in his early twenties strolled by then stopped to cast his eyes around the hawker stall. He came over to Alvin's table. 'Can I sit here?' he asked. 'The other tables are full.' He had on a Hawaii shirt of floral design and beige slacks.

'Sure,' Alvin said from over his steaming bowl.

'Thank you.' The man turned to the hawker's Indonesian assistant, 'One bowl of beef noodles, please. With extra tripe.' He flashed a smile at Alvin and said, 'You come here for dinner often?'

The guy looks like a Joe Sixpack. Alvin observed the man's parted hair plastered down on his head with cream and took in the pungent scent of his aftershave.

'No, I wanted a change of scenery. To eat something different. Chinatown's my regular spot.'

'I was supposed to go with a friend for some sexy Vietnam GROs tonight. They're the best in KL. But he had to cancel in the last minute.'

'How sexy is sexy?' Alvin poured more beer into his glass. *This is quite a coincidence.* After dinner, Alvin had intended to book a hot chick at a hanky-hanky spa too.

'It's a karaoke bar. Just a fifteen-minute walk from here. Customers can ask for bathroom services.' The man grinned at Alvin. 'Why don't we go there together? We can also play billiards and darts at the place.' The man's bowl of beef-ball noodles arrived, and he started to eat. 'We can split the bill down the middle so it won't dent our pockets.' He put down his chopsticks and extended his right hand toward Alvin. 'I'm Sam Chia. You are?'

It had been months since Alvin had held a woman in his arms. He clasped his hand and gave it an excited shake. It felt like a bag of nuts and bolts. 'I think that's a great idea, Sam. My name's Alvin Au.'

Sam's dry lips turned upwards in a sly grin. 'I'm a regular there, at Marigold KTV. I can tell you who their best GROs are, and who is most fun to play with.'

Alvin and his new-found friend ate their beef-noodles quickly and then rushed off together.

Soon, they found themselves sitting inside a karaoke room, ogling at the six fair-skinned GROs who stood before them. The thickset *papasan* – pink-faced and sporting a sinister-looking goatee – introduced the pleasure-givers to them.

'The first girl is Phuong; she's gives excellent bathroom service.' The GRO wriggled two fingers and smiled at them.

'The next one is Suzy; she offers super-high GFE.' The girl pouted her lips and blew them a kiss.

'Trang is the petite one. She's a sex commando. As good as the Viet Congs, if you know what I mean.' The *papasan* chortled at his feeble attempt at a joke.

'The fourth girl is called Julie, and she's our hot number because she speaks good English. And she's always eager to please.' Braless and wearing a halter top, Julie placed her hands under her saggy breasts and bounced them up and down a few times.

The hustler then pointed at a girl wearing a knee-length prom frock. 'Ngoc is new in this line. She is shy but is full of lust.' Ngoc smiled teasingly at them then hid a part of her face with her long hair, as if she were suddenly shy.

The *papasan* jerked his jaw in the direction of a lanky girl. 'The last one is called Mong, and she's a former car-show model. She arrived from Hanoi only a few days ago.' The girl hitched her miniskirt up to reveal her crotchless panties. Alvin's jaw slackened, while Sam's eyes grew wide.

'All the girls here are younger than twenty-five,' the *papasan* finished.

'I'll take Trang,' Sam said immediately. The sex commando stepped forward and sat on the settee beside him.

'I want Mong,' said Alvin, and he extended his hand to her. The former model smiled suddenly, revealing teeth that looked like a row of bombed houses. Alvin's insides churned. *Damn it! I've made the wrong choice. Kissing her would just make me chuck up.*

The GRO accepted Alvin's hand and plopped down next to him. *Well, she'll have to do for tonight,* Alvin comforted himself and slipped his arm around Mong's waist. She snuggled up to him.

The *papasan* and the other girls took their leave. With an arm draped over his sex kitten, Sam scanned the menu. 'What would you like? Order anything you want, darling.' He then looked up at the Myanmar waiter standing beside them, dressed in a bow tie and a black vest. 'Budweiser, big bottle, and a sirloin steak, please.'

Three hours thus passed, with lots of eating and drinking and fondling and petting and French-kissing.

Sam, who ate like a starved lion and drank like a man stranded in a desert, suddenly got up from the settee. 'Excuse me, Alvin, I need to pee.' He left the karaoke room and headed to the washroom.

The minute hand on Alvin's watch moved around half a circle, but Sam did not return. Alvin went to search for him but his new-found friend was not in the man's washroom or at the bar. He staggered down the hall to the reception. 'Oh, that handsome guy wearing a Hawaii shirt? He left about half an hour ago,' a girl wearing a bunny-ear head band informed him.

Shit, that bastard was a freeloader! What should I do now? Two GROs booked for three hours would burn a four-hundred-ringgit big hole in his wallet. And that was excluding the booze, the chow, the room rental and the *papasan*'s tip. *Should I slip away quietly?* Alvin considered it. It would be a new and exciting experience for him, a risk he had never taken before in his life. *How else will my life be enriched if not by new experiences?*

Alvin looked around. He did not see any bouncer nearby. The three waiters at the reception had their backs turned towards him, their attention focused on the tables. The bunny-girl he had spoke to was looking down at the bar's reservation book. *Great, the coast is clear. Here goes ...* Alvin began to slink away towards the twin swing-door and was about to push it open when a hand grabbed his shoulder.

'Sir, your bill has not been paid.' The goateed *papasan* gripped his wrist and started to pull him to the cashier counter with the strength of a bull.

Alvin gulped, shuffling along with the man. 'I'm sorry, I forgot. I guess I have had too much to drink.' He produced his credit card to the bunny-girl at the reception. He then picked up the ball pen chained to the counter by a spiral cord and waited for the slip.

'Sir, your card's been rejected.' The bunny-girl shoved his credit card back to him grimly.

Shit. He had forgotten to make the minimum payment for two months. Alvin retrieved his card and dug into his pocket for his wallet. 'I'll pay cash then.'

The goateed *papasan* stretched out an open palm towards Alvin. 'My mandatory tip is thirty.'

Alvin counted the notes and handed them over. Only eighteen ringgit was left in his wallet after the payment. He would need the services of an ATM to pay for the cab back home.

Stepping outside the karaoke bar, he broke into a smile. He realised that he had remembered to save his PIN into his hand phone. *Smart move.* He ambled to an ATM kiosk on Bukit Bintang Road.

Alvin entered the kiosk, took out his wallet and fished out his ATM card. When he stood in front of the machine, an 'Out of Order' message stared back at him. He moved to the next machine. The message leered at him again: 'Out of Order'.

He tottered out, feeling helpless. *Maybe I could phone one of my former workmates and ask for him to pick me up.* He decided against this immediately. They were all a bunch of back-stabbers and brown-nosers. Two years ago at the New Year's Eve office party, he had gotten drunk and crashed out in the washroom. When he had staggered out several hours later, he had found himself naked from the waist down with only a paper cup covering his genitals. They had all laughed at him, had thought that their immature prank was hilarious. *To hell with them! Those bastards deserve to fry in hell*!

Swaying on the kerb, Alvin looked around, unable to decide what he should do. He dreaded sleeping in his studio again and having to wake up with aches all over his body. There was a taxi rank ahead. He made his way there slowly and climbed into the back of the first one he found. 'I've only eighteen ringgit left. I want to go to Air Panas Road. Will this be sufficient to cover the fare?' he asked the driver.

'I don't know. Depends on the meter. I'll let you know when the meter hits eighteen, and you get out. Is that OK with you?'

Alvin thought about it for a moment. Perhaps eighteen would bring him pretty close to home. He could walk the remaining distance. 'Sure.'

'Payment first.'

Alvin tossed the money onto the front passenger seat, then leaned back and closed his eyes.

After what seemed like ten minutes, the driver pulled over outside Tawakal Hospital. 'Here's where you get off.'

'So fast? Are you sure that your meter's accurate?'

'Take a look yourself!' The driver pointed to the meter. 'After midnight, fares carry a fifty percent surcharge. Get out! Get out!'

Alvin crawled out of the cab. He stared ahead at the road. *Jesus Christ! I am almost three miles away from my place.* He started to tramp ahead, his legs shaking like a washing machine on a spin cycle. His feet carried him in an unsteady, weaving pattern past Chiao Nan Chinese Primary School, a petrol station, another petrol station, then past Galleria Complex. Sweat started to trickle in rivulets down his back. He sat down on the iron bench of a bus stop. Resting his hands on his knees, Alvin lowered his head and wheezed for several minutes. He heard a dog howl in the distance. Finally, when he had caught his breath, he wiped away the sweat on his forehead with his handkerchief and resumed his journey, tottering past the shuttered doors of hardware stores, past the rusting accordion doors of seafood restaurants, past Setapak Police Station, past Courts Megastore, past Christ Lutheran Church, past a showroom with gleaming cars parked inside it. At occasional intervals, he saw gangs race down the road on underbone motorcycles, spitting road dust and carbon monoxide onto him. *How many miles more? Possibly two.* His feet burned as if the kerb was molten lava, and a fireball seemed stuck in his chest. He sucked in and ejected air in hot gasps. He pressed on.

As he turned the corner of Air Panas Road, he saw his condominium block ahead.

He kicked off his shoes quickly when he entered his condo and went straight to the fridge in the kitchen. He carried out a six-pack of beer, put it on the living room table and flung himself on the couch. He popped a can and gulped it down. After finishing the sixth can, he sprang into the shower to wash away his sweat. Then, still dripping with water, he clambered to the bedroom and threw himself on the bed.

Saturday 10 April

The clocked showed 3:15 p.m. The pale man was seated before his computer. He pressed a button. The CD-ROM bay slid open, and he placed a CD onto it. It was a Japanese bondage movie, one of his favourites.

He clicked 'Play' then turned down the volume of the speakers so that his neighbours would not hear the sounds. He leaned back on his chair, reached for a can of beer and took a long swig of it. As he watched the porn star gag and tie-up the woman, the pale man started to grind his teeth, in anticipation of what was about to happen. The porn star then brought out a long whip, and the pale man's muscles quivered in delight. *Yes, the whore needs to be punished. She should be taught a lesson.*

When the film was over, he remained seated there, staring blankly at the screen. He thought about the girl with the big breasts he had seen in Central Market two days ago. The veins on his neck bulged out with rage. *That bloody bitch! How dare she insult my beloved Mama?* It was odd that she did not understand Cantonese. *Is she a foreigner? Why was she dressed like that?* He remembered her tight pink dress and her huge breasts popping out of it. *Is she a prostitute?*

She must be. If she were a prostitute, she deserved to be punished, just like the woman in the film.

Whores are evil. They all needed to be punished. His mind returned to that fateful day in February. The day he had finally snapped. The day he had finally decided to start killing them.

The pale man had been driving back from work. 'Here's a traffic update. Tun Razak Road is badly jammed because of an accident involving a lorry and a motorcycle. All motorists should avoid that area if possible. Try to use alternative routes. Now, let's get back to some more music. Coming up is the K-pop song "After School" by Diva!'

The pale man switched off the radio. He didn't like that Korean song. He threw a glance at the rear view mirror, squinting at the glare of the bright headlights. A long stream of vehicles was trailing behind him. He gazed at the slow-moving vehicles ahead of him, their brake lights blinking on and off. *Shit! What bad luck! It might be better to stop for a drink till the traffic is all cleared up.* He threw a glance at the radio clock. It was 11:15 p.m. Earlier, he had performed a clown show at the anniversary dinner of a senior couple, for a crowd of ten cheering grandkids. He had pocketed five hundred ringgit in cash as payment. He could now feel his wallet bulge against his hip pocket. *It wouldn't hurt to spend a bit of it at a pub.*

He turned into Bukit Bintang Road and then onto Tong Shin Road, managing to find a place to park his car. A ten-minute stroll took him to Bukit Bintang Hill, the city's infamous nightlife hotspot.

As he strolled along the lively drag, a garish sign caught his attention: 'Asahi Beer Promotion: RM18 for a big bottle'. The sign was placed outside Blue Melody Pub.

He entered the pub and found himself in a room the size of a volleyball court. A heavy cloud of fag smoke and grease fat hung in the air. The section near the entrance was taken up by an L-shaped bar and several tables. The rear end of the bar consisted of a small dance floor and a tiny platform where a DJ was playing loud and fast music. He had passed the bar and stood about twenty paces from the DJ box, watching. When the prancing DJ turned to his right, he had a moustache and wore a half-shirt. When he turned to his left, he had one bosom, displayed red lips and had on a half-dress. *Eh? That's interesting.* The pale man watched the DJ's amusing antics for some more time before returning to the front and settling down on a bar stool.

'Give me an Asahi beer,' he said to the barmaid.

The barmaid immediately whipped out a willybecher filled to its brim and then placed a small plate of fish fritters in front him. 'The *keropok* is on the house,' she said.

After the pale man had paid the barmaid and thanked her for the snacks, he sat there, munching the fritters and gulping down the beer. He had watched the small group of people jittering on the dance floor, shaking their bodies to the pulsating music. He scanned the faces of the dancers, and he had not liked what he had seen. *Ugh! All of them are bald grandpa boners and beer-bellied uncle boners, and they are shamelessly cavorting around with these twenty-something girls.*

He had then gazed about at the nearby tables. A fair-skinned woman with an inverted bob hairstyle had suddenly caught his eye. She smiled at him. The woman was sitting alone. She had on a short-sleeved floral dress and looked to be in her thirties. The woman's slight resemblance to his mother – when Mama had been younger – had startled him, and he had gazed at the woman for a moment longer than necessary.

The woman got up, crossed over to the bar and sat beside him. She leaned in and whispered, 'I love to dance but I don't have a partner. Would you like to dance with me?'

'No. I don't know how to dance.' *Is she a prostitute?* The pale man grew wary. He looked away.

The woman smiled. 'How about a scotch and *sofa* then?' She placed a hand on his arm, and he pulled away quickly.

The pale man snapped his fingers at the barmaid. 'Scotch and soda for this lady.'

The woman pressed her lips together and looked away for a moment, scowling. Her drink arrived, and she took a sip. Then she climbed down from the swivel stool, shifted it closer to the pale man and seated herself on it again. She tried making some idle chitchat. He had sat there, only half-listening, gulping down two more bottles of beer.

When the DJ started playing a slow song, she asked him again, 'Come on, let's do this dance, a slow dance. I can teach you. Even a three-hundred pound guy with a gimp can do it. It's easy.' She tugged him off the bar stool and started to take him to the dance floor. His inhibition and caution had been dissolved by the beer, and the pale man followed the woman. She put both her hands on his hip.

'I'll be the lead dancer,' she said. 'So drape your hands over my shoulders.' Soon, they were swaying to the music, holding each other close, and when the dance ended, she hugged him. 'Thank you for this dance. I gotta go.' She started to walk away from him.

The pale man returned to his bar stool. *Maybe this whore isn't like the others*, he had thought to himself. But as he raised his knees to put his feet onto the stool's foot rest, he had noticed something: the bulge in his hip pocket was gone. He quickly got down and stuck his hand into his right pocket. His wallet was missing. All the cash was gone. *The damn whore has stolen it*! He dashed out of the pub, looked around and saw the woman rushing away.

'Hey, you! Give me back my wallet!'

She began running on the pavement, pushing past several pedestrians. *Holy shit! How can she run so fast on pumps*? He went after her with all the speed he could muster.

The pale man kicked off his slip-on sneakers and held them in his hands as he ran. He pounded his bare feet on the pavement and finally caught up with the woman. He grabbed her from behind. 'Where's my wallet?'

The woman turned round with blazing eyes. Her leather pump kicked hard into his groin. He felt as if his testicles had burst open.

'A molester!' The woman screamed. 'Help! A molester!'

The pale man sunk to his knees, clutching his groin with both hands and doubling over in pain. He heard footsteps rushing towards him.

'What happened?' a gruff voice asked.

'He grabbed my breasts from behind. But I kicked him.'

'A pervert, eh? Shall we call the police?'

'No, I don't want to go to the police station. It's such a hassle. Can you beat him up to teach him a lesson he'll never forget?'

'It'll be our pleasure, Miss,' another voice said.

The heel of a heavy boot landed on the side of his face, throwing him to the pavement. The blow stunned him. Next, the toe cap of a leather brogue rammed into his left rib, and the pale man heard the *crunch* of his bones breaking. Pain was stabbing into his chest. As he rolled over, he realised that blood was pouring out of his face, from an open gash on his cheek. He looked up and saw the woman just standing there, smiling, watching the mob beat him up.

You evil bitch! Damn these prostitutes. They're evil. I'm going to kill them all! Every last one of them! He had promised himself before blacking out on the street.

The pale man continued to stare into the computer's blank screen. He was smiling to himself. He had kept the promise he made that day. He had already killed three whores, had given them what they deserved.

And he will not stop until he had punished them all. He especially wanted to kill the big-breasted hooker he had met at Central Market, the whore who had dared to insult his Mama.

* * *

The New Peng Hwa Food Court was packed. Chu stepped onto the perron to enter the building but then stopped for a moment. He gave the place an once-over. *Shit, the city's full of sleaze, if you looked in the right places.* Scattered inside the food court were jabbering johns, prattling prostitutes and babbling busybodies. The combined stench of cooking food, cheap dishwasher detergent and cigarette smoke was potent enough to suffocate someone to death.

He moved towards a middle-aged woman seated at a wooden counter. The woman frequently jabbed at the cash register to collect payment and dispense change. Her pixie short hair and floral print dress lent her a friendly demeanour.

'Yes? What do you want?' she asked as he approached her. Behind the woman was a glass cabinet stuffed with packs of cigarettes, tiny boxes of condoms and bottles of Kwan Loong medicated oil. Above the glass cabinet was a round wall clock: it showed 9:10 p.m.

'Have you ever seen this man here? Or this woman?' Chu produced the sketch of the suspect and the photograph of the murdered victim. 'The man came here frequently. He probably even bought cigarettes from you. The woman freelances here.'

The cashier peered at the images through her thick glasses and shook her head. 'I'm too busy to notice any of the customers. Can you please ask the girls?'

Chu moved to one end of the counter. He stood there, leaning back and scanning the tootsies seated at the different tables. He spotted a buxom young woman sitting alone. She had huge breasts and appeared to be the type the killer seemed to go for. *Perhaps he had hired her before?*

Chu made a beeline to her table. When he neared the China doll, she glanced up and stared at Chu with large curious eyes. The curves of her body were surprisingly ample for her slender figure.

'Hi, can I sit here?' Chu asked.

The hooker waved to a chair beside her, and he sank down. 'Can you help me, please? I'm an insurance claims investigator.' He placed the sketch and photo in front of her. 'Have you seen any of them?'

The hooker's eyes crinkled a little. 'The woman's dead, isn't she? And who's the man?'

'Yes, she died in a car accident. The man's the suspected driver in the hit-and-run. Have you seen him before? Has he hired you before?'

The woman visibly stiffened. 'Insurance investigator, my foot! You're a policeman, aren't you?' Her eyes filled with hostility, and she sprang to her feet. 'I can't help you, I'm sorry.'

'Pretty girl, relax! No need to get jumpy. I'm from the criminal investigation department, yes, but not the anti-vice division. I'm not here to create any trouble. I just need some information.'

She swung her bag over her shoulder and pushed the chair she had previously occupied towards the table. 'Why don't you talk to Ouyang Lifu? He might be able to assist you.'

Chu stood up. 'Who's he?'

The woman started to walk away, and Chu trailed behind her.

'He's the dragon master of the Red Centipede Society. He controls this food centre.'

'Where do I find him?'

'Ouyang Traditional Massage, Gajah Road. You can't miss the big neon sign,' she said, still walking away from him. Then, suddenly, she stopped and her eyes flitted around the other tables. 'That's all I have to say to you. Now leave me alone, please.' She quickly moved away from Chu again.

Within minutes, the police inspector was walking up the staircase leading to the first floor of Ouyang's massage centre. At the landing, he pressed a bell. While waiting for the door to open, he noticed a CCTV staring down at him from above the door. Chu fished out his police card and displayed it to the camera. He pressed the bell again then spoke into an intercom he found on the wall. 'I'm from the police.'

A voice crackled back through the intercom. 'What do you

want?'

'I want to talk to Ouyang Lifu,' he said, slipping his police card back into his pocket.

The wooden door opened a crack, and Chu swung it wide to let himself into the room. The sweet fragrance of huanghuali floated towards him as he stepped in. He observed with some surprise that the room was decorated with high-quality furniture, all of them expensive and antique pieces. He knew for sure they had been acquired by illegal means. The tiger-skin rug spread out on the floor was enough to throw Lifu in jail.

Chu approached the gaunt man with sunken eyes seated at an ornate wooden desk. 'I'm Detective Inspector Daniel Chu. C.I.D.'

The man did not bother to rise. 'Yes, Inspector, I'm Ouyang Lifu. What can I do for you?'

Chu produced the photo and held it up for Lifu to see. 'This prostitute was murdered in her apartment. Did she work for you?'

'Go to hell! I'm a legitimate businessman. My reflexology centre's registered. My reflexologists carry work permits. I've nothing to do with prostitution.'

Chu tossed the photo onto the desk, stepped forward and jabbed a finger in Lifu's chest. 'Listen here, you bloody pimp! Not only are you ugly but you're stupid as well. I'm trying to help you, don't you understand? A killer's running around loose. Three prostitutes – all of them China dolls – have been murdered. If news gets around about this killer, your girls may get too scared to work. That would be bad for business, don't you think so? We should catch this—'

A door at the far end of the room burst open and a thug leapt into the room. He held a wooden nunchaku in one hand. 'Are you alright, master?' He swung one end of the nunchaku menacingly in a circle.

His face expressionless, Lifu waved his man away. 'Don't push your luck too far, Inspector,' he said, turning to Chu and looking him in the eye. 'Take a seat and talk nicely to me if you want my help. Show some bloody manners, if your parents have taught you any.'

Chu stepped away from Lifu. Hot rage shot through his body. He curled his hands into fists and sat down. *Damn it! I want to tear out this opium snake's throat with my teeth*! But he knew that wouldn't help him. He needed information about the killer, and this man had it.

The flesh-peddler set his eyes on the photo again. 'Yes, Xiaoqian worked in New Peng Hwa but as a freelancer. She was there for only a month. Then she moved to another food court. Either on Yew Road or on Gelang Road. Anyway, check with the dragon master of the Green Scorpion Society. His name's Liu Yenshan. He controls both those eating-places, the bloody devil.'

'Where do I find him?'

'Green Angel Spa. It is located beside Amigo KTV.'

'Where's that?'

'At the site of the former F&N factory, on Sungei Besi Road. It's now a commercial site called Fraser Business Park.'

Chu wrote down the information in his notepad. 'Did Xiaoqian have any enemies?'

'I hardly knew her. But I'll tell you this. If anyone's capable of murdering his own girls, it's Liu Yenshan.'

'Why do you say that?'

'He has a criminal record. Please do your own homework,

Inspector.'

Chu took out the suspect's sketch, unfolded it and placed it beside the victim's photograph. 'I would like to know if you or any of your boys have seen this man. He's the prime suspect. He might have been hanging around your food court.'

Lifu reached into his pocket for his mobile phone. 'Big Dog, quickly get our boys here.'

While waiting, Lifu grabbed a red box with 'Djarum' printed on it in gold. He pulled out a clove cigarette from it, attached an ivory holder to its end and lit the butt. Lifu picked up the sketch and held it in front of him.

'His appearance is a bit familiar. Could be Yenshan's red pole.' He tossed the sketch back on the desk.

'Red pole?'

Lifu tilted his head and blew out a few smoke rings. 'A red pole is the enforcer of rules, regulations and business practices.'

'Enforcer? That sounds like a hatchet man.'

Lifu did not answer. He took a long drag from his cigarette.

The door bell rang, and Lifu leaned sideways to push a button under his desk. The wooden door swung open immediately, and six thugs entered the room. They appeared to be in their mid-twenties and early thirties. Among them was a midget with exophthalmic eyes; not taller than four feet, he wore a do-rag with its ends tied at the back of his head. His low-ride jeans revealed a dirty navel. Another thug sported blond hair, and a silver ring dangled from his one ear. The punks gathered in a tight half-circle around them, facing Lifu.

'Inspector Chu is here to track a suspect,' Lifu said, moving his gaze from one henchman to the next. 'He has a sketch of that man.

Possibly, this man has been hanging around our food court. Have you seen him before? All of you take a look at this.' He picked up the sketch and handed it to the ruffian standing closest to him. The photofit was passed around. All of them shook their heads.

'My men have given you their answers, Inspector. I'm sorry but I cannot be of further assistance to you.' He turned to the blond thug. 'Big Dog, show the inspector the way out of here.'

Chu returned to New Peng Hwa but could not find an empty table. A singer wearing a red sleeveless dress with tassels was singing into a mike: 'All the single ladies, all the single ladies …' He leaned against a steel pillar near the food court's entrance and watched her. She was now gyrating to her amateurish version of Beyonce's hit number, her hands placed on her hips.

A string of women in skimpy clothes walk around him. Chu suddenly felt aroused. Lust swelled in him, and his loins began to ache. *Yes, sir, why not make full use of my presence here? Hell, I am just a cop, not a saint.*

His eyes scanned the gaggle of tootsies around him. He was looking for the curvy China doll he had spoken to earlier. He couldn't stop thinking about her slender body and big breasts. He couldn't find her. *She isn't here anymore.* He decided that he would have to make do with another girl.

A small bottle of beer and twenty minutes later, Chu was walking up to Ace Electronics Building with a young, voluptuous girl.

Sunday 11 April

Alvin took a gulp of beer from the stein and glanced at his watch. It was 10 p.m. Four big and full bottles of Heineken stood in front of him. A plastic plate with the oily dregs of some *char kway teow* had been pushed aside on the table. He had stayed away from alcohol since morning because he hadn't really needed to steady his nerves. He had been fine. Until now, that is.

After eight hours of staying sober, his muscles and bones seemed to have turned to dry sponge. He needed to restore some life in him again. He let the contents of the stein wash down his throat, then poured himself another stein and downed it too. His body sucked in the beer eagerly, like desert sand does water. He drank some more, gulping it all in. Finally, he was down to the fourth bottle. The beer was starting to settle within him, was warming his gut.

Oh God! Am I an alcoholic? He stopped drinking suddenly to consider this. *No, that's nonsense*, he answered himself. *I am just a fairly heavy social drinker, that's all.*

Now, feeling a tad less torrid and a notch steadier, Alvin looked out the entrance of the food court. Cars and motorbikes were moving by, and people were traipsing up and down the kerb. Did these people know what was going on in New Peng Hwa? Did they know that the place was filled with raunchy hookers and horny men? Alvin had driven past the infamous food court so many times, had heard about what happened in there, yet had never dreamed that he would be sitting here himself one day, looking for sex.

But it had been months since he had held a woman's body, had touched her warm and tender skin. He needed this.

He spotted a girl walking down an aisle towards him, swaying her hips. Her eyes moved to the left, to a group of men sitting at one table, then to the right, to another table, scanning the room for potential customers. She was now ten paces from Alvin, and he waited to catch her attention. *Wow, she has such beautiful eyes. Like those of a cat.* He wanted to smile at her and give her the glad eye.

'Meisu!' a voice suddenly called, and the woman turned to look at a man waving his hand at her. She walked towards his table and settled down beside him.

Alvin's heart sank. He had missed his chance with her. He would have to pick another woman. A few other women strutted past his table. One of them caught his eye. She had killer legs. She wore a low-cut halter top and a skirt that was cheerleader short. It swirled as she walked towards him, revealing the full length of her smooth and toned legs, right from her slim ankles to the flare of her upper thighs. *These legs are an artist's dream.*

As she neared Alvin's table, he greeted her, 'Good evening, Miss.'

The hooker smiled. 'Hello, my dearest. Why are you sitting alone?' She took a seat next to him. 'My name's Yingying. Want a date with me?' Her mouth looked soft and wet and provocative.

'Sure. I'll pay you one hundred for a full hour. You can pay for the room.'

The woman scowled. 'That's not how I work. My price's one hundred and fifty. My room's in the opposite apartment.'

I have to do it in a smelly apartment room in Ace Electronics Building? Alvin cringed. If the police raided the place, he would be trapped like a rat. It was best not to take the risk.

'How about a motel nearby?' he asked.

The smile returned to her face. 'That's fine with me. But the room will cost you thirty extra. You have to pay for it.'

'OK.' Alvin finished his drink in one long swallow and stood up, supporting himself on the back of the chair. His legs felt like they had run a marathon. Alcohol and sadness gripped at his temples like a set of iron claws. He let go of the chair and started to stagger away.

Outside the food court, the hooker held his arm as he stumbled to the kerb. 'Are you sure you can walk?' she asked and pointed up the road. 'Springtime Inn is over there, on the other side of the market.'

Monday 12 April

Oh God, please let me be in my condominium. Alvin rubbed the sleep out of his eyes. He was aching all over, and his head felt heavy. In the past two years, he had found himself waking up on lawns, park benches and picnic tables, even in public washrooms, stairwells and sidewalks. He peeled open his eyelids with great effort and looked around him.

He was on his couch in his condo. *Thank God.* An empty 350-millilitre bottle of budget brandy lay on its side on the living-room table. He sat up, and the walls spun around him for a moment. He stepped out of his clothes and hauled himself to the bathroom. For ten minutes, he splashed around in the shower and then he changed into fresh work clothes. He tottered to the kitchen to prepare breakfast.

Two cups of hot coffee with a splash of brandy put him back in shape. He ate a sandwich and tried to remember what had happened the previous night. He had an image of a hooker offering her arm to steady him as they had walked across a deserted drag. He had an image of a garbage dumpster as they had entered a dark alley behind the motel. *What did the motel room look like?* He couldn't recall it at all. He had an image of the hooker kissing him on the cheek, but when he had tried to kiss her lips, she had pushed his face away. He had an image of the hooker removing her dentures to perform oral sex on him.

Jesus Christ! Was she that old? Alvin shuddered a little. *What did she look like?* He couldn't remember. *Did I have sex with her?* He couldn't remember. *How much did I pay her?* He couldn't remember.

Suddenly, his palms were sweaty. He dashed to the living room. His clothes lay in a crumpled heap on the floor. After fumbling in the pockets of his trousers, he pulled out his wallet and opened it. He counted the notes. The cash was still there. The old-lady hooker had not stolen from him. He heaved a sigh of relief.

* * *

Alvin had entered his studio at noon. He had been painting for over two hours, and his stomach was growling. His hands were beginning to tremble as well. *Where should I go to for lunch? Could I do without alcohol today?* Alvin told himself that he could surely go without having a drink that day.

But it would be better if I drank a little, not too much. You know, just to keep me going. He could gradually reduce the amount of alcohol intake, day by day, until he could stop altogether. He gazed out the entrance. *How many times have I said this to myself?*

A year ago, a big bottle of beer made him drunk; today it sobered him up. His eyes glazed over the canvas before him. If he were alcohol-free he couldn't hold a brush. Alcohol will uncork his imagination, make him more creative. He had made his decision. Drinking a bit of alcohol will help him work better. *Now, where should I go to get some lunch and a quick drink?* He was sick of eating chicken rice at Zhing Khoong Coffee Shop. He searched his memory and remembered the backpacker inn beside the Sri Mahamariamman Temple on Tun H.S. Lee Road. It had a café downstairs that served Western food and liquor. He closed the studio and walked over to the joint.

His lunch consisted of a plate of 'Chicken à la King' and a 350-millilitre bottle of malt whisky.

Back in the studio, he resumed painting. He found himself in high spirits again and humming a tune. The alcohol felt warm in his gut, and he felt light in his limbs. A middle-aged woman, dressed in a blue sheath dress with lace sleeves, walked in. A string of pearls the size of grapes hung around her neck. *Whoop-di-doo! A loaded customer, finally!* A brown-skinned girl walked in behind the woman, carrying two big shopping bags. *She is probably the rich hag's Filipina maid.*

'Can I help you, madam?' Alvin asked the woman with a bright smile.

'I'm looking for a few pieces to decorate my new house,' she said. 'Please, don't allow me to interrupt you. I'll look around and pick whatever I want.'

The rich woman walked along one wall, looking at its display of oil paintings, then took down two pieces from their hooks. She gently placed the paintings on the floor, leaning them against Alvin's desk. The woman then ambled to another wall, her eyes travelling from one end of it to another. She lifted two acrylic pieces off their hooks and placed them with the other paintings she had selected.

'There ... These four pieces will suffice. They should add zing to my bungalow's architecture. It's Tudor. My poppy got a London architect to do the design. The interior walls are sky-blue,' she informed Alvin. 'Well, what do you think?'

Alvin stood up, walked a few paces from his desk and looked down at the paintings. He burst into a fit of loud laughter. 'You're so ignorant of art! These pieces and their genres are a misfit for Tudor architecture. You're all fur-coat and no knickers, aren't you?' Alvin was almost doubling over with laughter.

'Buggering hell!' The woman's eyes were wide and furious as she stared at Alvin.

Alvin composed himself quickly. *What the hell have I done? I shouldn't have said all that to her*. He cursed himself for speaking without thinking. The bloody alcohol had loosened his tongue.

'I'll be damned if I'm buying anything from you after what you've said.' The woman was still fuming as she and her maid left his studio.

Alvin stood frozen for a few moments. He then walked over to the paintings the woman had selected and returned them to their places on the walls. He had just screwed up a ten-grand sale. He plodded back to his canvas with a heavy heart. His posture sagged and his hands felt lethargic as he tried to paint. He knew that his schoolboy howler wouldn't have happened if he hadn't been drunk. The alcohol was getting to him. He was losing control.

That afternoon, while Alvin was still reconciling himself over the morning's indiscretion, a tall and fair-complexioned man with piercing eyes drifted into the studio. He wore a pair of crisp charcoal-grey trousers with old-style button-clasp suspenders. As he walked along one wall of the studio and looked from one painting to another, the man chuckled loudly to himself.

Alvin got off his chair and approached the man. 'What's so

funny? Care to share the joke?'

The tall man turned to glare at him. 'The landscapes are charming, but they're not good,' he said. 'You're merely copying what you see in nature, not interpreting it.' He swept an arm over a row of canvases. 'Most of your acrylics are amateurish. The moods and subjects clash. Also, there's no consistency in your technique. A few even looked like they were done by an Alzheimer's patient.'

The man's words stung Alvin like a swarm of bees.

'This one here.' Taking a step forward, the man pointed to an abstract work. 'Where's your artist's statement? This piece deserves a statement. I don't understand the symbolism at all.' The man shuffled over to another wall. As he passed by Alvin's framed diploma, his eyebrows shot up. 'By golly, you've a qualification in art? I thought you were self-taught.'

'Are you qualified to critique my art?' Alvin managed to murmur.

'I own the Island Glades Gallery in Penang. I've a degree in Art History from John Hopkins University.' He turned toward the door. 'I am sorry to say this, but your work lacks potential. I would suggest that you quit painting and try your hand at something else.' He nodded. 'Good day then.' The art critic ambled away.

Alvin felt nauseous. His chest suddenly felt tight, as if something heavy had just crashed into it. The walls were closing in on him, and he was finding it difficult to breathe. He closed the studio and rushed over to Pink Panda Pub. He walked straight in and ordered a Planter's Punch.

The barman served him two as it was 'Happy Hours'. He looked behind the bar and caught sight of rows and rows of liquor bottles placed inside a cabinet. He felt himself getting tempted by the booze and looked away, then moved to the end of the bar.

A large mirror hung from a wall there, and as he looked into it, a man with a hollow ashen face and vacant eyes stared back at him. The man in the mirror had stopped thinking of his ambitions and his success, had lost interest in making plans for his future. He had failed as an artist. His prospect as a potential husband to any woman was zilch. He was turning into an alcoholic. His whole life was slipping out from under him. He tipped his head to swallow the last gulp of Planter's Punch, and then ordered a gin-and-tonic. *Why not put an end to this farce once and for all?* After all, he couldn't find a reason to keep on living. And if he died, he wouldn't have to worry anymore about failing as an artist or getting rejected by women.

Alvin tried to push these thoughts of suicide to the back of his mind as he finished his drink, but they refused to stay there. The little voice in his head was only growing more persuasive, and it kept insisting that he end his own life. He looked at his watch. *The evening rush hour would be over now. Time to head home.*

On the drive home, he picked up several bottles of brandy, whisky and vodka at an all-night restaurant on Genting Kelang Road.

When he reached home, Alvin loaded the bottles into the fridge, then took out a few slices of leftover pizza and popped them in the microwave oven. When the oven dinged, he took out the slices and sat down in the kitchen to have them.

As he ate, the thought of suicide kept ballooning in his head, growing big until it filled his brain, overwhelming his other faculties until it seemed to be the only logical thing to do. *Hell, that's it then. It's time for me to quit once and for all. But how should I kill myself?*

He immediately switched on his laptop and placed it on the

dining table. He performed a Google search for 'suicide methods' and unearthed a list of sites that suggested the different ways in which he could take his own life. Hanging. Carbon monoxide poisoning. Plastic bag over the head. Drowning in bathtub. All the ideas seemed grisly, too painful. He wanted a method that was highly lethal but inflicted very little pain. Drug poisoning seemed to be a good option. It seemed easy and painless. Secobarbital Sodium and Pentobarbital produced peaceful deaths when taken in large doses. *Fantastic! But how will I buy these drugs without a prescription?*

He was checking the websites of pharmacies to see if he could order the drugs online, when his hands began to shake. The craving for more alcohol was beginning to grip his head in a wrestler's hold, and the pressure was mounting by the second. It was time for his evening binge. *What? So soon? I shouldn't. I had just had three drinks*! He tried to resist the urge, but it was cutting into his veins, digging into the marrow of his bones. He sprung to his feet, turned to the fridge behind him and grabbed three bottles of vodka.

He carried them to the living room table and sank into the armchair. His thoughts were scurrying about in his skull like rats. They scurried and scurried and, finally, it came to him. The best way for him to take his own life – he would drink himself to death. It would be a perfect death, like that of a sex-addict in the arms of a prostitute. *What a way to go.*

By the time Alvin had emptied the three bottles of vodka, he lay on the couch in a pool of his own urine, in a state of near delirium, still thinking of his death.

The next morning, he woke up at 10:20 a.m. and shuffled to the washroom for a shower. While the water flowed over him, he propped himself upright with one hand pressed against the wall and closed his eyes. When he felt clear-headed enough, he stepped out. He cleaned up the couch, prepared half a cup of Nescafe and topped it to the brim with whisky. The caffeine and alcohol helped revive him, and he ambled to his regular grocery store to ask for as many empty cardboard boxes as they could give him.

When he returned home, he opened his bedroom closet, took out the clothes Karen had left behind, folded them neatly and put them into one of the empty boxes. He then went to his book case, cleared away his novels and magazines, and stacked them in another box. Then he unplugged his TV, lifted it off the cabinet and placed it near the living room door. When he was finished packing up the things, he looked up the contact information of old folks' homes and orphanages on his laptop. 'Hello? Is this the Happy Sunshine Senior Citizen Home? Yes, I would like to donate a TV, some books and a box of clothes. Would all this be useful to your residents?'

He paused and drew a long breath. 'Well, I'm migrating abroad. Can I come over in the afternoon?' A pause. 'Sure, you're welcome.'

He then dialled his landlord's number. 'Hello, Mr. Arumugam? Alvin here. I would like to terminate my tenancy. I won't be paying next month's rental, so just utilise my deposit. It's good till the end of May.' A pause. 'Well, I got a job in Penang. Yes, sure, everything will be cleared up. OK, thanks, bye.' Another loose end tied up.

Alvin went into the kitchen and opened the wall cabinet. Inside was a stack of plates and bowls and some cutlery. He closed the cabinet and looked around; he made a mental checklist of the things he had to get rid of. The fridge had to stay. He needed it to keep his liquor cold. But the crockery, electric toaster and electric iron could be disposed of soon. He went to the shoe rack, glanced inside and took note of a pair of sneakers and a pair of running shoes inside. A schoolboy might find the running shoes useful.

I have a lot of cleaning up to do before I leave this world. He carried the TV and the other boxes to his car in three separate trips. Then he drove off to drop the items at the senior citizen's home.

Tuesday 13 April

Chu strode over to Green Angel Spa, housed on the ground floor of a commercial block in Fraser Business Park. He stepped towards the mirror door that opened from the inside. *Hah, a two-way mirror. When the Johnny Laws approach, the gorillas can lock the door and keep them out.* That would give the whores enough time to scuttle away. *Damn, these pimps are devious.*

Chu stepped in, and a man with ferret-like eyes closed the door for him. The police inspector walked over to the reception counter, where a middle-aged and lumpy-jawed woman sat, dressed in a grey jacket and a red scarf.

'I want to talk to Liu Yenshan, the owner.'

'May I know why?'

Chu flashed his police card. 'I'm Inspector Daniel Chu. I need to ask him some questions.'

The receptionist lifted a telephone and spoke into it, 'Mr. Liu, sorry to disturb you. An Inspector Chu wants to see you. Hmm ... Alright.' She put the phone down. 'Please go down this corridor and then turn left. It's the last room down the hall.' The tone of her voice was cold and reproachful, like that of a mother superior chastising her nuns.

Chu walked down a long hallway, past several rooms with curtained glass doors. He could hear the slapping and striking sounds of palms against the bare backs of the customers coming from a few of the rooms. The corridor branched into two, like the reception had informed him, and Chu took the left turn. He stopped outside a room with 'Management' printed on its door.

Chu rapped on the single-panel flush door; the door felt like solid hardwood under his knuckles. As the door opened, a black-and-tan Rottweiler stood up and greeted him, baring its teeth. The beast stood more than two feet tall. Suddenly, the Rottweiler's head flew towards him, and it reached the end of its chain, its jaws snapping where Chu's groin had been only a second ago. The brute was held back by the chain, but it lunged at him again, and was stopped again by the chain.

His heart racing, Chu took a step back and collided into somebody. He turned to face a handsome man trying to move past him. He wore a black vest over a long sleeved shirt.

The Rottweiler shook its head vigorously to try to slide out of its collar, and the metal license clanged.

'Down, Fredo!' the man shouted to the dog.

The dog immediately lay down on its stomach, its eyes still staring at Chu viciously.

'Stay!' the man ordered.

Chu threaded gingerly past the mutt.

'I'm so sorry about Fredo,' the man said. 'Come on in, Inspector.' The man walked to a leather Chesterfield swivel chair behind a desk and sat down. 'I'm Liu. Now, how can I help you?'

The man was in his early thirties, and he had small, glinting eyes and a wide grin that seemed too innocent to be true.

Chu settled down into an armchair, heaving a huge sigh. 'What's this vicious dog doing in your office?'

'My spa doesn't accept credit cards. So I keep quite a bit of cash in here. Though I've a very tough Chubb safe, Fredo is additional security.'

Chu gave the dog an uneasy look then turned back to the man. 'Well, Mr. Liu, I'm here because I'm investigating a case. And I believe that you may be able to assist me with it.' He took out the photograph of Caiqin and handed it to the spa owner. 'Do you know this girl?'

Liu held the photo between his forefinger and thumb, gazed at the image for a moment then returned it to Chu. 'I've never set eyes on her before. Who's she?'

Before Chu could answer, there was a knock at the door. A brown-skinned girl entered, carrying a porcelain pot, its outside engraved with the painted motif of a stylised scorpion, two porcelain cups and a plate of prawn crackers on a metal tray.

Liu sat upright. 'Ah, tea is served.'

She placed one porcelain cup in front of Chu, the other in front of her boss. She put the prawn crackers and the pot between the two men.

'Come, have a drink, sir. This tea is called Yunnan Pu-er. It's excellent for lowering cholesterol.' Liu stood up and poured steaming tea into both their cups. The aroma of wood and mushroom wafted towards them.

Chu lifted his cup, blew at it and took a long sip of the tea. 'The girl in the photo is Xiong Caiqin. Her working name is Xiaoqian. She's been murdered. Did she work for you?'

'Did Ouyang Lifu tell you she's one of my girls?'

'Let's just say I've my sources.' Chu put his cup down.

'Lifu and I are friendly competitors, Inspector. He'd say anything to get me in trouble.' Liu smiled. 'Inspector Chu, let me tell you something about China dolls. They are like birds of passage. Just like the raptors in Tanjung Tuan, they come to feed here, and then they fly away. They do us no harm, and we don't harm them. It's a win-win situation, really. The client and the lady get what they want. They can do their happy tango. The dolls get paid, and so do we. So, I'd be bloody stupid or downright insane to slaughter the mother hen that lays the golden egg. Do you understand what I'm getting at, Inspector?'

Chu nodded. *Hell, this conversation isn't going the way I want it to.*

Liu paused to take a long swallow from his cup. 'I'm sure Lifu also told you of my food centres?' He grinned. 'Or maybe you've already heard of them? They are quite popular.'

Chu sipped at his tea, said nothing.

'Well, we should look at them as transit points for ambitious women wanting to improve their financial standing or to help tide them over a bad spot.' Liu munched on a piece of prawn cracker. 'Try one, Inspector. This is a famous brand made in Pangkor.' He gently moved the plate toward Chu. 'They are crispy and full of flavour, especially served fresh from the frying pot.' He washed down the crackers in his mouth with a gulp of tea. 'Anything else you need to ask me, sir?'

Chu pulled out the photofit of the suspect from his back pocket and spread it in front of Liu. 'Is this man one of your employees? Has he worked in any of your establishments, either in the present or the past?' He picked up a cracker and chewed on it while Liu started down at the photofit, considering it.

Liu shook his head. 'Definitely no. Is he a wanted man?'

'He was the last man seen with Xiaoqian.'

'You can look around in my food centres – Pudu Food Court on Yew Road and One Stop Food Centre on Gelang Road. Meet my men, see them with your own eyes. None of them even vaguely resemble the sketch.' He took out a letter opener shaped like a dagger from a wire-mesh container and fingered it. 'As a matter of fact, Inspector, I run a tight ship. Never have any of my boys misbehaved. Discipline is strict in my organisation. The penalties are severe. You get what I mean?' He replaced the letter opener, leaned forward and said. 'Can I make a photocopy of this? I'll pass it on to my boys and instruct them to keep a lookout for this suspect.'

'Thanks for your help, Mr. Liu.'

Liu nodded, then lifted his phone and spoke into it. 'Miss Tan, come here, please.'

A curvy girl sashayed into the office. 'Make a copy of this, thank you.' Liu handed the sketch over to her.

Chu's eyes swelled in their sockets as he took in Liu's secretary. She had red, pouting lips and breasts as big as pomelos. A silver pendant in the shape of a scorpion nestled in her bare cleavage. She took the sketch and turned to leave the room, and Chu's eyes followed her, an intense heat coursing through his veins when he saw that her mini dress had a cut-out back.

The voluptuous lass returned a while later and handed both copies to Liu. He returned the original to Chu. 'If there's nothing more, Inspector, you'll have to excuse me.' He turned to his sexy secretary. 'Miss Tan, please show the good inspector the way out of here. You may wish to explain to him the services we offer.'

The secretary took Chu outside and accompanied him down the corridor, explaining the benefits of Shiatsu massages, Swedish massages and traditional Thai massages. As they walked in step, Inspector Chu couldn't help but stare at the secretary's chest.

* * *

Alvin hopped out of his car. He was in the parking lot of New Peng Hwa. He strode to an empty table near the entrance and sat down. He wanted to be certain that he spotted that tall voluptuous girl when she arrived, that he booked her for tonight.

As he sat there eating a plate of braised duck with pig intestines and drinking two bottles of Anchor beer, she entered. Alvin waved his hand at her, and she steered towards his table. His mouth broke into a warm smile.

'*Ni hao*, you speak English?'

'Yes, of course.' Her eyes met his in a coquettish stare, causing his breath to snag in his throat.

The way her clothes hugged her body mesmerised Alvin. He gazed up and down her figure. From her slim ankles and up her shapely legs, to the hem of the pencil skirt that ended at her milky thighs. From the curve of her hips, to her breasts that stretched tightly across the fabric of her ecru halter top, to her smooth shoulders, left bare by spaghetti straps, and then to her feline face. Time seemed to stand still for Alvin as he took in all this. The woman waited beside him, watching him with a teasing smile.

He pulled out a chair for her. 'Come, please take a seat.'

The woman smoothed her skirt and set herself down beside him, crossing her legs at the ankles. Alvin leaned toward her, and she reciprocated.

'You want to book me?' she asked. Her hair brushed his face, filling him with the jasmine and rose scent of her perfume. The next instant, she drew back. 'Sorry, your breath smells like sour barley.'

Alvin sat up straight. 'Oh dear, this is embarrassing.' A pause and a smile. 'Yes, I want to hire you. You're Meisu, aren't you?'

'How did you know?'

'I overheard someone call you by your name. I was here on Sunday. I am Alvin.'

He agreed to her price, quickly finished his drink, and then walked with her to Loveboat Motel. When they had gotten themselves a room, they gargled with mouthwash, then showered and dried themselves and headed to the bed, naked. Alvin pulled Meisu to him.

Their pelvises pressed together; their tongues danced as their lips met; their hands ran over each other's body. The second hand on Alvin's watch ticked two circles, and they kept kissing and groping one another.

Meisu disengaged herself suddenly and turned to lie on her side beside her client. She propped up her head on one hand and looked down at Alvin's flaccid manhood. 'Darling, does that thing work or not? We can't be hugging for an hour.'

Alvin sighed and turned away, unable to look at her. 'I'm sorry, can we just talk?' He felt hot embarrassment rise up from his gut and radiate through his body, reaching his cheeks. 'I can tip you if necessary.'

'Whatever. It's your time. Are you always like this?'

'Sometimes.'

'You're too young to be impotent. Do you drink too much? Excessive alcohol damages the nerves and blood vessels in the manhood. I read that somewhere.'

He turned to look at her again. 'Doesn't matter to me anymore. Nothing matters.' He gave a slight shake of the head. She frowned, but did not press him about what he meant.

'Can we talk about something else now? Where're you from?'

'China.'

'Yes, I know that. Which province?' He cast a downward glance at her body, and found himself filled with desire. He was desperate to have her.

'Guilin. It's in Guangxi Province.'

He started to stroke her hips then ran his fingers down her thighs. 'Beautiful place. I've seen pictures of Guilin online. What did you do in Guilin?' The curve of her hip was about seventy degrees. *She'll make a great life model for a sketch.*

'I was an independent tour guide.' She flashed him a wry grin. 'Come to Guilin, and I'll take you to a place that serves horse-meat noodles, roasted dogs and bamboo rats stir-fried with ginger. You can get all this and more at the restaurants in Zhenyang Lu,' she said, laughing. 'Now tell me a bit about yourself.'

Alvin wished she would tell him some more about herself. *I am being too hopeful. Which China-doll hooker would be willing to reveal her personal details to a client*? He tried again anyway. 'Free tour services for me?'

'My charge is fifty US dollars a day. So, what kind of work do you do?'

'I'm a painter. I've a studio in Central Market.' He looked away from her for a second, to let out a burp.

'I like art,' Meisu said, suddenly interested. 'I've gone to the Central Market before. Strange that I didn't see your studio.' She manoeuvred herself into a sitting position, placed the fluffy pillow against the headboard and leaned back on it. Alvin's eyeballs looked upward, taking in her perky breasts and her full lips, now spread into a wide smile.

'You probably missed it. Most people do. It's in the annexe, behind the main building.' Alvin sat himself up, too, beside Meisu, and wrapped his arm around her slender waist. 'Why are you doing what you're doing here?'

'My tour guide earnings are irregular. I wanted to come here so I could earn enough to go to university.'

'How long have you been in KL?'

'Almost two weeks.'

'I don't understand this idea of selling yourself to get an education. When you graduate and get a good respectable job, your past may come back to bite you in the ass,' Alvin said, caressing her hips.

'Lots of things cannot be understood. For instance, I can't understand why men come over to New Peng Hwa to hire women.'

Her sarcasm caught him unaware. 'I can't speak for other men but I went there for a reason,' he said defensively. 'I'm divorced, and I've not had sex for four or five months now.'

A pain suddenly pulsed between his eyebrows. 'I'm getting sick of living. I am very tired of life.' He uttered the sentence word by word, as though pulling a flower apart, petal by petal. 'I just want to indulge in a few flings before I … Before I …' His eyes welled up as he tried to cross the space between his intentions and his words, but this river was too broad to traverse, its water too cold to tread.

Meisu took his hand in hers. 'Would you like to tell me your troubles?'

Alvin confided in her about his problems, told her about his failure as an artist and as a husband.

She listened patiently, and then kissed him tenderly on the cheek. 'Don't blame yourself, Alvin. None of this is your fault,' she said, her voice filled with sympathy. 'Bad things happen to everybody. It's how you respond to them that defines your character. Ending your life is not the solution to this. Life is precious. You can't throw away yours so easily. You can choose to wallow in perpetual sadness and end your life like a coward. Or you can rise above the pain and treasure the most precious gift you have – life itself. The storm will pass.'

Alvin took a deep breath and stared at the ceiling, letting her words sink in. Then, suddenly, he was overwhelmed with the desire to be hugged and held, and he fell into his companion's arms, burying his head in the dark curtain of her hair. Meisu embraced him and stroked the back of his head gently.

When he felt composed again, Alvin pulled himself away from her. Meisu smiled at him. 'Well, sorry to do this, but I think your time's up,' she whispered.

Alvin nodded and returned her smile. He observed how Meisu was unlike the crude prostitutes he had met in the past.

They got dressed and left the motel. When they approached the New Peng Hwa Food Court, Alvin turned to her, 'It was interesting talking with you, Meisu. You've helped me look at my life and my situation from a difference perspective. I would like to meet you again. Can I have your mobile number, please?'

'Sure, I'll give you a miss call.' She took out her mobile phone from her handbag. 'Your number please?' She pressed the nine digits given by Alvin, typed in his name and pressed 'call'.

As they started to walk away from each other, Meisu waved her hand in a brief farewell. 'Come again when you've time,' she said, flashing him a warm smile.

While Alvin drove home, thoughts about Meisu fluttered about in his mind like a flock of birds. In his bedroom, he could still smell her on his clothes, the jasmine scent of her hair and the sweet smell of her skin. He could still taste her in his mouth, and he was filled with a deep desire to be with her again. He gulped down a 350-millilitre bottle of whisky and went to sleep wondering when he'd see her again.

Thursday 15 April

Alvin stationed himself at New Peng Hwa sharp at eight o'clock. He was dressed in a brown short-sleeved shirt, dark jeans and black slip-ons.

'One bottle of Tiger, make it a big one,' he said to the dumpy Indonesian waitress. The drink arrived in a jiffy, and the waitress prised off the cap, poured the brew into his glass. He walked over to the stall selling Thai food and asked for seafood *tom-yam* and white rice.

Back at his table, he fished out his cell phone and tried calling Meisu, but he found that her mobile was switched off. He left her a voice message: 'Hi, I'm Alvin. I'm waiting for you at the food court.'

The evening stretched on, and the minute hand on his watch had finished two full circles. He had eaten the food and had drunk two more bottles of Tiger. He was almost ready to give up and leave, when his mobile phone rang.

A jolt of excitement ran up Alvin's spine when he heard Meisu's voice on the other end. 'Hello, Alvin? I'm on the way. I was engaged with a client. Sorry to keep you waiting.' By the time she had hung up, the chirping and fluttering birds had returned to Alvin's mind.

Ten minutes later, Meisu walked into the food court, wearing a strapless fuchsia dress and matching stilettos. Alvin raised his hand and wriggled two fingers at her; at the same time a man seated at the table next to Alvin rose to his feet and waved at Meisu.

The man shot Alvin a venomous glance. 'Hey, mister, I saw her first!' The man was probably in his early twenties, and had a broad barrel chest and the face of a bulldog.

The painter glared back at him. 'I booked her earlier by phone.'

'So what? I'm her regular customer.'

'Well, Mister, that doesn't entitle you to skip the queue. Your parents never taught you any manners, huh?'

'What did you say? Don't you dare insult my parents!'

The bulldog-faced man flung his glass of hot Chinese tea into Alvin's face. He stepped forward and grabbed at Alvin's shirt. His other hand waved a pudgy finger in front of Alvin's nose. 'Whether you like it or not, I'm jumping the queue. Any objections?'

Meisu approached the two men. 'Let go of him!' she shouted at the bulldog-faced man. 'I don't want your business! Not today, not ever again. Any objections?'

Many pairs of eyes from the other tables stared at the three of them, but no one wanted to get involved.

The bulldog-faced man tightened his hold on Alvin. 'See, it's your fault! Now, she has rejected me.' He looked at Meisu, and gave her a brief offended look, then turned back to Alvin, raising his fist. 'Because of that, I'm gonna spray your throat with your own teeth!'

Alvin's heart skipped a beat. He floundered for words but they couldn't come to him. Then, suddenly, from a nearby table, a man dashed towards them and delivered a blow into the ribs of the bulldog-faced man. The goon gasped, released Alvin and doubled over. The man who had hit the goon quickly cocked his elbow and drove it into his back.

He then reached down, grabbed the bulldog-faced man by his arm and yanked him up. 'Listen, you punk! You better behave or I'll put you in the bullpen. Now sit down and be a good boy. You understand?'

The bulldog-faced man nodded and returned to his table glumly, massaging his ribs.

Alvin took out his handkerchief and wiped away the Chinese tea from his face and neck. 'Thank you for your help,' he said to the man who had saved him.

'It's good that you were here. Usually, Big Dog or some other bouncer's here to take care of such things, but they are missing today,' Meisu informed the man.

'No problem at all.' The man sat down at Alvin's table, then motioned for the two of them to join him. 'Can you give me a minute of your time, please? I think you could be of assistance to me.'

Alvin and Meisu sat down facing the man, confused.

'What can I do for you?' Alvin asked.

'My name's Inspector Chu,' he said, displaying his police card. 'I've here because I'm investigating a murder.'

Alvin noticed Meisu's eyes widen with recognition and wariness. She rose to her feet and began to walk away from them quickly. Alvin got up, too, and rushed after her, but Meisu turned around and said, 'No, you stay here and talk to the cop. Hear him out, find out what he wants. I'll come back when he's not around.' Before Alvin could ask her any questions, she was walking away again.

Alvin returned to the table. 'Yes, Inspector, what were you saying?'

From his pocket, Chu took out the photofit of the suspect and shoved it across the table. 'I'm looking for this man. He can help me investigate a criminal case. I believe he comes here often. Have you ever spotted him?'

'He's the suspect, isn't he?' Alvin looked down at the sketch. 'I'm sorry, but I'm afraid I haven't seen him before. I've only started to come here quite recently.'

Chu retrieved the photofit from Alvin. Then, he took out his name card and handed it over. 'Well, if you spot the guy in the sketch somewhere, call me.' The inspector rose to his feet. 'Can I have your name card?'

Alvin gave it the policeman then shook hands with him.

When the inspector had walked out of the food court, Meisu slipped out of the ladies' toilet and made her way back to Alvin's table.

'What was that all about?' she asked, settling into a chair.

'Oh, nothing important. He was just looking for a wanted man, asked me whether I'd seen the suspect.' Alvin placed a hand on Meisu's shoulder. 'Are you OK? Why did you leave so abruptly?'

Meisu shrugged. 'I just hate cops. They are trouble.' She then reached out to touch his arm. 'And I'm sorry about that man. He is one of my clients. He's not a bad man, just possessive and sensitive.'

'Forget about him.' Alvin smiled at her. 'Meisu, tonight, I would like to book you for three hours. Dinner first, then we go to a hotel. I know a delicious restaurant near Pudu Plaza. We'll go in my car, and I'll drop you back here. That's fine with you?'

'Sure. That will cost you ... One hundred and eighty multiplied by three ... So, five hundred and forty ringgit. Are you sure you can drive?'

'Sure. The restaurant's only ten to fifteen minutes away.'

She flashed Alvin a mischievous grin. 'Are you sure you're up to form tonight?'

Alvin smiled. 'You'll find out later.' *Hah, she is in for a big surprise tonight.* For the past two days, he had been popping horny goat weed and ginkgo biloba pills. The pharmacist had assured him that they would work like magic.

* * *

The artist drove Meisu to Pudu Plaza, parked the car and held her hand as they walked across the road to Lam Fatt Seafood Restaurant. From the menu, he ordered steamed grouper, braised mushroom-chicken, stir-fried Chinese broccoli, a big bottle of Carlsberg and a pot of Oolong tea.

Within minutes, a Myanmar waiter brought them the beverages on a metal tray. Meisu used chopsticks to grip and pick out two cups from a plastic bowl of steaming water. While she filled them to the brim with tea from the pot, Alvin poured his beer into a stein and took a long swallow of it.

'How long have you been a painter?'

'Almost two years. I left my former employer because I wanted more freedom.'

'What kind of art do you do? I am pretty good at art too, but I was never encouraged to pursue it as a career.'

'I do all kinds of art. Everyone has different taste in art, and I believe that an artist has to cater to a broad market. It's a good thing you did not become an artist though, Meisu. It's not easy to make it in this field.'

'So, do you stay alone here? Any family or friends?

'Nope. No-one. I've a brother but he's in Singapore.'

'Makes you feel lonely, doesn't it? Living alone …'

'Yes, Meisu, horribly lonely.'

'I understand how you feel. I live alone, too. My flatmate got arrested and deported. Sure, I've the company of customers on most nights, but that's different. It's not the same as having friends or family around you. Or living with a man, someone you love.'

'Do you have a boyfriend back home?'

'No. I've gone through a series of not-too-good boyfriends. Nothing worked out. One even hit me. I guess I am unlucky in love. '

'Yes, I understand. But don't worry. Someone as beautiful as you is sure to find love soon.' He smiled and reached for her hand, pressed it reassuringly.

A part of Meisu revelled in Alvin's open admiration of her. She suddenly thought about Master Ong's prediction. *Is he the chosen one for me?*

The food was brought to them by the same waiter. Meisu dunked the forks and spoons into the plastic bowl of steaming water and dried them with a piece of tissue. She then passed a fork and a spoon to Alvin. He speared a chicken drumstick and passed it to Meisu's plate. 'Try this. The meat's smooth and succulent. This dish's their specialty.'

'Thanks.'

Alvin took another gulp of beer and served himself some Chinese broccoli.

'Why are you always drinking? Do all artists drink so much?'

Alvin gazed into his glass for a moment. 'No, not all artists do. Obviously this is a habit I picked up because I feel depressed. Now it has become a small vice, part of my diet. Recovery from depression takes time.'

'I think I know how to cheer you up.'

'How?'

'I could tell you my real name.' She chewed on the chicken meat. 'Mmmm ... You were right. The braised chicken is good.'

'You would tell me your real name? That's wonderful!' Alvin leaned forward, his eyes gleaming with curiosity.

'You're the first man in *Jilongpo* to know. My name's Jin Ailing. But I still prefer that you call me Meisu.' She smiled at the artist. 'Jin is a Manchurian surname. My grandfather fled from Manchuria when the Japanese invaded in 1932. My parents were born in Yangshuo. Sadly, my Papa died in a scooter accident when I was a child. Then my Mama got a job in a knife factory in Guilin and remarried. I, too, was born there. I've my grandpa's genes. That's why I'm tall.' She sipped her tea. 'So, Alvin's your real name?'

'Yes, my full name's Alvin Au. You're the only child?'

'The one-child policy was implemented in China in 1979. I was born in the year of the Snake.'

'Wow, you're good at history. I'm a Monkey.' He grinned at her.

'So, did you have a happy life in China?' Alvin cut a piece of the grouper and served it to her.

'No. I had a very unhappy one,' she said, poking at the grouper with her fork. 'I was molested by my stepfather. Luckily, he died early, because of heaving drinking and smoking.' She gave a slight shake of her head, then put down her fork and looked away. 'Then, my Mama died too. She never had a good life, the poor woman. She died of breast cancer when I was sixteen or seventeen, and I was taken care of by my auntie and uncle after that. Luckily, they treated me well.'

Her eyes welled up as she remembered it all. Alvin handed her his kerchief. 'Thanks,' she said and dabbed at her eyes with it. When, she returned the handkerchief to Alvin she noticed she had left her black mascara stains on it.

'Oh, I'm so sorry, your hanky is stained.'

'Forget it, Meisu. Don't worry about it,' he said as he folded it and stuffed it back into his pocket.

Alvin and Meisu were silent for several moments. He took a long swig from his mug then looked her in the eye. "You know what I'd like to do? I'd like to paint you, Meisu. Would you like to pose for me?'

She laughed. 'What'll you do with a painting of me?'

'I want to give it to you. When you go back to Guilin, you'll have something to remember me by.'

'Oh, that's so sweet of you, Alvin. You're a kind person.'

'So are you, Meisu. I quite like you. Can you come over to my studio tomorrow afternoon?'

'How long will it take?'

'Three sittings of two to three hours each will be sufficient.'

'Hmm … OK. What do you want me to wear?' *Alvin is treating me like a lady, not a piece of meat as most men do.* She felt a warm feeling spreading through her body.

'Anything you like. If I might suggest so, light colours complement your complexion.'

'Thank you.' Meisu placed her hand over his thigh and smiled. 'Now, if you have finished eating, perhaps we can proceed to the next stage of this evening's programme?'

Meisu was quite surprised when Alvin could have sex with her that night. After a night of passion and more conversation in the hotel, Alvin dropped her back at New Peng Hwa.

'I will call you soon, Meisu. I am eager to meet you again.' Alvin hugged her goodbye.

Meisu watched as Alvin left the food court a satisfied man, healed and happy, with the ghost of his inadequacy behind him.

Friday 16 April

The pale man picked up a sheet of paper from his fax machine, which sat on a writing desk, along with a computer, a Styrofoam wig stand and several bags of plastic kazoos.

He read the message aloud: 'The clown must be completely bald. He must perform ten magic tricks and illusions on stage. Then the clown must set up a station for face-painting. The rest of the performance should be a thirty-minute walkabout to distribute balloon animals and stickers printed with our company's logo.' The pale man stroked the back of his head, playing with his hair, considering the job offer.

Then, he took out his cell phone and pressed a speed-dial number. 'Hey, Max, it's me. Do you've a white hoodie at the store?' A pause. 'How come when I need supplies, you don't have them?' Another pause. 'So, how about a bald wig? You have one? OK, I'll come over now.'

The man put the phone back into his case pouch and grabbed his car keys. Soon, he was at the clown-supplies store.

'This is a one-size cap and will fit your head right. It won't slip off.' Max flashed him a reassuring smile. 'Just trim your hair at the sides and back. Then it won't stick out of the cap.'

The pale man drove uptown to his regular hairdressing salon and parked his car at the front. After putting his parking ticket on the dashboard, he locked the car and walked up the sidewalk to the salon. *Bloody hell, it is closed.* He looked at the day and date on his watch. It was the sixteenth, a Friday. But of course. These Pakistani barbers always closed early on Fridays, so they could go to the mosque for prayer.

He remembered that there was a barber shop in the next block. *Well, since I've already parked my car, I could just walk there.* A nice Hakka noodle stall was also close by, and he could grab some lunch there.

He climbed up the stairs to the barber shop. As he pushed the door open, a metal bell hanging from it rang loudly to announce his arrival.

'Handsome man … Come, sit down, please,' greeted a huge woman, a cigarette dangling from her mouth. 'You're so lucky today. Our best girl is not engaged at the moment. I'll get her for you. Come … come …'

The salon was empty, and the pale man was the only customer. On a couch by the wall sat two middle-aged women barbers, reading magazines.

The pale man sat himself atop a chair. He watched uneasily as a woman with cantaloupes for breasts stepped out through a door at the end of the room and moved towards him.

'You want any drinks? We've Chinese tea, beer and soft drinks.'

The pale man shook his head curtly. 'I want a trim. At the back and sides. Please cut them short.'

'How about a shave or a shampoo?'

'No need for all that. I'm in a hurry.'

The barber draped a plastic sheet over the pale man. From a drawer in the styling station, she pulled out a pair of scissors and a comb, and started to snip at his hair. The man stared at the woman barber in the mirror. She had a crooked nose that bulged in the middle.

She took a step backward to inspect the trim. Then, suddenly, she smiled at him. She leaned forward and rubbed her breasts against the back of his head.

The pale man turned to her, shocked, and she giggled and whispered into his ear, 'Wanna have a good time in the karaoke afterwards? It's just behind the shop.'

The man's face darkened and heat flushed through his body. 'No! I'm not interested.' His fists clenched in rage.

'Come on, it won't cost much in tips.' Again, the barber stuck out her chest and rubbed it against the pale man's skull.

A volcano now blazed inside the pale man. He yanked the white sheet away from his neck and jumped to his feet. 'You bloody bitch!' he screamed.

He landed a blow on her face, then grabbed the barber by the throat with both hands.

'Help!' Her face was turning red as she gasped for air. 'Help me.' She raised the arm that held the pair of scissors and tried to plunge them into the assailant's chest. The pale man ducked to the side, then continued to choke her.

Two other barbers rushed towards them and dragged the pale man away from the woman. The door at the end of the room swung open and out dashed the huge woman who had earlier greeted the pale man, her cigarette still clamped in her mouth. She was holding a broom, ready to use it as a club. In her tow was a thickset man with the face of a gorilla and a neck as big as his head.

'Big sister, he choked me!' the barber screeched, holding her neck, gasping for breath.

'Yes, I saw it too. This man's a raving lunatic!' added another woman barber.

The pale man lunged again towards the woman, but her workmates held him back. 'This woman's a prostitute. She was disrespectful to me!' Spittle was beginning to build at the corner of his mouth.

The huge woman grunted, 'No need to be violent with my girls. If you don't want to karaoke with her, pay up for the haircut and leave.'

The pale man clenched and unclenched his fists.

'Add another fifty as compensation. She needs to buy Sing Foong San medicated powder to calm her fright.'

The pale man paid the seventy ringgit to the huge woman, and the broom went back to being a broom, and all the woman barbers went back to lounging on the couch.

As the pale man walked back towards his car, he could still feel the barber's cantaloupe breasts against his skull, soft and heavy, rubbing against it again and again. He wanted to slice them right off.

* * *

From Jamek Mosque, the muezzin's call for Friday prayer floated across the confluence of the Gombak and Kelang Rivers. In Alvin's studio, Meisu sat on a high-backed chair facing the painter. She was sitting about five feet away from Alvin, her body turned at a quarter angle to him. She was dressed in a floral print dress with laced sleeve-cuffs. Alvin had positioned her near the entrance so light would fall on her.

'Please tilt your head a little more,' Alvin said from behind his desk. He had moved it to the centre of the room. A wooden easel with a linen canvas stood on the desk, and around it were a clutter of brushes, bottles of turpentine, a palette and tubes of oil paint.

'Am I showing my good side?' she asked. 'You know, Alvin, in ancient China, only aristocrats had their portraits painted.'

Alvin smiled at her then picked up a charcoal pencil. 'Please relax your face, Meisu. Great art is about subtlety.' He started to move his arms over the canvas. Two matronly women in calf-length dresses who were walking past the studio entrance stopped to gawk at the painter and his subject.

'Why not take a picture of me?' she asked, yawning. *I hope the afternoon naps I am sacrificing are worth it. In any case, these sessions would give me an opportunity to bond with Alvin.*

'When I observe you like this, I can better interpret the range of gestures and characteristics that uniquely reflect your traits and mannerisms.' Alvin explained. 'But, if you're impatient, I can do a drawing now then finish the painting using a photograph.' He pulled open a drawer at his desk. 'I've a Fujifilm instant photo camera here.' He pulled out a camera and held it before her.

'No, that's OK. Let's see how this goes,' Meisu said, and she saw Alvin put the camera back into the drawer.

'Sometimes, I get sleepy in the afternoons.' Meisu smiled. Her eyes shot a sideward glance at the two matronly women. They were walking away from the studio.

'How much does it cost to get a portrait done?'

Alvin stared at her for a moment then looked back at the canvas. 'For you, it's free.'

'Yes, you told me earlier. I mean how much for your commissioned paintings?'

'Four thousand for a three-by-two feet.'

'Other paintings? How much do they sell for?'

'Depends on the size and medium.' Alvin was engrossed in the canvas. 'Oils and acrylics are more expensive than water colours.'

Meisu was tempted to ask how many paintings he usually sold in a month but decided that it would sound tactless. 'Are you drawing my face now?'

'I'm outlining your features.' He paused. 'You've fascinating eyes.'

'Is that what attracts you to me?' Alvin was not physically attractive to her but that wasn't too important to her. She was more worried about financial stability and compatibility.

'I appreciate symmetry and the right proportions. Creating a portrait is like giving birth to a baby. Don't you think so?' He paused. 'So, do you like children?'

'Having children is not a priority in life.' She shrugged. 'Besides, I think children bring out the incompatibles in couples.'

Alvin smiled as he squeezed some oil paints onto a wooden oval palette. 'Is the smell of paint bothering you?'

'No. It smells like linseed oil.'

'When you go back to Guilin, will you hang my portrait in your home?'

'When I go back to Guilin, will you still remember the moments we are sharing now?' she asked

They both grew silent for a moment. They smiled at each other.

'Can we be friends, Meisu? I mean can I go out with you without paying your escort fees?'

She smiled again sweetly. 'Sure, Alvin, we're friends.'

Two hours thus ticked away. Meisu noticed that Alvin's hand holding the palette was trembling slightly. Alvin moistened his upper lip with his tongue, then the lower lip.

'Are you getting tired?' she asked him.

'A little. Can we go for lunch? If you don't mind a short walk, there's a Chinese soup restaurant on Pudu Lane. They've several varieties of double-boiled soup.'

'I love soups.' Meisu stepped down from her high-backed chair. Alvin opened a drawer at his desk and took out Meisu's handbag, which she had left there for safekeeping, and returned it to her.

She took out a compact from her handbag and powdered her face. In her heart, she felt a storm of emotions brewing. She felt drawn to Alvin. He was a nice man and a talented painter. Yet she disliked drunks. They reminded her of her stepfather. Nevertheless, as she started towards the open door, she realised that his presence gave her joy. *No man is perfect*, she reminded herself. *I can change him. Once we're together, I will make him give up drinking.*

Monday 19 April

Outside, the sky was dull with odd patches of brightness. Detective Inspector Daniel Chu was sitting at his desk and looking out the window, contemplating his investigation so far and planning his next move to track down the serial killer. He considered the various pieces of information from the three case files and tried to mesh them together to find any clues. But that didn't work.

He turned to his side, 'Sergeant June, do you have any leads on the Xiong Caiqin murder case? What's the progress so far at your end?'

June swivelled her chair to face her superior. 'I'm afraid I've no new leads, despite staking out Pudu Food Court and One Stop Food Centre for more than a week. I even checked the photofit of our suspect against the mug shots of all the Chinese criminals released from prison in the last three years. No match.'

Chu pressed his back against his chair and sighed. 'Did you manage to interview any prostitutes?'

'Yes, I spoke to a few. None of them has seen anyone resembling the photofit. I don't think they've any reason to lie.'

'Have you contacted the Henry Gurney School in Malacca?'

'I had to go to Malacca because their records are not computerised. They gave me access to their physical files.' June got up, advanced a few paces and sat on the edge of Chu's desk, crossing her legs and leaning towards him. *Hell! She is trying to flirt with me again. I don't need this now.* Chu pushed his chair back a little, away from June.

June frowned. 'I've gone through the records of juvenile criminals released between 1997 and 2001. I worked backwards with the assumption that the suspect is thirty years old. Only one juvenile sex offender was released during those years, but he's not a Chinese.'

'Hmm ... So, it looks like we don't have any new clues to work on. And our killer has no criminal record.'

'All three victims were killed in the early hours of the morning. The killer is probably jobless or self-employed, doesn't hold a regular nine-to-five job.'

'And he speaks English. Could be a small-time trader. Definitely not a menial worker though. These facts only narrow down the profile of the killer. I think we should talk to Anthony's client, the one who acted as marriage broker between Xiong Caiqin and him. What do you think?'

The sergeant held his gaze for a moment. 'We'll be wasting our time in that direction. He did her a favour. Why should he then kill her? I've another suggestion.'

'Yes?'

'Why don't we lure the killer out of his hole? On my next surveillance, I will dress like a hooker. You know, fishnet stockings, miniskirts, that kind of stuff.'

'Good idea. But there's one problem.' Chu tried to suppress a smile. *Holy Crap! She will be the ugliest hooker in KL!* 'How will you deal with johns who will want to hire you?'

'I'll just tell them that I only take overnight bookings, and charge two thousand ringgit for each one. The exorbitant price will put them off.'

'We need to wire you up for your safety.' Chu pointed a finger at her. 'Also, we should get you some back-up. That would require approval from Sofian.'

'Forget Sofian. We don't need gadgets or men to do this. I can keep my mobile phone switched on while you listen in on yours. Backup's not necessary because I won't be exposed to any danger. First, I'll be carrying my semi-automatic. I'll hide it somewhere on my person. Second, the killer won't attack me on sight if he maintains his *modus operandi*. When the killer comes up to me, I'll signal you.' She thought about it for a moment. 'I'll put a cigarette between my teeth and light it. Then you can move in.'

Chu listened to her with rapt attention then nodded. 'Let's lay the trap at Pudu Food Court first. He'll probably come there for his next hooker. The first victim was murdered at San Peng. That's within walking distance from One Stop Food Centre, and it is very likely that the first hooker was picked up from there. The second victim was killed in Chinatown. The third victim probably street-walked at Sayur Road, where there're a lot of hawker stalls that are open late. Since, the serial killer hasn't picked up any hooker from Pudu Food Court yet, he'll most probably try there this time. If he doesn't turn up there, we can try at Alor Road, another popular hangout spot with street-walkers.'

'Great idea. We don't need to go early. All three victims were killed between two and three in the morning. So, the best time to set the trap would be after midnight.' June got off Chu's desk, smoothed her skirt and returned to her chair. She turned to look at Chu, grinning. 'Give me a few days to get the sexy-hooker clothes. I'll beg, borrow or steal if I have to.'

* * *

Alvin punched a button at the ticket dispenser, and it spat out a chit with a number. He looked at the queue machine display above the bank counter. There were eight customers ahead of him. About a dozen people sat scattered on the rows of seats before him. He plonked down on an empty seat and waited his turn impatiently.

Earlier in the morning, Meisu had sat in his studio for two hours and posed for him. Then, they had lunch together at a nearby café. His sirloin steak tasted great, had been juicy and tender, and he had washed it down with a 350-millilitre bottle of rum. As he had walked back to the Central Market, with Meisu beside him, the usually drab streets of Chinatown had taken on the bright colours of a theme park: the smiles of the women selling flowers outside Malaya Hotel had broadened into half-crescent moons; the stained aprons of the street hawkers had resembled exquisite works of Abstract Expressionism; the hoarse hollers of fruit-sellers sounded like the words of a rock-and-roll song; the cheap sweat-shop sewn clothes displayed in the crammed stores had looked like the pieces of haute couture one might see on London's Bond Street.

'Raise your hands! Drop the gun!' A hoarse voice jolted Alvin from his reverie.

Alvin turned around. Loud gasps burst from several women,

and they clutched their handbags tightly. At the door of the bank, a heavy-chested man wearing a plastic Mickey Mouse mask and a dark t-shirt was pointing a pistol at the head of the security guard, a thin Nepalese in his early twenties. At the same time, another man wearing a Spider-Man mask ran up to the counter and handed a bag to the female teller, a trembling middle-aged woman.

'Gimme the money! Quick!' He pointed a sawn-off shotgun at her, and she filled up the bag from the cash till until it was empty. 'Pass the bag to that fat guy next to you!'

The woman handed the half-filled bag to the teller beside her. The robber in the Spider-Man mask shouted, 'Fill up the bag!'

Alvin saw the security guard raise his arms above his head and drop his shotgun to the floor with a clatter. The man in the Mickey Mouse mask kicked the weapon away. 'Lie down!' He kicked at the back of the guard's knees, and he dropped face down on the floor. The other robber looked from the tellers to the seated customers. 'Nobody moves!' Everyone sat still with pale and terrified faces.

Alvin stared at the robber with the Mickey Mouse mask. He remembered going to an amusement park once with his Papa and Mama. He had seen a life-sized Mickey Mouse there, donning the red-and-black costume and a pair of big mouse ears, dancing and kicking his legs in time to cancan music. The mouse's big yellow shoes had flown off its feet mid-dance and headed toward the faces of two spectators, who had tried to dodge but had been hit by the footwear anyway. Everyone at the amusement park had burst into laughter.

Alvin smiled to himself at the memory.

'What's so funny?' The robber in the Mickey Mouse mask had spotted Alvin. He was staring at him.

'Nothing.' Alvin burst into a fit of laughter. He covered his mouth with his hand.

The robber in the Spider-Man mask stepped away from the cashiers and toward Alvin. 'You wanna die?'

'No.' Alvin laughed until he shook like a tree caught in a monsoon.

'Are you laughing at me?'

Alvin thought of the dancing Mickey Mouse again, of his flying yellow shoes. 'Hahaha! No.'

'Damn you!' The last thing Alvin saw was the butt of a shotgun coming at him.

Tuesday 20 April

The squeak of wheels on polished tiled floor woke up Alvin. He opened his eyes and light exploded into his eyes, searing them like a branding iron. The smell of disinfectant and stale food settled in his nostrils, and a dull ache thumped in his skull. Alvin looked down at himself. He was wearing a green short-sleeved gown that reached down to his knees. The fabric felt coarse, and three stiff knots of it pressed into his back.

He turned to the left and saw a grey-haired, emaciated man lying on a bed about five feet away. The man whistled and wheezed as he breathed. Alvin rolled to his right and saw a brown-skinned man fast asleep on a bed, his arm connected by a tube to a plastic bag that hung from an intravenous stand A portly woman wearing a *tudong* was slumped in a vinyl chair next to his bed, fast asleep and snoring, her pudgy hand resting on the man's thin one.

Footsteps sounded in the corridor outside. A dark-skinned woman in a white pinafore and a fair-skinned man with a stethoscope hanging from his neck walked up to Alvin's bed. It took a second for Alvin to register that the man was a doctor and the woman a nurse. The doctor looked like he was in his thirties. He wore square Retro-

Nerd spectacles.

The nurse handed a plastic cup to Alvin. 'Drink this.'

'What's this?'

'Some medication to sober you up.' She smiled. 'It tastes excellent.'

Alvin came to a sitting position, held the cup with both hands and gulped down its contents. He grimaced as the medicine's pungent taste made his tongue curl. The doctor walked to the foot of the metal bed and pulled out the clipboard that was attached to it.

Then, clipboard in hand, he moved to the side of the bed. 'What's your name?'

'Alvin Au.'

'What's your occupation?'

'Painter.'

'House painter?'

'No, I'm an artist. I do paintings.'

'Where do you live?'

'Begonia Court, Air Panas Road.'

'What year is this?'

'Why are you asking me all these questions?' Alvin was getting annoyed. 'Twenty ten.'

The doctor's face was expressionless. 'What month is this?'

'April.'

'What day is this?'

'Depends on how long I've been here.'

'Today's Tuesday. An ambulance brought you here yesterday afternoon. According to the bank's police report, you were hit unconscious by a rifle butt. Remember?'

Alvin fingered the side of his head. 'Oh, yes, now everything's coming back to me.'

'Luckily, the X-ray didn't show any fracture,' the doctor said.

'What's the time?' Alvin just remembered Meisu.

'A little after 11 a.m.,' the nurse said. *Jesus Christ, I have missed today's portrait session with her.*

'You can leave,' the doctor said. 'You seem fine but try not to drink so much. Your alcohol level was very high yesterday.' He pulled out a pen from his breast pocket and scribbled onto the clipboard. He then returned the clipboard to its former place at the foot of the bed, turned and walked away.

'Your clothes are in here,' the nurse said, pointing to a small cupboard beside the bed. 'You've to go to the discharge counter and sign a form.'

Half an hour later, Alvin got himself a taxi outside the hospital gate. He leaned back and tried to switch on his mobile phone but the battery was dead. He desperately wanted to call Meisu.

Back in his condo, he took a quick shower and changed into fresh clothes. He then dialled Meisu's number on his hand phone.

'Meisu, I'm so sorry. Something happened to me yesterday afternoon. I just got home.' A pause. 'Where're you now? Uh-huh … Shopping in Chinatown? That's great.' He looked at his watch. 'Listen, can we meet for lunch? Give me about an hour to get to the studio.' Another pause. 'I'll explain everything to you when we meet. Yes, OK, see you then.'

* * *

Alvin and Meisu met at Precious Old China restaurant on the

mezzanine floor of Central Market. They sat side by side, surrounded by antique furniture and under the light of chandeliers, and as they ate, Alvin recounted what had happened to him at the bank. Meisu's caring words helped comfort him.

A waiter served them a plate of *kuih pie tee*. Alvin put down his cutlery, scooped a mixture of turnips, carrots and fried cuttlefish onto Meisu's plate. 'Try this. It's a delicacy originating from Penang.'

'Thanks.' Meisu chewed the snack slowly, relishing it, then swallowed. 'I don't think you should live alone anymore, Alvin,' she said, holding him with her gaze. 'Why don't you move into my apartment? I've a spare room.'

'As a lodger?' Alvin's mind went fuzzy for a moment. *I really do like Meisu, but isn't it a bit too soon for her to speak of us living together?*

'No, as a friend. But give me whatever you can to help me pay the rent.'

'Why should we stay together?'

'So we can take care of each other.' Her words opened a flood-gate in him. *Is this the start of a new beginning for me. How wonderful it would feel to be cared for by a woman again.*

His heart started to beat a little faster. 'Are things moving a bit too fast between us?'

'Alvin, we are both living alone. And we are both lonely. I don't know what's going to happen between us in the future. But I'm willing to take this step and see where it takes us.'

'What about my rented condo?'

'Let go of it.' She put down her fork and spoon and wiped at her mouth with a tissue. The tone of her voice was half-plea, half-command.

'Meisu, I'm alive today because of you. Since I have met you, I've been taking each day as it comes. And I'm finally feeling happy and alive. What if we get deeper into this relationship, and then things go wrong? What if you get busted? Or deported? My world would fall to pieces again.'

'Let's not look too far ahead. If the worst happens, take over my apartment.'

Alvin kept silent and chewed his food. He wanted to ask her about his drinking, if she knew he needed to have a few drinks every day. He wanted to ask if she was OK with that. But he decided against it.

'I know you're a drinker,' Meisu said as if she had read his mind. 'And you know my profession. Let us just be ourselves, with all our faults and weaknesses.'

'So, we just live our own lives?'

'Yes.' She placed her hand over his shoulder, and he felt like an iron stuck to a magnet. He had made up his mind.

'When do you want me to move in?'

'Up to you. Even today is fine with me. I'll get the room ready, spread a new bed sheet, mop the floor and make spare keys. The room's furnished. You only need to pack your clothes and come over. But try to arrive before I leave for work at 7 p.m. That suits you fine?'

'Sure. Let's just do this now and hope for the best.'

Wednesday 21 April

Alvin pushed the canvas away from him. He rested his folded arms on the table and dropped his head onto them. He closed his eyes to rest them. He had worked nonstop since 10:30 a.m., and now it was late afternoon. He had taken double shots of rum with his cup of Aik Cheong Cappuccino before he had left home, so his hands had not started to tremble yet. His stomach rumbled though, and he knew he had to get himself a bite to eat soon.

'Look what I've got for you!'

Alvin raised his head and opened his eyes to see Meisu before him, dressed in a short pink dress, cradling a rectangular wrapped package with both her arms. Alvin smiled fondly at her.

Yesterday, he had moved into her condominium. He had arrived at her door with a wheeled travelling bag and a shoulder bag, and Meisu had greeted him with a smile. It was the first time he had seen Meisu without make-up and dressed in a casual collarless t-shirt and slacks. She had still looked so beautiful. She had led him to the spare room and switched on the air-conditioner.

'Here are the spare keys.' She had handed them to Alvin. While Meisu had been busy getting ready for work, Alvin had unpacked his clothes and hung them in his new closet. He had walked to the kitchen with his shoulder bag, taken out several bottles of his liquor and put them in the fridge, had then entered the bathroom and placed his toothbrush and toothpaste on the plastic ledge of the mirror, along with Meisu's.

By the time he had finished unpacking and setting up his things in his new home, Meisu had become ready to set out for work.

'I'll be back around two or three', she said. 'There's no need to wait up for me. In case you missed it, there's a cafeteria in the first block, on the left.'

She had kissed him goodbye and left the apartment. Alvin had eaten dinner at Leisure Mall. And when he had returned home, he had opened himself a bottle of whisky. He had followed it up with two bottles of vodka before staggering into his new bedroom and falling asleep on his new bed.

'I've got you a gift, Alvin, and I think you'll love it.' Meisu walked up to his desk and put the package by his feet, tore away the brown-paper wrapping and shook the open end of the cardboard box to the floor. The folded components of an easel slipped out with a soft thud.

'Wow, a box easel!' Alvin got to his feet, excited.

'Yes, and it's made of bamboo. Harder than oak and comes with telescopic legs.' She loosened the bolts and spread the easel's tripod legs, setting them up on the floor. 'The salesgirl said it can be adjusted to various configurations for different applications.'

'Let me do it,' Alvin said, moving forward to the easel. Tears of joy ran down his eyes. He didn't bother to brush them away.

'When the legs fold, it becomes a table easel as well. There's also a pull-out drawer to store your paints and brushes.' Meisu smiled at him.

When Alvin had assembled the easel, tears were still trickling down his face. 'Oh, Meisu, this is the most wonderful present. So is the person who has given it to me.' He ran his hands down the frame and stroked its edges and back. 'Must have been expensive.'

'If you've not eaten, let's have lunch.' Her smile was soft and gentle.

'How about going to that soup restaurant again?'

'Is that all you have to offer me in return?' She giggled. 'That's fine.'

They left the studio, and Alvin locked its shutter door. They walked out of the building into an overcast sky. Standing on the kerb, they looked for a gap in the fast flowing line of cars and motorbikes before them.

'So, just now, were you resting or snoozing?' Meisu asked.

Alvin did not meet her eyes. 'Trying to re-energise myself,' he said simply.

They crossed the street, holding hands, and then walked side by side on the sidewalk. 'Business has picked up again. I got a commission to do two portraits for a big shot. The work's worth twelve grand. They're four-by-three-feet, and the client has already paid a deposit.' His insides broke into a small celebratory dance. 'I'm clearing off my other works-in-progress so that I can start work as soon as possible. I'm sorry, Meisu, but your portrait will have to wait. I hope that's OK.' He shot a sideward glance at her and saw her nod.

'When did you get home yesterday night?' he asked.

'Around 2 a.m. I bathed, changed, had supper, and then slept half an hour later.'

They were now treading past stores selling pickled cabbage, preserved black beans and sun-dried meat. A salty aroma stung their nostrils.

'Do you always take a late supper?' He held Meisu's slender waist and steered her up the carpeted side staircase to the restaurant. 'This morning I saw an instant-noodle wrapper and a plastic bowl in the trash can.'

'Sometimes,' Meisu said. 'I try not to though, since I am afraid of gaining weight.'

A thought suddenly struck Alvin: *If she threw the wrapper into the waste can, she must have seen the empty liquor bottles I put there too.* He felt uneasy. He was afraid that she might say something, might stop him from drinking. *Sure, she must have seen it. But it does seem a good sign that she has not mentioned it to me yet.*

* * *

Meisu entered New Peng Hwa Food Court at her usual time. She ordered a plate of sweet-and-sour pork with rice for dinner, and then settled at a table near the entrance. A petite Indonesian waitress brought her a can of Coca-Cola and a glass half-filled with ice. Meisu poured the soft drink into the glass and sipped it from a straw, scanning the hordes of prospective customers milling around tables, their wallets bulging in their hip pockets. Her hand phone rang: it was Lawrence Leow.

'Hello, Lawrence. How are you?' The sweet-and-sour pork arrived, and Meisu tucked her phone between her shoulder and ear as she took out some money from her purse to pay the waitress. 'I'm fine. Want to meet tonight?'

A pause. 'You've a business proposition for me? Big money? Is it a gangbang?' She giggled. 'Sorry, I don't do that.' Another pause. Meisu frowned then took a sip of her coke. 'An old lady? What does she want me to do? I hope it's nothing too kinky.'

The waitress handed her the change, and Meisu put the money in her handbag. 'I'll be taped? Lawrence, I'm not a porn star and I don't intend to be one.'

When Lawrence tried to explain further, she cut him off. 'Why don't you come over and explain it to me? Hmm ... OK, thanks. See you.'

A short while after Meisu had finished eating her dinner, she saw Lawrence walk over to her table. He was dressed in a casual grey t-shirt and dark jeans. 'Chinese tea,' he said to a passing brown-skinned waiter.

Meisu smiled. 'What's this big proposition of yours?' she asked as Lawrence sat beside her.

'A middle-aged woman wants to file for divorce. And while she's at it, she wants to take her husband to the cleaners. She wants to film her husband making love to another woman, and then claim that she's cheating on him. This is where you come in, Meisu,' he said, grinning. 'It's an overnight session for three thousand. The wife will use the video CD to threaten the husband. Their divorce lawyers may look at it. That's all. Your identity's not important to them. But you've to make sure the victim's face is seen clearly in the video.'

'Who's this rich man?'

'I can't reveal his name yet. But he's a big shot, the vice-president of a bank. He is in his early fifties, a Chinese.'

'Let me ask you a few questions before I decide, OK?'

Lawrence nodded. She glanced at her ice-filled glass sweating on the table, thought for a moment then looked up at him again. 'Why doesn't the wife just install a secret camera in the room?'

'She doesn't know which room he'll be using. But she knows which hotel her husband brings his prostitutes – his ladies – to. It's always Sheralux Hotel. It's near that Lexington place, where you met that Arab, Mr. Yasser."

'I see. Why doesn't he go to a spa? Or a KTV?'

'This fella's a public figure. A very popular guy. He cannot be seen in these sorts of places. He'll ruin the bank's reputation, and the board of directors will sack him.'

Meisu's brows drew closer, and she took a long sip of her cold drink. 'There're a few details I still don't understand. Like why can't the old man book the room himself?'

Lawrence shrugged his shoulders. 'Perhaps he trusts his P.A?'

'Where do you come into the picture?'

'His personal assistant always books the room. He's my friend. The old lady bribed the P.A. to help her in the setup, and he asked for my help with picking a girl who could pull this off. I chose you because your specs meet the old man's taste – you're bosomy, fair and speak good English.' He let out a long breath. 'Now, are you interested? If not, I can always ask someone else.'

'If I accept, what exactly do I have to do?'

'It's all very simple, Meisu. Once the old man arrives, he will be allotted a room. You'll have to message the room number to the cameraman. Your job is to let the cameraman into the room and let him hide in the closet. After the act is over, you'll have to let him out again. That shouldn't be a problem if you can get the client to go into the bathroom, so the cameraman has time to slip in and out of the room.'

Oh, Lord Buddha. Timing's crucial in this set-up. Things can go wrong, and there's quite a bit of risk involved too. I might as well ask for more money. 'A hidden one-man audience will be watching me?' She wrinkled her nose. 'That's embarrassing. Make it four thousand.'

'Impossible. The old lady won't agree. There's no market price for this sort of thing. Besides, the three thousand comes only from the old crone. And then there's your usual fee from the client too. He's generous, and he will most likely pay you two thousand for this.' Lawrence shook his head at her. 'Don't act difficult, Meisu. Other girls will be more than happy to take me up on this offer.'

'And how much are you getting for setting this up?'

Lawrence grinned, revealing his crooked teeth. 'Very little. It's more like helping out a friend.'

A scruffy-looking waiter in an apron served Lawrence his glass of Chinese tea. 'So, you want the job or not?' Lawrence turned to press a fifty-sen coin in the waiter's palm and looked back at Meisu.

The food court was filling up, and the crowd was getting louder, drunker.

'When's the booking?'

'Tomorrow. The old bugger wants to meet at 10 p.m.'

'OK. Are you sure the closet's big enough for the cameraman?'

'Yes. Sheralux's a five-star hotel. The room is big. Everything is big there.'

'Payment procedure?'

'The cameraman will pay you once he's inside the room.'

'Fine, I'll do it.' *This is a lucky break for me! If I get this right, I'll be able to send my cousin the fifteen thousand yuan he asked for, without feeling the pinch. And if I do screw up with the cameraman, the client will still pay me. So what's there for me to lose?*

Lawrence fished out his cell phone from his pocket. 'I'm sending the cameraman's phone number to you now.' He pressed a few buttons. 'He's called Steven, is in his late thirties and is quite tanned for a Chinese. Be early and give him a call when you arrive in the lobby.' He took a few gulps of his Chinese tea. 'The P.A. will give your contact to the old fellow. He'll call you when he gets there.'

He flicked his wrist to look at his watch. 'I guess that settles this arrangement.' He rose to his feet. 'Good night. And all the best.'

After Lawrence left, Meisu went about her business as usual. She picked up four customers, serviced them and received payment for the same.

It was almost dawn when Meisu returned home. It had been a good night. All four customers had tipped her generously.

As she walked to her bedroom, Alvin came out in his pajamas, his hair tousled and falling over his forehead. He crossed the kitchen and trudged towards her, smiling mischievously, both his hands held behind his back.

'Close your eyes,' he said. 'I bought you a gift. I hope you like it.' His eyes were heavily lidded, his face flushed, his breath smelling of stale hops.

He is drunk again. Is it too late to change him? Meisu closed her eyes for a moment. 'Can I open them now?'

'Yes.'

She opened her eyes to see that Alvin held in his hands a Seiko watch with a sleek and sparkling stainless-steel bracelet. 'Oh, thank you so much!' Meisu leaned in and kissed the corner of his mouth. 'You didn't have to wait for me to give me this,' she said as he handed her the watch and the satin box it came in. 'You could have left it on the table with a note.'

'I wanted to see your face when you got it. Do you like it?'

'Of course, I do.' She looked at the watch again. *Oh shucks! This watch is too expensive to be worn while I am working. I'll wear it only on special occasions.* She put it carefully in its satin box and closed it. 'Thank you, Alvin. This is so nice of you.' She hugged him and wished him goodnight.

Alvin's such a dear, tender man, she thought as she walked into her room, smiling to herself. *If only he'd stop drinking ...*

Thursday 22 April

Meisu had reached Sheralux Hotel on Sultan Ismail Road. 'Hello, Steven?' she said into the mouthpiece of her cell phone. 'I'm Meisu, I'm in the hotel lobby. Where're you?' Her stomach tickled as if she had swallowed a handful of fuzzy caterpillars.

'Are you wearing purple dress with a bowknot at the waist?'

'Yes.'

Meisu looked around her. From the ceiling hung a chandelier, dripping glass tears, spilling its golden light across the polished marble floor. A bellboy glided past her, pushing along a bird-cage luggage cart. A few guests, dressed in casuals, stood at the gleaming marble counter of the hotel's reception, while more than a dozen others sat scattered on the lobby's plush chairs. A white-gloved doorman hovered at the glass entrance, greeting anyone who walked in.

'Just remain seated and wait for your client. I'm at the pillar across the lobby.'

Meisu looked in the direction of a large square pillar with a potted solitaire palm on one side, and saw a man seated there in an upholstered armchair, holding a phone to his ear. He was of average build and wore a striped shirt and khaki slacks.

'Yes, I see you,' she said. 'Did you bring the payment?'

'Of course. It's C.O.D. when your mission-impossible is accomplished.' He chortled at his joke. 'Text me the room number, OK? I need about ten minutes to grab a room here. Turns out only guests can use the elevator in this hotel. Anyway, when I'm outside your door, I'll message you. Then, you let me into the room. We've to work fast. Understand? Let's keep our fingers crossed.'

At 10 p.m. sharp, Meisu's client called her. She told him what she was wearing, and he was able to identify her without any difficulty. He walked to the divan and sat down beside her.

'Hello, I'm Carrick,' he said, smiling. 'I've collected the room key.' His voice was deep and gruff. He was of average height and had a receding hairline, big round eyes with yellowish whites and a mouth of gleaming white teeth. 'Have you had dinner yet? Would you like to go for a bite?' He was dressed expensively, had on an Ermenegildo Zegna jacket and a pair of Prada leather shoes.

'Thanks, but I'm not hungry.'

They walked to the lift. Inside, Carrick swiped the card key at the reader and pressed '12'. As the doors closed, the strong smell of his cologne filled the confined space of the lift. Carrick gazed into Meisu's eyes, smiled and gently ran his fingers over her face. 'You're so beautiful. You've exceeded my expectations.'

The twin doors opened, and they stepped out. 'Room 1206,' he said, looking to the left and right. 'That way, baby.' He pointed to the right.

A short walk brought them to the deluxe room. They entered it, and Carrick tapped on the wall switches. Illuminated under the dim ceiling lights was a king-sized bed with a padded headboard. On its side were two bell-shaped table lamps with scalloped edges, a two-drawer dresser with cabriolet legs and a gilded wall mirror placed above the dresser.

Meisu looked around the room, taking in a closet with louvered sliding doors and a round coffee table with two Chippendale armchairs on one end, and a LED television and a mini-fridge on the other.

'Here, let me help you with your jacket,' Meisu said, taking a step towards her client.

He turned his back to her. 'Thanks, baby.' He unbuttoned the jacket, pulled out one arm, and let Meisu slip the jacket off of his other arm.

She walked over to the closet, slid open one of its louvered doors and hung the jacket on one of the wooden hangers inside. *Great. The doors don't make a squeaking noise when they open. And there's ample space for a man to stand inside.*

'Take a seat, please,' Carrick said, pointing to an armchair. 'I'm going to switch off the lights. There's no need to be alarmed. I just want to check if the room's OK.'

Meisu watched with some surprise as the man turned off the lights and pulled out a small torch light from his pocket. He moved to the dresser and examined its wall mirror, shining the torch's light at it from a few angles. Then he touched the mirror with his forefinger and looked at its reflection, leaning into it.

He then moved towards the bathroom. Meisu immediately took out her mobile phone from her handbag. She texted '1206' and fired away the SMS then placed her phone on the table. Several moments later, Carrick came out with an empty toilet-paper tube in one hand, still holding the torchlight in the other. He put the tube over his one eye like a telescope and flashed the light over the room's wall.

'What're you doing, darling? Why don't you come to bed?' *Heavens, this guy is being so careful. I hope I don't get caught.*

'A small glimmer can indicate the lens of a mini spy camera.' He moved across the room, scrutinising every inch of the wall, and then proceeded to do the same with the other walls of the room.

When he was finished, he tossed the empty toilet-paper tube into a waste basket beside the dresser. He then moved to the foot of the bed and shone the torchlight upward at the ceiling. 'Sorry about this. Just one more detection test. Then I'm done.'

He moved across the room to switch on the lights, and then took out his mobile phone and made a call. 'David? Just hold the line, please.' He walked to the dresser facing the bed and waved the cell phone around it. 'Why are you playing James Bond?' Meisu was starting to worry now. She feigned a giggle, although her heart was pounding inside her chest.

'I'm testing whether there's an electromagnetic field in the dresser. An electromagnetic field will produce clicking noises during a call.' He moved to the closet and conducted the same test on it. Then, satisfied, he spoke into the mouthpiece, 'Thanks, David, that's all.' He put the cell phone back in his pocket.

'Sit down, please. Let me take off your shoes, darling.' *Damn it, fifteen minutes have already passed! What is the cameraman doing? Why hasn't he sent me a message yet?*

Carrick sat on the edge of the bed and stretched his legs. Meisu got down on one knee, unlaced his shoes and peeled off his socks. As she was stuffing the socks into the footwear, she heard her phone vibrate. She had just received a message. Her client shot a sideward glance at her cell phone but said nothing.

Meisu rose, flashed him a coy smile and started to unbutton his shirt. 'Darling, can you please take a shower?' she said. 'Please take your time to scrub yourself. I like clients who smell good.'

When she had stripped Carrick naked, he walked to the bathroom with a whistle. The door slammed shut.

Meisu kicked off her shoes, flew to the hotel room's door and opened it. The cameraman scampered across the room to the closet, slid open the door and entered. Meisu gestured for him to give her the money, and the cameraman dipped into his pocket, produced a bulging brown envelope and handed it over. He then pulled the door shut, leaving only a half-inch gap for his camcorder lens. Meisu took a peep at the contents of the envelope and scrambled across the room to put it in her handbag. She could hear Carrick turn off the shower in the bathroom. She quickly switched on the tableside lamps, tapped off the ceiling lights and started to undress.

Friday 23 April

Alvin sat facing a canvas, a neat line of tiny paint pots placed across the desk before him. His finger pinched around a reed brush, dipped it into a pot and started to dot on the canvas with mathematical precision, putting hundreds upon hundreds of minute dots there.

He leaned back and gazed at his work, pleased with it. The scene showed the island of Pangkor. Fishermen made out of infinitely graduated points of colour stood out like miniature toy soldiers. The canvas was done completely in bright colours. Living with Meisu was filling him confidence, a sense of well-being, and this showed in his work.

His cell phone rang. It was her. He carefully put the brush away and answered it. 'Good afternoon, Meisu.'

'Alvin, how's work?'

Alvin massaged his left shoulder with one hand. 'Good. I sold two acrylics this morning, but without their frames. Where're you?'

'At home. I got back at ten this morning. I had an overnight booking.'

He transferred the cell phone to his left hand and massaged his right shoulder. 'No wonder I couldn't hear the buzzing of the air-con in your room.'

'Alvin, I've made some extra money yesterday, and I was wondering if we could take a short break? Maybe spend a night in Genting? I've heard about that casino, and it sounds exciting. We could go there tomorrow. We can even catch a performance in the evening. I can pay for the hotel room if you want me to. What do you think?'

He swiveled around in the chair, considering the plan. 'No, I'll pay for it. That's a great idea. I need a break too. I'll call and book a room right away.'

'Should we drive there or take a taxi?'

'The journey's only an hour from the foot to the peak. Driving there's better. On the way, we can stop for some delicious wild river fish at Bukit Tinggi.'

'Excellent. I'm going to the bank now. I need to wire some money to my cousin in Guilin. Bye.'

Alvin was smiling as he put his cell phone away. *This is going to be a great getaway. It will be nice to spend a whole day with Meisu, without any clients or other distractions.* He reached out for the can of beer on his desk and took a swig from it.

Saturday 24 April

Alvin, dressed in a formal brown jacket and dark pants, and Meisu, dressed in a long chiffon dress, entered Casino de Genting. They held hands as they walked by the rows of slot machines that filled one side of the room. The place was as big as a grand ballroom. A series of gaming tables filled the other side of the casino. Shimmering chandeliers hung above the heads of gamers, and a cloud of stale cigarette smoke hung in the air above them. Occasional bursts of announcements of wins at the slot machines intermittently drowned the steady stream of the piped-in muzak.

The tables were packed with excited gamblers. Behind one row of people were herded a second and a third row, all of them awaiting their turns, some of them stretching a hand through the first row of gamblers in order to deposit their stakes. Alvin and Meisu moved to the roulette table where a male croupier and a female croupier, both of them in shiny vests and bow ties, were stationed. A tall man, whose legs seemed to begin at his chest, finished his game and vacated a seat.

'Grab that seat, Alvin.' Meisu pulled out some cash from her handbag and handed them to him, 'And, here, get some chips too. You do the betting for me. Maybe your hands are luckier than mine.'

The croupier passed some red chips to Alvin.

Meisu scanned the board. 'Which bet pays the most?'

'Zero. Thirty-five to one.'

'What are the lowest pay-outs?'

'Red, black, even and odd, one to eighteen, nineteen to thirty six. One to one.'

'Stake ten chips on zero, please.'

A stout woman with a flabby chin turned sideways and said to Alvin, 'Sorry, I don't mean to interfere. But zero just turned up.'

Meisu shouted from behind Alvin, 'Nonsense. Stake, please. It's my money.' She flashed the stout woman an annoyed look.

'Bets open!' the female croupier announced.

Alvin pushed ten chips on zero.

The male croupier spun the wheel and flipped the ball in the rim. After several seconds, the ball started to hop along the notches of the revolving wheel.

The male croupier waved his hand over the table. 'No more bets!'

The ball hopped and bobbed for a while, then finally came to a stop. 'Twenty!' called the croupier. He placed a marker on number twenty on the green betting table, then collected the losing bets and paid the winning bets.

'Shit!' Alvin slapped the table with his palm.

Meisu put a hand on his shoulder. 'Please stake on zero again. Ten chips again. I believe my luck is good tonight.'

Alvin turned around to see her holding the locket around her neck, blowing at it and praying. 'Big win, big win.' She muttered, peering over his shoulder.

The croupier spun the wheel, and after it began to slow down, he announced, 'No more bets!'

'Zero!' called the croupier.

'See! I told you!' Alvin turned to see Meisu's smiling face.

The croupier shoved two piles of chips to number zero.

'How many chips should I receive?' Meisu asked.

'Three hundred and fifty chips.'

'Let's continue. We're on a winning streak!'

'What shall we stake on?' Alvin asked, mopping his forehead with his palm. He was starting to sweat. His hands were trembling. A sudden craving for alcohol was gnawing at his insides. He had not consumed any liquor during lunch and dinner, partly to impress Meisu and partly to start tapering off his drinking, and the withdrawal was getting worse. His old friend was nudging him hard.

'Zero again, zero again! Stake one hundred chips this time.'

Alvin tried to distract himself. 'Why not play safe? Bet on either red or black?'

'No, no, Alvin. I like high risk, high return.'

Once more the croupier invited the company to stake and prepared to turn the wheel. With shaking hands, Alvin betted one hundred chips on zero and turned to look at Meisu's face for a moment. He could see she was sure of winning. He hoped she was right.

The wheel revolved and stopped, and the ball dropped into one of the notches.

'Zero!' announced the croupier.

'Yay!' Meisu clapped her hands in glee.

Alvin's stomach suddenly twisted in agonising knots. His bile rose to his throat, and he lowered his head and puked, spraying garlic, soy sauce, morsels of grilled beef and pieces of chicken on the carpet.

The other gamblers gasped in disbelief and moved away from him. 'Get a cleaning lady! Some bastard vomited!' a security guard standing nearby mumbled into his walkie-talkie.

'Ladies and gentleman, we've to close this table for a while,' the croupier announced. He threw Alvin a look of contempt.

'Oh, I'm sorry, everybody,' Alvin said, wiping his mouth with his handkerchief. 'I ate some food that disagreed with me.' He turned to Meisu. 'I need to go to the room to rest.'

'Sure, you go ahead and rest. I'll stay and continue with the other games. Put your hand phone beside your pillow in case you don't hear the doorbell. I might be pretty late.'

Meisu's words surprised Alvin. *I didn't know gambling was so important to her?* He noticed that although her tone was gentle, an undercurrent of annoyance frothed beneath its surface, frustration that her gambling pleasure had been disrupted by him. This was a side to her he hadn't seen before.

Alvin staggered out of the casino. Heads turned to look at him as he made his way back to the hotel room, the front of his shirt stained with vomit, smelling of stale food. He dashed to the bathroom and put his head over the toilet, and again his stomach wrenched. When there was nothing left in his gut to retch out, he plucked a few sheets of toilet paper, wiped his mouth and pulled the flush lever.

He walked over to the refrigerator in the room. Inside were two bars of Kit Kat, two packets of pistachio nuts, two bottles of mineral water, two 170-millilitre bottles of whisky and two 170-millilitre bottles of gin. He took out two bottles of whisky, and then plopped down into an armchair and switched on the TV. He finished the first bottle in a few swallows. He watched a musical programme while he sipped from the second bottle. When he had finished the second one, a surge of relief coursed through his veins. He moved to the dresser top, took the PVC guest services directory and flipped through its pages.

Great, a pub is listed among the F&B outlets. I can reserve the gin in the fridge for tomorrow morning then. He left the room and headed to the pub. An hour later, after treating himself to two bottles of beer and a plate of lamb chops, he returned to the bedroom, showered and changed into his pajamas. He leaned against the headboard of the bed to watch TV, his cell phone placed beside him on the side table. A few hours later, the doorbell rang, and he got up to let in Meisu.

She entered the room, kicked off her shoes and unzipped her dress, letting it fall to her knees.

'Did you enjoy yourself?' Alvin slipped back into the bed.

Her face beaming, she unhooked and removed her bra, letting it drop to the carpet. 'Of course! I played blackjack, *tai sai*, poker and mini baccarat. Overall, I won more than two thousand. Luck was on my side, Alvin.'

As she walked towards him, she frowned. She sniffed at the air a few times, crinkling her nose. 'Darling, we need to have a talk regarding your drinking problem. Not now, but over breakfast tomorrow. I don't want this habit to become a thorn in our relationship.'

Alvin's froze for a second. His heart sank to his toes. 'I thought you said we should accept each other,' he mumbled. 'Warts and all. In fact, I'm trying my best to cut down.'

'When we're in love we fall under all sorts of illusions,' she said, stepping out of her panties. 'I didn't realise you're such a heavy drinker. You're almost an alcoholic.' She picked up her dress and undergarments and walked over to the closet to hang them in there. She turned to look at him, her lips pursed together in anger. 'It was such an embarrassment to me when you vomited in the casino. What will everyone think of us?'

'Yes, you are right about illusions. I don't know a lot of things about you, either. For instance, I didn't know you have a passion for gambling. Is this your first time in a casino?' he said, his voice brimming with sarcasm.

She slipped on a short-sleeved nightgown, and then a knitted sweater over it. 'It's not a big deal, Alvin. Back home, I used to visit illegal gambling houses to play card games. I grew fond of it. In any case, I gambled with my *own* hard-earned money. So what's wrong with that?'

Alvin blanched. 'Nothing.'

Meisu walked towards the bathroom. At the door, she turned to look at him. 'Tomorrow after breakfast, I'm going to the casino again. I'd like to try the slots. If you'd like to join me, please make sure you're feeling better.'

'Aren't we planning to take in some sights tomorrow? Maybe browse the stores?'

She did not answer him. She entered the bathroom and closed the door behind her. A sudden coldness welled up inside Alvin. *Alas, her alter ego has surfaced already. She's acting so arrogant with me. Gone is the sweet and understanding Meisu.*

Alvin's desire to have sex with Meisu left his mind quickly. He closed his eyes, willing himself to fall sleep.

* * *

Chu, dressed in khaki slacks, t-shirt and denim jacket, strode across the open car park towards the Pudu Food Court. As he approached its entrance, he fished out his hand phone.

'Hello, Sergeant June? Where're you now? I'm almost inside the food court now.'

'Will be there in ten minutes.'

Chu stopped on the pavement outside the food court and surveyed his surroundings. *Where would be a good place for June to station herself?* Two lampposts, about forty paces apart from each other, stood outside the food court. A long-haired and horribly plump hooker was squatting under one, while two floozies with short hair, lean and possibly in their mid-twenties, were chatting under the second lamppost. A man stood near them, his beer gut straining against his t-shirt; he was leaning on a moped, smoking a cigarette and watching the hookers. Chu noted that the light spilling out from the food court along with the light coming from the lamp posts was enough to illuminate the place and reveal the faces of the hookers and passers-by to him. This would be an ideal place for June to lure and trap the killer.

He walked along a gap in the row of motorcycles parked at the entrance and entered the food court.

All the hawker stalls were closed for the night, and only beer and soft drinks were being sold by the establishment's operator. A string of hookers took up some of the tables inside; a few sat alone, others were engrossed in chatter with their clients. A glittery curtain hung over the stage at the far end, and a few men were streaming in and out of it.

Chu settled at an empty table near the entrance. 'A glass of black coffee with ice,' he said to the Myanmar waiter who came to his table. He needed the caffeine to stay alert. He watched as the obese long-haired hooker got up, vacated her spot and walked inside. Chu's eyes trailed her as she proceeded to seat herself at a table. *Hmm, she must be tired. Sergeant June could take her spot under the lamppost.*

Chu continued to survey the food court's entrance. A taxi pulled over to the side of the road in front the food court, and a woman stepped out. She was busty and had on fishnet stockings, a miniskirt and a leopard-print top. As she came closer to the entrance, he recognised her and almost gasped in shock. *Christ, the woman is June! What a startling transformation! Obviously, she is wearing a heavily padded bra.* June spotted Chu and made a beeline towards his table. She sat down, grinning, and said, 'Well, do I look convincing?' She winked at him. 'Am I sexy?'

Chu swallowed hard. 'Yes, you look perfect for the part.' A pause. 'Now, I don't think the killer will attempt to pick up any girl inside the food court.' He gestured to the lamppost nearest to them with a jerk of his jaw. 'Station yourself there. Signal me when he approaches you. Keep him engaged in conversation so that I have time to slip away and get close to him. I don't want to dash out and make it obvious, or he'll take off.'

June fished out a lighter and a pack of cigarettes, held them in one hand and rose. 'OK, let's hope our sting operation works.' She walked over to the lamppost on high heels, her butt swaying from side to side.

The minutes ticked by agonisingly slow. Chu finished sipping his coffee then ordered a Coke. When he saw a man approach June, his muscles tightened in readiness. However, a few moments later the man walked away, and he relaxed again. Chu got up, stood at one side of the entrance and looked around. The beer-bellied man, now sitting on his propped-up moped, was talking to a woman. *Damn, the porker weighs two-hundred pounds easily.* A skinny man moseyed up to the pavement, stood there and started to eye June and the hookers. Anxiety fluttered in Chu's chest. Then the man walked inside the food court. Chu returned to his table.

A maroon car cruising down the drag pulled over outside the food court and drew level with June, its engine still chugging. Her back facing Chu, June took a step forward, leaning forward slightly to talk to the man. Then she stepped back again. Chu watched the scene with unblinking eyes, the muscles in his neck corded. He couldn't see the man in the car very clearly, but could make out that he was pale and scrawny and with long hair. *Damn it! What if he was our suspect? I hadn't expected such a situation.*

A second passed. Two seconds. Three seconds. June turned her head sideways to show Chu the profile of her face. A glowing cigarette hung from her lips. June had given him the signal – the man in the car was indeed their suspect. Chu got up and started to walk quickly towards the car just as June lowered her head again to talk to the man.

Chu watched as the suspect turned away from June and looked right at him. The wheels of the car screeched as it sped off.

'Stop! Police!' June shouted. She ripped her miniskirt apart, pulling at the Velcro that held together its sides, and snatched a Beretta Px4 Storm from a holster strapped to her inner thigh. She took aim at one tyre of the speeding car and fired twice. The two hookers screamed and began to run into the food court. The car continued to speed away. She had missed.

Chu ran up to the beer-bellied man, who was sitting on the moped, his eyes wide with shock. 'I'm a policeman! Follow that car! I'll pay you fifty ringgit!'

'OK, brudder!'

The beer-bellied man's moped immediately sputtered to life. The police inspector leapt aboard, and they sped away, leaving behind a cloud of exhaust fumes.

The suspect sped through a traffic red light and entered Tun Razak Road, with the scooter in hot pursuit, their riders not wearing helmets. The beer-bellied man whizzed down the road like a Grand Prix motorcycle racer, overtaking cars and motorbikes, weaving in and out of the divider line. Chu clung to his shoulders tightly, the wind blowing in his face. *Will I be able to draw my gun from my shoulder holster and shoot at the car's tyres?* He was spared that difficult task as the scooter eventually couldn't catch up with the car. After about two kilometres, the car could no longer be seen, and Chu returned to the food court.

He saw that June was seated inside, waiting for him. Chu paid fifty ringgit to the beer-bellied man.

'Wow! What a thrilling experience!' the man said as he walked away, grinning.

Chu took out a small comb from his back pocket, brushed his hair and settled down beside June. 'We lost him. Did you see the registration number?'

'No, I didn't. By the time I had taken out my pistol, he had sped away. And the car's backlights were switched off. I called HQ and they said they'd alert all patrol cars in this area.'

'Fat chance they'll catch him. Are you sure he was the suspect?'

'Yes, he resembled the photofit.'

'What did he say to you?'

'He asked whether I was a working girl. I said yes, and he asked me to get into the car to discuss my rate. But I told him to come out instead. He was reluctant to do so and became impatient. I tried to stall him by talking dirty with him. I think he became suspicious when he saw you approaching.'

'Damn! We had our chance and we blew it.' Chu banged his fist on the table.

June rose to her feet. 'At least we know that he drives a maroon Kia Spectra. Well, that's assuming the car is not stolen.'

Sunday 25 April

Alvin awoke to the smells of fresh toast, chicken sandwiches, coffee and orange jam. Meisu was sitting at the dining table, stirring a cup of coffee with one hand and holding two slices of toast in the other.

'Morning, *bao pei* [darling], have something to eat.' She had on a beige jacket, a shirt dress and dark jeans. 'I called room service as I didn't want to disturb your sleep. I know you're feeling too lazy to go out.'

She turned to look out the window. Sitting on the ledge, a sparrow shivered, drenched in dew drops. Beyond, thick mists swirled around the sky like water colour glazes on a Chinese painting.

Alvin got out of bed, lumbered to the bathroom and came out a minute later. He settled on an upholstered chair opposite Meisu and started to eat a chicken sandwich. He half-filled a cup with coffee and added a sachet of sugar, then stirred the contents. He swallowed the bite of sandwich drily. 'I'd like to take a nap after eating,' he said and took a gulp of coffee. 'Then I'll pack up our things. You go ahead with your gambling. Just remember that we've to check out at twelve. On the way down, perhaps we can stop at Chin Swee Cave Temple for a vegetarian lunch?'

'Great. I'll meet you at the lobby. At twelve.' She swept the bread crumbs off the table to the carpet and sipped coffee from her cup.

Alvin took another bite off the sandwich, chewed and swallowed it with great difficulty. He got up and went to the mini bar, and took out two bottles of gin. He returned to his seat, unscrewed one bottle and poured a splash of it into his cup of coffee. He let out a relieved sigh as he sipped the drink. 'Hmm ... The sandwich finally tastes good,' he chuckled. 'So does the coffee.'

'Alvin, you need help.' Meisu frowned at him. 'As I said yesterday, you've a drinking problem. If you stop, you develop withdrawal symptoms that are horribly severe. It seems that you can't even function normally.'

'Come on, darling, I just need something to carry me through the day. I'm trying to taper down my drinking and can only do it gradually, right?' He raised the two bottles of gin. 'I'll only drink two bottles today. Only two. No more.' He set them down on the table with a thud. 'I swear to you that I'll gradually stop. I just need more time. Please bear with me for the time being, OK?' He pumped his fists into the air feebly. 'The will to reform must come from within, right?'

'I'm glad you said that. There's a clinic in Leisure Mall, third floor. There's a doctor there, a consultant physician – Dr. Leonard Leong. I spoke with his nurse as I happened to pass by the clinic last Friday. She said the doctor can prescribe sedatives and detox plans to help treat alcoholism. I could book an appointment for you with him.' Her voice flattened. 'A friend also suggested an Alcoholics Anonymous club that meets up in a church at Sentul. You can get the address from the Internet. They have open meetings every Monday. So, we have two options you could try.' She wiped her mouth with a serviette.

'Why are you doing all this?'

'Because I care for you, Alvin. How can I stand by and watch you drink your way to destruction?'

She's doing so much for me. She must really care for me, Alvin realised. He sat up straight, suddenly feeling confident. 'OK, I'll go consult that Dr. Leonard Leong.'

'I'll fix an appointment for you then. Does the following Monday work for you? Will 2 p.m. be fine?'

'Sure. Thanks for your concern, darling. I'll make a note of this in my diary.'

'Another thing. I'm flying to Bangkok tomorrow morning. I want to renew my visa. I'll be riding a cab to the airport with a friend. Her name's Yehua. You haven't met her. She's a nice person. We'll be there for two or three days. I'll return via Penang and take a taxi back.' She rose to her feet and smiled. 'It's now time for some more fun at the casino. See you in the lobby afterward.' She leaned toward Alvin and let him kiss her cheek.

* * *

The pale man entered his study and saw a paper curled up at his fax machine. He plucked it out then strode to the living room and sat down on the couch to read it: 'Please give your best quotation for a one-hour clown performance at a Mother's Day party on May 9, 2010. The venue of the party is my residence at Ukay Heights. The timing is between 8 p.m. and 10 p.m. My requirements are as follows: a close-up magic show, balloon twisting and stand-up comedy jokes. No. of pax: 6 adults and 8 children. Please call Mr. Li at his hand phone no. 017-2810244 if you require further details.'

He looked at the words 'Mother's Day' again. They suddenly released a torrent of emotion in him. He crumpled the sheet of paper with his hands, and his body racked with sobs as he recalled the day he had lost his Mama, only two days after she had confronted his Papa outside Daisy Motel & Cabaret.

When he awoke that morning, he heard retching noises in the master bedroom. As he entered the room, he saw Mama laying there, her chest heaving breathlessly, her eyes staring up blankly at the ceiling.

He stood at the side of the bed and shook her. 'Mama, what's wrong? Are you ill?'

In a voice filled with despair and agony, and between gasps of air, she said, 'I've consumed paraquat. There's no antidote. So don't call an ambulance.'

He hugged her and climbed onto the bed beside her. He held her tightly, sobbing. 'Mama! Please don't leave me … What will I do without you?'

'Go stay with your uncle. He'll take care of you. I've some money in my savings account. I've written the PIN and other details for you.' She pointed to a piece of paper she had placed on the bedside table beside her.

His mother turned sideways to look to him and her face, as pale as steamed Hainanese chicken meat, startled him. 'Take good care of yourself. Be a good boy.' She suddenly clutched at her stomach and groaned.

'Mama! Don't leave me, please. Let me call Uncle. He can help us.' He had got up to rush to the phone, but his mother pulled him back. 'No. It's too late. There's no use now … Call him when I'm dead and tell him that I want a cremation.'

'Shall I call Papa?' he mumbled, sobbing, feeling helpless.

'No! Never! He shouldn't even come to my funeral.'

'But Mama—'

'He wants nothing to do with us. All he wants is that damn whore. She stole him from us. She was after his money. The old fool! He fell for her charms.' Then, suddenly she pushed her son off the bed with one hand. She leaned over the edge and vomited. A splash of white gooey liquid fell on the boy's feet. 'Oh, god, the pain's unbearable.'

She coughed. She was panting heavily. 'Just let me die. I'm so ashamed that I lost my husband to a worthless whore.' She broke into sobs. 'Where did I go wrong? Why did he leave me?' she asked, holding his hand. 'Is it because I'm old compared to that cheap young whore? Is it because I am not as attractive as her? I was a good wife to him. Son, am I a good mother to you?'

'Yes, Mama. You are the best mother.' He got down on his knees and wept. 'I love you Mama. I will always love you.'

'Prostitutes are evil, son, they came from hell. They deserve to die. They should be sent back to hell.'

'All whores must die.' His mother had repeated these words over and again. Her eyes closed, and she was frothing from her mouth. He watched wide-eyed in horror, his knees trembling. His mother's left eye twitched uncontrollably and her upper lip curled.

'Mama! Mama! Don't die, please!' He gripped her stiffened fingers, until they had gone limp against his. He closed his eyes and wailed, tears flowing down his face like a river. He had lost his mother forever. He had lost his family forever. And that filthy whore was to blame. She had done this to him, to his Mama, to their family.

As the memories of that terrible day faded slowly from his mind, the pale man leaned back against the tattered couch. He un-crumpled the fax message, smoothed it with his hand, folded it twice, and then put it in his shirt pocket. Wiping away tears from his eyes, he lifted himself to his feet and moved towards the long shellacked altar that stood in one corner of his living room. He kneeled before a small rectangular wooden block engraved with golden Chinese characters, splayed his hands in front of his knees and knocked his forehead against the tiled floor. With mechanical precision, he executed the ritual three times.

He then stood up and fastened his eyes firmly on the ancestral tablet. 'Mama, I'm sorry, but I failed yesterday. I wanted to send another whore back to hell, but I couldn't. I almost got caught by the police. Please don't be angry with me. Shall I try again?'

A voice whispered inside his head:

Of course, my son, you must never give up.
Don't let one failure stop your good work.
Your work is never done until all prostitutes have been sent back to hell.
They're evil! They break up families. They ruin marriages.
The worst are the big-breasted whores.
They're irresistible to men who are weak.
Like your good-for-nothing Papa.
Kill them first.
Kill them all.
All whores must die.

Moving to the other end of the altar, the man pulled out three joss sticks from a cylindrical metal container, lit them for his mother and sank to his knees again.

'Yes, Mama, I shall not stop now. I must learn from this failure. I had a suspicion that the whore was a cop. She behaved like one. Thankfully, I am smarter than her. Mama, I am going to try again. Please protect me from the bloody cops and grant me success this time.' He bowed his head reverently. Then, he rose to his feet and planted the joss sticks in a metal urn.

He re-entered his study and sat at his writing desk. He took out his scrapbook from a drawer and flipped through its pages. He went through the 'before' photos of his victims, which showed the skimpily dressed hookers sitting at food courts or other pick-up joints with their customers. He then went through the 'after' photos of them, which showed their bloodied mutilated bodies and their pale faces and blank eyes after their deaths.

He turned to a page that had no pictures: the words 'Fourth Victim' had been written on its top. He pounded his fist at the empty page a few times. 'This page will be filled up soon. This time I will not fail.' He snapped the scrapbook shut and returned it to the drawer.

He flipped out a butt from a packet of Kent in his shirt pocket and caught it with his lips. He drew a matchbook from his shirt pocket, plucked one match away and dragged the red tip across the sulphur strip. A crackling hiss morphed into a snap of flame, then immediately caught the end of the waiting fag. He inhaled then blew out a long trail of smoke towards the ceiling. The white fumes swirled under the slow-rotating fan; his eyes followed the thin clouds as they floated toward a mantleshelf, where three large and clear glass jars with metal clamp lids were arranged in a row, proudly like trophies. Inside each jar was stored a pair of breasts, preserved in formalin.

The sight of the three jars reminded him of something. He took out his hand phone. 'Golden Health Pharmacy? Hello, Miss Sin, it's me. I need another big bottle of formalin.' A pause. 'Yeah, my kid brother's got another biology dissection project.' Another pause. 'That's great. I'll come over tomorrow to pick it up. Bye.'

Tuesday 27 April

Alvin stopped by his letterbox at the back foyer of the building to see if there was any mail for him. He pulled out four envelopes of assorted sizes, and then walked back to his studio. He sat at his desk and opened them. Two contained sales brochures from insurance companies, and one was a request for donation from a Thai monk in return for Da Ma Cai lottery predictions. He crumpled and threw them into the wastepaper basket.

Inside the fourth envelope, he found a glossy card, about eight-by-four-inches in size:

Ken Koh cordially invites Mr. Alvin Au
to the official opening of 'The Sands of Time' Exhibition
Venue: Ken Stellar Gallery, Jalan Ara, Kuala Lumpur
Date: Saturday 1 May
Time: 8 pm
Dresscode: Smart casual
RSVP: +603-22829999

Alvin called the host from his cell phone. 'Hello, Mr. Ken Koh?

I got your invitation. Thank you so much. How big is this event?'

'Three hundred pieces by fifteen artists. Don't miss this. There'll be great networking opportunities – museum professionals, institutional collectors, art critics, auctioneers, they are all coming.'

'Any press coverage for it?'

'Nope. Those bloody hacks will probably mention the exhibition in just one miserable sentence. But the president of the Malaysian Society of Professional Artists will be there.'

'That's wonderful. Can I bring my girlfriend?' In his mind's eyes, Alvin could see the looks of envy the other male guests would give him when he made his entrance with Meisu.

'Sure, I'm looking forward to meeting her. Shall I go ahead and put your name on the confirmed list?'

'Yes, of course. Thank you, bye.'

Alvin dialled Meisu's number. 'Hello, darling. Everything's fine with you?'

Static crackled on the line but her voice was audible. 'Yes, Alvin, I'm OK. My visa should be ready by tomorrow.'

'Good. And how do you like Bangkok?'

'Bangkok's a nice place. I like it. My friend Yehua's with me right now. We're eating mango sticky rice at a roadside stall.'

'That's great. Listen, Meisu, I've just received an invitation to a function. It's an art exhibition.' He leaned back and smoothed the back of his hair with his left hand. 'It's this Saturday evening. I would like you to come along.'

'That'll be wonderful. I should be back in KL tomorrow evening. Do I need to wear an evening gown for the event?'

'That's not necessary. Dress code says smart casual. Waiting to see you tomorrow, darling. I love you. Bye!'

Everything's going my way now. He smiled gleefully. He pulled open a left side drawer, rummaged through its contents and found what he was looking for: a plastic box of his name cards. *I will hand these out like confetti to the guests at the event.* From his trouser pocket, he took out his metal name-card case and filled it with as many cards as he could. His life was finally picking up again.

Saturday 1 May

Alvin and Meisu arrived at Ken Stellar Gallery sharp at 8:00 p.m., but couldn't find any parking. Tight rows of cars already lined both sides of the drag near the converted double-storey bungalow. He finally parked his Myvi at the corner of an adjoining road, more than a hundred metres away from the place, then took Meisu's hand in his and strolled toward the gallery with her. Alvin was dressed in a formal grey-and-blue checkered shirt and pleated khaki pants, while Meisu had on a silken black sheath dress with cap sleeves.

They entered the open gate and walked under a scalloped red canopy erected at the bungalow's front, and then through the doorway. At one side of the gallery was set up a long line of tables draped in silken white sheets and laden with plates of cheese nachos, chicken *yakitori*, canapés, spinach *samosas*, cuttlefish balls and pretzels. A mish-mash of aromas swirled around them. On another table stood bottles of expensive wine and a few glass punch bowls filled with colourful mocktails and cocktails. Two bow-tied waiters were filling up plates with the finger food, setting them on silver trays and taking them to the guests.

With heightened senses, Meisu watched as Alvin lifted his chin, squared his shoulder and walked in with confident strides. 'Ah, this is perfect. So many important guests. Great food. Great drinks. And a lovely lady by my side. I can look forward to a lovely night!'

The gallery had been turned into an open and brightly illuminated space, all its walls covered with canvases in expensive frames. Meisu observed admiringly that the place was an impressive display of sophistication and wealth.

A waiter materialised and offered Alvin a glass of wine, which he accepted, while Meisu lifted from the tray a highball glass containing a soft drink. She surveyed the crowd and saw clusters of men and women standing around, immersed in animated chatter, sipping drinks from their glasses.

Meisu watched as a balding man with a beaked nose popped out from a cluster of men and walked toward him. He wore a classy Hugo Boss sports jacket and dark flat-front pants that fell over his polished shoes.

'Welcome, Mr. Alvin Au!' he said, smiling.

'It's an honour to be here.' Alvin extended his hand, which the gallery owner pumped vigorously.

'And who's this charming lady here?'

'Mr. Koh, meet my girlfriend, Jin Ailing. She's a student at Omega University College in Cheras.'

'How do you do, sir?' Meisu smiled and threw an appreciative glance at the walls. 'Your gallery is magnificent. I've never seen so many beautiful paintings before.'

'Thank you. Come on, Alvin, there's someone you should meet. Let me introduce you to the gentleman.' While he searched for the man amidst the crowd of guests that filled the room, Alvin took three big gulps of his wine and gave his empty glass to a passing waiter, and Meisu picked a rolled bacon skewer from the waiter's tray, popped it into her mouth and placed the toothpick back onto the plate.

'Ah, he's over there. Come on, you both.' Ken steered them over to a chunky man with a full-face beard; he was talking to a little man with a flat face and bloodshot eyes.

'Charles, please meet Mr. Alvin Au, a good friend of mine and an expert at oil portraits.' The bearded man nodded at Alvin and Meisu. The gallery owner turned to Alvin. 'Mr. Charles Chee is an art critic and publisher. He owns the magazine *Singapore Art World*.' Ken smiled at the little man beside Mr. Charles. 'That's Mr. Eddy ... err ...' He snapped his fingers twice. 'Sorry, I just had it at the tip of my tongue. Ah, yes, Yap. Mr. Eddy Yap. He's an art supplies retailer.'

Handshakes were exchanged, and the men plunged into a discussion about the economics of the art industry and how to educate the public to appreciate paintings. Meisu simply stood beside Alvin, sipping her drink and watching the men talk, trying to follow them.

Eddy, the art supplies retailer, didn't join in the conversation either. Silent and sipping his glass of wine, he turned his attention towards Meisu. He looked at her closely. 'Hmm, you look familiar,' he said to her. 'Have we met before?'

'I don't think so, Mr. Yap,' Meisu smiled and shook her head.

Eddy snapped his fingers at a waiter, placed his empty glass on the tray, grabbed another glass and emptied its contents in one swallow. With furrowed eyebrows, he continued to stare at Meisu. 'Ah ... I got it now. I remember you,' he suddenly said, grinning. 'You call yourself Meisu. You work at the New Peng Hwa Food Court. You tried to pick me up once, but I declined. You were too expensive.

Remember?'

Meisu blanched. She looked away. Eddy chuckled quietly, and then pulled her a few steps away from the others. 'How did you get invited here?' He threw a sly glance at Alvin. 'He's your boyfriend?'

'I'm afraid you're mistaken. I'm not Meisu.' She moved away, her skin tingling. She turned around momentarily to glance at Eddy's sneering face, and then paced away to a nearby wall, pretending to look at a row of paintings. Ten agonising minutes passed before she saw Alvin walk up to her with a quizzical look on his face.

'Hey, darling, what're you doing here?'

'Alvin, I'm sorry. Let's leave this place,' she whispered to him. 'Eddy, that horrid pipsqueak who was with that bearded man, knows me. He recognised me from New Peng Hwa.'

Alvin coloured, then looked around. Some of the guests were staring at them, and a bevy of ladies were trying to muffle their giggles and whispers as they averted their eyes away from Meisu. A couple of men whistled softly as they walked past them. Meisu saw that Alvin's cheeks had turned a deep red, as if they had been scalded by boiling water. He took Meisu's hand and led her out of the gallery.

On the drive home, his cell phone rang suddenly. Ken's angry voice crackled in through the hands-free earpiece: 'Mr. Alvin Au, your conduct is a disgrace! How could you bring a prostitute to my prestigious function? I don't want to have anything to do with you anymore. Please don't step foot in my gallery again. Do you understand?' Before Alvin could reply, Ken hung up.

Meisu watched anxiously as Alvin bit his lower lip and switched off his cell phone, his chest heaving, his knuckles turning white as he gripped the steering wheel.

'Are you ashamed of me?' Meisu stared at the road with unblinking eyes. She could feel them welling up with tears. There was only silence from Alvin.

'Do you regret falling in love with a prostitute?'

A long silence. 'No.'

Alvin turned to face her for a moment. He brushed her hair away from her face, touched her cheek. He then looked back at the road ahead. 'Let's just forget about tonight, OK?'

He remained silent for the rest of the drive. And when they reached home, he headed straight to the fridge and took out two bottles of beer. Then he walked into his bedroom and closed the door behind him. Meisu heard the bolt slammed home.

A flush crept over her cheeks as she entered the master bedroom. She flopped down on the bed and buried her face in the pillow. *He's finding solace in alcohol. I don't blame him. Tonight's my fault. Damn it. Was it fate that made me a prostitute?* She lay motionless for almost five minutes, pondering over the question, then got up and went to the bathroom to wash off her make-up. She changed into a nightgown, and then walked to the kitchen wall cabinet. She remembered having bought a bottle of cough medicine last week when she had been afflicted with a slight cough. She unscrewed the bottle's cap and took two long swallows. *This will help me to sleep through the night.* She returned to the bedroom and shut her eyes, allowing the cough medicine to slowly numb her senses.

Sunday 2 May

With the signal light of his car blinking, the pale man turned left, tapped the brakes, and deftly wedged his car between two others. He lowered the car's back windows a little to allow the air to circulate, then switched off the engine and waited.

When a scruffy man walked over to the driver's door, the pale man slipped him a five-ringgit note. In return he got a parking chit and displayed it on the dashboard. He waited until the scruffy man had walked away. Then he put on a baseball cap, opened the door, got out and climbed into the back. He settled into the seat and turned to look out the back windshield. He had parked right outside the entrance of the New Peng Hwa Food Court. It was dark inside the car, and he was not visible from the outside; but he could clearly see the hookers and their johns sauntering up and down the perron of the food court, only twenty feet away.

Now, who will be the next whore I send back to hell? From a pouch bag, he took out his camera and switched it on. He selected the 'Night Mode' option then set the lens to its maximum zoom position. He looked into the viewfinder: petite huskies, lanky tootsies, pear-shaped floozies and curly-haired tarts streamed in and out of the building, but none interested him. The minutes ticked away.

Suddenly he saw her, and his heart skipped a beat: a hooker with huge breasts was walking down the steps with a young handsome man. He focused on her face and let out a low whistle. *Bloody hell, it was her. This was the same bitch I had met at Central Market. The one who had screamed at me and threatened to call the security guard. The one who had insulted my loving Mama.* Resting the camera on the headrest of the backseat for stability, he took several shots of her face, of her curvaceous body, of her ample bosom.

An hour later, he was back in his study. The pale man watched as his colour laser printer spat out four colour printouts of the whore. He took out his scrapbook and turned to the page that had the words 'Fourth Victim' scrawled on the top. He pasted the printouts there.

As he looked at the whore's cat-like eyes and high forehead, hatred glinted in his saucer-like eyes, and madness seized him like a rabid dog.

Monday 3 May

Alvin's client, a small pinched man who smelled of amber wood, stepped into the studio at 1:30 p.m. The painter rose to his feet and smiled at him, but the client's eyes were flinty. About ten days ago, the man had commissioned Alvin to paint two portraits of himself and of his family.

'Good morning, sir! Are you here to deliver your latest photographs? You could have just called. I would have picked them up from your office.'

'No, I'm not here for that, Mr. Alvin Au. I've come to discuss to something else.' The client paused, seemingly searching for the right thing to say. Alvin held his breath. *What is he going to say? Is it bad news?*

'Mr. Au, there's a certain charm in the portraits you do, and I admire that.' A pause. 'However, as much as I like and respect your work, I also believe that an artist and the way he conducts his life in public must be respectable. I don't think it'll do justice to have my family portraits created by an artist who doesn't display the highest level of proper conduct and decorum.' Another pause. 'Well, I attended Ken's exhibition last Saturday. You didn't see me but I saw you and your ... companion, from afar. After you both had left, lots of unpleasant remarks were passed around. About her. And you.'

Alvin shook his head uncomprehendingly. 'But those are two separate issues ...'

His client cut in. 'I'm sorry. I really am. But I have decided to cancel my commissions. Please issue a cheque to refund my deposit.'

Alvin's head buzzed as he walked under a cloudy sky to the coffee shop at the end of Hang Kasturi Road. He deliberately sat at a table at the back of the shop, crammed into a corner near the toilet. He wanted to be alone. He wanted to prepare for another struggle with himself, with his emotions, with his thoughts.

'Waitress! Beer! A big bottle!' he yelled. His rudeness shocked the waitress; the meek brown-skinned girl spun around look at him, her mouth wide open.

Alvin didn't apologise. He simply stared back at her. He didn't care what anyone thought about him anymore. He felt as if he were on the verge of death now. *Alcohol is the only thing that can make me feel alive again.*

He looked at his watch and realised he had missed his appointment with Dr. Leonard Leong. *Well, does it really matter anyway?* He ordered a plate of chicken rice and ate it hungrily. When he was done, he sat there drinking his beer. He asked for a couple of more bottles. The more he drank, the less pain he felt. He was becoming numb, his head and eyelids growing heavier with each sip he took. He thought again of Meisu. He knew he would incur her wrath by having missed the doctor's appointment. Yet, he might be able to salvage the situation. He could attend the Alcoholics Anonymous meeting that night. *That would be another waste of time.* A voice inside him laughed mockingly. *But I must go*, he answered it. *For Meisu. It would make her happy.*

He staggered to his feet, paid at the counter and went to the sink to wash his face. An hour later, a taxi dropped Alvin outside the Church of St. Alphonsus in Sentul. He paid the driver, and then walked through the wrought-iron gates and down a gravel path leading into a small hall attached to the side of the church's building. A sober wooden signboard greeted him: 'AA Kuala Lumpur'. Alvin pushed open the door and stepped in: eight or nine people were sitting in a circle, all of them facing a middle-aged man whose skin looked like elephant hide – an obvious result of the ravages of alcohol.

In a throaty voice, the man was saying, 'To me, alcohol became just another beverage. Like tea or coffee. So, for breakfast, I drank alcohol and ate *roti canai*; for lunch I guzzled alcohol and ate *chappati*; and for dinner, I sipped on alcohol with *naan*. My weight dropped to eighty pounds.' The men sitting around him nodded solemnly in understanding.

The middle-aged leader sitting at the centre of the circle stopped talking when he noticed Alvin. The rest of the group also turned their heads to look at him. 'Ah, we have a new friend. Please take a seat, my brother. Let me finish, and then I'll let you introduce yourself.' The other alcoholics turned back to the leader.

The minutes rolled by, and the man was wrapping up his talk. It would be Alvin's turn to speak soon. He suddenly felt as if a large pit had opened up in the centre of his stomach and that these curiosity-seekers were about to probe his innards. He began to panic. He wasn't sure anymore if he wanted to confide in these strangers about his problems. He sprang to his feet and ran out of the room, without looking back at the alcoholics.

Alvin returned to Opal Condominium, freshened up under a cold shower, raided the fridge and carried a bottle of rum to his bedroom. He lay in bed, taking long sips from the bottle. His thoughts returned again to the disastrous party at the gallery, to the way everyone had looked at him and mocked him and judged him there, to the client's refusal to buy his paintings anymore. He realised that Meisu's profession was becoming a liability to his career and his reputation. Perhaps, he could pay her a lump sum and ask her to discontinue her work. Yet, on the other hand, he didn't have much savings stashed away. He continued to drink, confused about what he had to do. He felt utterly helpless, as if he were standing between a cobra and a crocodile.

Tuesday 4 May

Meisu looked at her watch: it was 12:15 a.m. She looked out the entrance of the food court. *Oh, thank goodness, it has finally stopped raining. It's been pouring for almost three hours.* What a rotten night it was. She had never seen New Peng Hwa so empty. The rain had laid a pall over the city, forcing all the johns to stay indoors. She had only picked up two clients, much below her nightly average of five.

She slumped back in her chair. Having nothing else to do, she turned her attention to the two men sitting at the table next to her, chatting and gorging on plates of noodles. Earlier, Meisu had solicited them for business, but they had simply smiled and shook their heads at her. They were now immersed in animated chatter over dinner. One of them, a butterball with pouched eyes, was saying, 'In 1881, there was a great flood in the town, and one morning, people suddenly ran around screaming that a tiger was loose in the waters. They were running for their lives.' He laughed, his mouth full of food. 'The flood had washed a tiger onto a road. It eventually retreated into the jungle.' His thin-haired, long-nosed companion chortled. 'Hah, those were the days. Do you remember this? In 2007, Merdeka Square's basement car park was completely submerged.' He pursed his lips at the memory and continued, 'KL's location sucks. It's smack at the confluence of two rivers. When they overflow, the drainage system can't cope with it. All our mayors keep claiming that they have implemented flood controls. But today's drainage system isn't any better than it was during Kapitan Yap's time.'

Meisu rose to her feet. She was bored out of her mind. *Screw this. What is the point of listening to such idle talk about the history of Jilongpo?* Some fresh air and a late supper might help refresh her. She left the food court and sauntered down Pudu Road, then turned into a narrow street, packed with bright stalls and pedestrians. A signboard said 'Sayur Road'. She remembered that a client had brought her there once after a quickie. He had told her the road's moniker was 'Glutton Street'. Meisu suddenly realised that she was hungry. *It all looks delicious, the clams, prawns and crab sticks.* She walked over to a stall and ordered herself a bowl of seafood congee.

Meisu was almost done eating when she noticed something. Several metres ahead, standing under a brightly illuminated advertising billboard, was a petite brown girl dressed in a tank top and denim shorts. She was leaning against a lamp post, scoping the road for potential customers. Curious, Meisu decide to wait and see if the girl would get lucky. After a few moments, a silver sedan pulled over to the side of the kerb beside the brown girl; she immediately approached the car and bent against the car's window. After a few moments of conversation and negotiation, the brown girl suddenly hitched her top up to reveal a round breast. A hand came out from the driver's side and squeezed the girl's breast. Meisu almost did a double take; she couldn't believe what she had just seen. The hooker walked round to the passenger side, opened the door and sat down. The car then drove off. *Shit, business is so bad tonight that a fellow sister has to resort to such cheap tactics to get customers.* Meisu looked at her watch again. Only two hours were left before she had to head home. She started to walk back to New Peng Hwa Food Court.

After traipsing a hundred yard or so down the street, she noticed a brown-skinned man standing with arms folded on his chest and looking around. 'Are you working?' he asked her in English.

Meisu did not answer him. She recalled that Yehua had warned her about picking up non-Chinese clients as they might be undercover cops. The man started to follow her. 'I'll pay you three hundred for a short-time.' Meisu continued to walk. Trailing behind her, the man said, 'I'll also pay for the room. And the taxi, if necessary.'

Meisu stopped and turned to the prospective customer. She studied him: mid-forties, thick spectacles, a bit stoop-shouldered, a beer gut, brown moccasins. No hint of being a cop. She was eager for the money. 'OK, three hundred and fifty. You pay for the motel room.'

The man smiled. 'That's great. Agreed! I'm Johan. Which hotel do you usually use?'

'Loveboat. It's just round the corner.'

After the act, the man got off the bed and wore his clothes. Meisu got dressed too. When they were done, Meisu asked him for her payment. The man produced a wallet from his pocket, flipped it open, but didn't take out any money from it. Instead, he flashed a card in Meisu's face. 'I'm from the Immigration Department. You've violated your social pass.'

Meisu's chest muscles tightened, her scalp crawled. The lawman placed his wallet back in his pocket. 'So, how shall we settle this?' He grinned maliciously at her. 'Either you can give me coffee money, or I'll arrest and deport you.'

The bloody bastard! I should have heeded Yehua's advice. 'I'll pay you one hundred.'

The man scoffed at her. 'One hundred? That's just insulting.'

'How much do you want?'

'One thousand.'

'Please, I don't have one thousand ringgit with me. Business is bad tonight.'

The man grabbed Meisu's handbag from the side table and opened it. 'I'll take everything that's in here then.' He dipped his hand inside and extracted a bundle of notes. 'I'll let you keep twenty as taxi fare.' He grinned again. 'See how kind I am.' He tossed the handbag on the bed and turned to leave the room. 'It was my pleasure making your acquaintance.'

Meisu dragged herself back to New Peng Hwa. She found herself an empty table and flopped down, tired, still shocked at being cheated and robbed. *Bastard. I can't believe he took all my money.*

She had barely composed herself when two boys, barely seventeen, approached her. The first boy was pudgy-faced and had little black beady eyes. The second boy had a big nose; a pompadour of wiry hair sat on his forehead.

The pudgy-faced boy sat down beside her. 'How about a threesome, baby?'

'Sorry, I don't do that.'

'Hey, baby, we've got money.' The pudgy-faced boy took out his wallet and opened it to display more than a dozen fifty-ringgit notes. 'How much will it take for you to do it?'

Shit, this must be the pocket-money his Daddy gave him. 'One hundred and eighty. But one at a time.'

The big-nosed boy smile and nodded. 'That's fine. Where's your room?'

After the encounter with the immigration officer at the Loveboat Motel, Meisu decided to avoid the place for the night. 'Springtime Inn, behind the wet market.'

The pudgy-faced boy started to count out the money. 'Three hundred and sixty. Here you are.' He handed it to her.

Hah! Payment before even entering the room! Such naïve schoolboys! Meisu smiled to herself. Fifteen minutes later, they were inside the lobby of Springtime Inn. 'Who's first?' she asked, holding the room key in her hand.

The boys looked at each other for a moment. 'Me!' said the pudgy-faced boy, grinning.

'Follow me upstairs.' Turning to the big-nosed boy, Meisu said, 'You can wait here. Come up when your friend comes back here.' The lad nodded then sank into the lobby's wicker sofa.

Once inside the room, the pudgy-face boy started to unlace his shoes. He looked at her. 'How about anal sex, baby?'

Meisu started to take off her clothes. 'Forget it. I never agreed to that.'

He kicked his shoes under the bed and smiled. 'OK, fine. But I want you to take a shower first.'

'Sure.' Meisu grabbed a towel from the side table and headed to the bathroom. When she stepped out, she saw that the big-nosed boy was in the room. He and the pudgy-faced one were standing together, both of them naked, grinning at her.

'Hey! I said one at a time!' She pointed to the big-nosed lad. 'You! Get out! Come back later.'

The young punks burst into laughter. They chanted in unison, 'Roses are red. Violets are silly. Bend over the bed. Here comes my willy!'

Before she could react, the boys were upon her. They dragged her to the bed and pinned her there facedown. She started to struggle and scream, but they slapped the back of her head. 'Shut up, bitch! Or we'll beat your brains out next time!' Then Meisu felt one of them crawl onto her back. A pain seared through her anus, as if it was being pinched by a crab's pincer, and Meisu couldn't help but scream.

Wednesday 5 May

Meisu held a wad of toilet paper with her left hand, wiped her bottom and rose from the commode. As she was about to push the flush lever, she peeped into the bowl: her stools looked crimson, were stained with blood. *Damn. This was such a bad night. I wish I could choke those bastards to death.* Such things had never happened to her before. *Has living with Alvin brought me bad luck?* Searing pain still shot through her rectum. A visit to a doctor was necessary. She flushed the toilet, stepped under the shower and started to soap herself. She cleaned herself up, and then changed into a knee-length skirt and a short-sleeved blouse.

She walked into the living room and sat at the table. The rays of the ten o'clock sun slanted through the window and painted a golden rectangle on the tiled floor. Alvin, still wearing his striped pajamas, was alternating between biting off from a baguette and sipping from a cup that reeked of whisky and black coffee. Meisu noticed that he was averting his eyes from her; he was staring instead at two black ants drinking at a cordial stain left behind on the table from last night.

Meisu took out a sachet of three-in-one coffee powder, tore it and poured the granules into a porcelain cup. Then she added some hot water from a flask and started to stir the contents.

'Not going to your studio?' The puppy of annoyance was starting to nip at her heels.

'No. There's no need to rush there. Besides, I'm not in the mood.' He looked up at Meisu, his eyes hard as stone.

'Did you meet Dr. Leong on Monday?'

'Yes, I did.'

'What did he say?'

'He said I'd live to a ripe old age. All I need to do is pop a pill to calm my nerves when necessary. Pretty soon, I'll be as sober as a coma patient.'

Meisu gritted her teeth. 'Stop lying, Alvin! I called his clinic. You didn't consult him.' She lifted the tea spoon from the cup and threw it on the table. 'What about the AA meeting? Did you attend that at least?'

'Yes, I lied. No, I did not attend it. So what? Why are you so concerned about my drinking anyway? What about your addiction to gambling? Isn't that bad? And what about the work you do? Let me be honest with you, Meisu. I don't like it, the fact that you're a prostitute. I don't like it because I care for you! Why don't you quit New Peng Hwa?'

'I told you I'm saving up for my future education, didn't I?' Meisu was fuming. *How dare he suggest that I quit? It is so unfair of him to ask me this. He doesn't give a damn about my ambition or my future finances. He only cares about himself.*

'Please, Meisu. Try to understand why I am telling you this,' he insisted. She turned away from him.

'I don't want to talk about my work, if you don't mind.' Alvin gave her an exasperated sigh.

'Your drinking is a separate issue, Alvin. Don't you understand that? You promised me you would stop! You promised to change.'

Silence.

'Are you listening to me?'

'No.' He paused, took a bite off the baguette and spoke with his mouth full. 'Things are getting complicated between us.'

'I should have known never to trust a drinker.'

'Yes. And a gambler cannot be trusted either.'

Meisu's insides turned with regret. She felt disappointed by Alvin's lack of empathy, by his lack of drive, by how stubborn he was. She realised that there were places inside him that she would never be able to enter. They were like closed doors.

Meisu took a gulp of her coffee and rose to her feet. 'I need to see a doctor. I was sodomised yesterday. I was also raped and robbed.'

Alvin remained silent and chewed on the piece of baguette. His indifference stabbed Meisu's heart like a knife. Her eyes welled up with tears as she walked away from him.

* * *

Chu was typing a report on the computer when his interoffice phone rang. He picked up the handset and heard a familiar voice growl at the other end: 'Superintendent Sofian here. I want you and Sergeant June to report to my office now.' Before Chu could reply, the line went dead.

He clicked the 'save' icon on the computer screen, then fished out his cell phone and jabbed the speed-dial button for Sergeant June Qwong. 'Hey, Sergeant, are you still in the cafeteria? Our boss wants to talk to us. Pronto.' A pause. 'Could you do me favour? Grab me a packet of fried noodles.'

Minutes later, June entered the room, carrying a plastic bag with a Styrofoam box. 'Your food, Inspector.' She handed the bag to him.

'Thanks. I'll need this for later. I'm doing a static surveillance on a house in an oil palm plantation today,' Chu said. As his fingertips brushed against hers, the corners of her mouth turned up in a coquettish smile.

The inspector shoved the package to a corner of his desk then rose to his feet. 'Come on, let's go. Sofian seems to be in a bad mood.'

'So, what's new about that?' June moved to her desk, pulled open a drawer and took out a spiral notepad.

Their leather shoes clacking on the corridor, the duo strode down to Sofian's office. As they stepped in, Chu noticed that his superior's forehead was crinkled with worry. That sweat dotting his brown skin further indicated that he was under stress.

'Sit down,' Sofian said bluntly. 'What took you so long?' He stared at June. 'You went to the cafeteria again, didn't you?' He shook his head and heaved a sigh. 'I just got a call from the China embassy. The ambassador's aide wanted to know – well, actually, he demanded to know – about the progress we've made in solving the murder of their nationals. Especially the last victim, Xiong Caiqin.'

Sofian flipped open the case file. He read through it silently, rubbing his jaw. 'Today's already May 5. The girl was murdered on April 6. One month has passed. And you're not even close to finding the killer?' His eyes blazed. 'Speak up, Inspector! I haven't got all day.'

Chu's throat became dry all of a sudden. *I have twelve other cases on my plate right now, and I'm sitting here wasting my time with this old fool.*

'Sir, I admit that off late I've not been concentrating on this case,' he finally managed to say. 'After the suspect escaped from our trap in Pudu Food Court, I knew he would lie low for a while. That's why I have slowed down the investigation temporarily. And since new clues have surfaced on the robbery and gangland-killing cases, I've been focusing my attention there.'

June piped in, 'This killer's cunning and cautious, sir. He won't be hanging around the pick-up spots for a while. That's why this case has been put on the backburner.'

Sofian glared at them. 'Earlier, I told you to release the photofit to the press, didn't I? But you refused to listen.' He pounded the desk with his hairy fist. 'The embassy people are putting a lot of pressure on me. The ambassador has made a threat to issue a travel advisory to their nationals, advising them not to visit Malaysia if the murder cases are not solved. And I know that a couple of the Opposition politicians will try to gain cheap mileage by creating a big fuss over this. They will claim that we're not doing our work.' He wagged a stocky forefinger at them. 'Listen here, both of you. Just because the killer's lying low, it does not mean you can take it easy. I want results soon. You understand?'

June leaned forward slightly and spoke in a lowered voice, 'If the heat becomes unbearable, sir, we could just rope in an illegal foreigner and pin the blame on him. Maybe a Bangladeshi drunk on *samsu* or a Vietnamese guy high on amphetamine.' She shrugged. 'We can beat him up until he can't stand the torture, and then force him to sign a confession for the murder of those China dolls.'

Sofian's eyes widened with shock. 'My goodness!' he said, sputtering. 'How dare you suggest such a thing to me? Do you want those Human Rights Commission assholes to come after me, Sergeant? We've enough problems already with the A. Kugan case.'

He gave them a grim shake of his head. 'No. No way. I don't want any more shit to hit the fan. Solve this case the proper way. And do it quickly.'

Friday 7 May

Meisu woke up to the buzzing of her cell phone. She groaned, looked at the alarm clock. It was 10:30 a.m. Her eyes still half closed, she picked up the phone and mumbled into it, 'Hmm, who's that?'

'Hello! Meisu? Are you awake? I'm Yehua.'

'Yes ... Good morning. What's up?'

'Meisu, something horrible has happened. Have you seen today's copy of *Hua Ren Daily News*?' Yehua was breathless, speaking quickly. 'A sex scandal is splashed on the front page. And there're two pictures about it on page three. The pictures show the couple in a compromising position. They are quite graphic. And very clear, too.' Yehua paused for a moment.

What does all this have to do with me? Meisu was getting impatient. She wanted to sleep for some more time.

'And, um, the girl in the papers resembles you, Meisu,' Yehua said awkwardly.

Shock slapped Meisu's cheeks, shaking away her drowsiness. She sat up straight. 'Me? What do you mean me?' She pressed her feet to the cold floor to make sure she was not dreaming.

'You and your customer are in the pictures. Naked in bed.'

'What? Naked? What the hell's going on?'

'Yes. And it gets worse. It seems someone's uploaded clips of this sex video on the Internet too. Everyone's talking about it.'

Meisu's mouth went dry. Her pulse started to race. 'Shit! OK, thanks for telling me, Yehua. I'll go get a copy of the paper now.'

She sprang to her feet and scuttled to the bathroom to wash her face. She changed into a t-shirt and shorts, rushed out of the condo, wearing flip-flops, her hair tied in an untidy ponytail. She headed to the cafeteria, which was located in another block, and pulled out a copy of the *Hua Ren Daily News* from the newspaper rack.

Her eyes almost popped when he saw the black and white photograph of Mr. Carrick on the first page. Beside it was a three-column news item:

Carrick Chuah Forced to Resign over Sex Video Scandal
In a national press conference, Carrick Chuah, aged 57, admitted that he was the man in the sex video that has gone viral online. He tendered his resignation as President of the Pan-Malaysian Chinese Party and Member of Parliament. The identity of his sex partner, believed to be a mainland China prostitute, is not known. Meanwhile, top Opposition leaders condemned the sex video as 'gutter politics of the worst kind'. (Continued on page 3)

Meisu flipped to page three. The first picture showed a smiling Carrick lying in bed, his face turned sideways on the mattress, his skinny buttocks raised in the air. Meisu was kneeling before him, her head between his legs. The caption read: 'Carrick Chuah getting his goolies licked.' A second picture showed the politician lying on Meisu's chest, snuggled between her massive breasts. Meisu saw that her face was completely visible and clear in this one, except for a thin black strip printed across her eyes. The caption read: 'Carrick Chuah eating China's sweet pears.'

Meisu closed the newspaper and pulled out her cell phone. 'Lawrence?' A searing rage was exploding in her stomach, was rising up her body until it was burning her brain.

'Hi, Meisu. How are you?'

'You bastard! You lied to me!'

'Huh? About what?'

'Come on, don't act so innocent!' She was controlling the volume of her voice with great difficulty. 'About that so-called banker you set me up with. He's a goddamned politician. Our sex video has gone viral online. And our pictures are in the papers!'

'Well, I just read about it. To be honest with you, Meisu, I didn't know his real identity either. My friend used me. I'm innocent as you are. If it's any consolation, you're hardly recognisable in the pictures. I'm sorry, really sorry.'

'I don't want to see your bloody face in New Peng Hwa again. I know Ouyang Lifu very well. He controls the food court. If I see you there again, I will get his thugs to break your legs.'

'Don't threaten me, you cheap whore! You can't do anything to me!' Lawrence's voice was suddenly loud and coarse. 'Damn you!' The line went dead.

Meisu felt helpless. She opened her locket and gazed at the golden rat inside. She made a wish to the gods: *please, let this storm pass over quickly.* She closed the locket, ordered some breakfast then hopped into a cab. She asked the driver to take her to a hair-dressing salon.

'Change my hair style, please,' she said to the hairstylist. 'I want a layered cut, a few different lengths of graduated layers, also more volume.'

* * *

Alvin lay in bed, tossing and turning, trying to sleep. But sleep eluded him. The graphic pictures he had seen of Meisu and Carrick in the newspaper continued to play in his head and torture him. He had read about the sex scandal last afternoon. He had immediately recognised Carrick's sex partner as Meisu; just to be sure, he had gone to a cyber café to watch the video on an anti-Opposition blog. His suspicions were confirmed. He knew for sure that it was Meisu.

Now, in his mind's eyes, he saw Carrick's rubbery lips pressed against Meisu's, his grubby hands running down her body. Bile suddenly rose in his throat. Alvin groaned, twisted the cap off a rum bottle, and gulped it all down. Two empty beer cans, squeezed shapeless, already lay on the side table. His head was throbbing. He knew he wouldn't be able to sleep. He got up and crawled to the living room, sat down there.

He fished out his cell phone. 'Hello? Poseidon Escort Agency? I want to book one of your girls.' A pause. 'Yeah, I want a China girl. How much for two hours?' Another pause. 'Here, take down my address. It's in Cheras. I would like her to come around one-thirty tonight. Is that possible?' He glanced at the round wall clock. 'When she's at the guardhouse, she has to call me. Do you understand?'

Two hours later, the fixed line phone rang. 'Sir, you have a visitor,' the security informed him. 'Shall I let her in?'

'Yes, she's my sister. I'm expecting her.' He put down the phone, moved to Meisu's bedroom door and turned the knob. It was not locked. He opened the door, entered and turned on the lights. Everything was as neat and orderly as in a museum. Nothing was out of place there, except for a few of Meisu's undergarments strewn on a chair. He threw them into her closet, and then switched on the air-conditioner.

Ten minutes later, the social escort arrived at the front door with a smile. 'Hello, *qing ren* [darling]. I'm from Poseidon.' She wore a tight halter top with low-cut denim shorts. A mop of curly hair framed her cherubic porcelain-skinned face. Alvin smiled at her and pointed to the shoe rack. 'Just leave them there. And follow me.' The escort slipped off her pumps and put them on the shoe rack.

'My payment first, darling, if you don't mind.'

Alvin took out his wallet and handed her the money. He then took her by the arm and steered her in the direction of the master bedroom. 'This way, please.'

When they had gotten undressed, Alvin flicked off the lights. He tugged at the cord of the side table lamp to switch it on, and then lay down on the mattress. 'Can we start off with a bit of massage?'

The escort looked around the room warily. 'Sure.' The door of the bedroom stood ajar, and a glow came from the ensuite bathroom. 'Why isn't the door locked?'

'There's no need to do that. I stay alone.' He pressed a button on his mobile: soft and romantic music gushed out.

The escort had barely pressed Alvin's torso for a few minutes.

'My arms are tired.' She sighed. 'If you're not taking me anywhere, can we just get on with the sex?' She fluffed up a pillow, plunked herself beside Alvin and drew in a deep breath, eyes staring at the ceiling.

Alvin moved forward to kiss her but she turned sideways to avoid him. *Bloody hell, the escort agency has sent a newbie to me. She just wants to lie there like a dead pig!*

Alvin leaned toward her again, but she turned away again. 'What's wrong with you?' he asked, gritting his teeth.

She did not answer him. She simply stared at the ceiling.

'Hey, I'm paying you good money. At least, do a bit of acting, can you? You want me to brush my teeth? Gargle my mouth? Spray my throat with peppermint?'

'I'm new in this line. I don't kiss customers.'

'Why not?'

'I just don't.'

'You don't like me?'

'No. It's nothing to do with that.'

Alvin threw a glance at the alarm clock on the side table. It was 1:45 a.m. already. *Oh boy, Meisu should be back any time now.*

'Come on, I'll pay you extra for it.'

'I'm not interested.'

Teeth clenched, Alvin grabbed a handful of hair and yanked it. 'I want kissing, you understand? You little whore!'

'Owwww, that hurts!' the hooker cried out, but Alvin grabbed her face between his hands and forced his mouth onto hers. At that moment, the bedroom door was whisked open from the outside. It was Meisu. Alvin felt nervous at first, but then his face broke into a smile when he saw the expression of shock on Meisu's face.

'Hello, darling,' he drawled. 'Come on in and meet one of your China sisters. You enjoy what you see? Yes, darling? Please answer me.'

Meisu's eyes widened. 'Damn you! You're doing this here? On my bed? You're way out of line, Alvin. You don't shit where you eat!' Tears started to trickle down her eyes. 'Just because I'm a prostitute, you think I've no feelings? I can feel jealousy just like any other human being. I get hurt too.'

The escort got out of bed quickly and started to get dressed. 'I guess it's time for me to scram,' she muttered to Alvin.

'Now you know how I feel, huh?' Alvin sneered at Meisu. 'Now you know what it's like to be in my shoes. The pain I've felt. Do you know your romp with Carrick is the talk of the nation? God knows how many thousands of people have watched that sex video. It's disgusting, Meisu.'

Fully dressed now, the escort scampered out of the bedroom, slipped into her shoes and rushed out the front door.

'Let's split up, Meisu. I'm sorry I came into your room and abused your hospitality.' Alvin got out of bed and started to put on his clothes. 'I don't deserve you. I'm sorry for getting my screwed-up life involved with yours.'

He stormed past Meisu and entered his bedroom, and came out ten minutes later with his luggage. Meisu was sitting in the living room now, staring at the floor. Without speaking a word to her, he walked out of her apartment.

Along Cheras Road he gunned his car engine angrily. After he turned right, onto Middle Ring Road 2, he sped even faster. He had gone only a short distance when a traffic cop astride a white Honda emerged from behind a huge tree, its trunk the size of an oil drum. With the blue light on his motorcycle beeping and his sirens blaring, the cop rode up to him and flapped his hand, asking Alvin to stop.

He pulled over, his palms sweaty. The cop propped up the bike on a side stand, walked over to Alvin's car and tapped the window. He sported a handlebar moustache and his skin was rough and bumpy like that of a pineapple. Alvin rolled down his window, a blast of wind hitting his face along with the loud *vroom* of passing motorcycles. He was not sure what he would say or do now.

'Step out of the car.' Alvin staggered out.

'Can you walk in a straight line?' Alvin leaned against the front fender of the car and smiled sheepishly.

The cop sniffed his nose, and then walked back to his bike. He came back with a breathalyzer. 'Blow into this continuously for three seconds,' he said, holding the tube in front of Alvin's face. Alvin obeyed him.

The cop looked at the reading. 'Aha, you failed!' He grinned, revealing buck teeth. 'That's a fine of five thousand. And the suspension of your driving licence.' He placed the equipment back into the side box of his motorcycle then approached Alvin again. 'I can help you, my friend.' He stroked one side of his handlebar moustache, smiling conspiratorially. 'Pay me one thousand now, and we can just pretend that the breathalyzer test never took place. Let's scratch each other's backs, shall we?'

'You corrupt bastard. I'd rather go to jail.' Alvin blurted out.

The cop scowled at him. 'That's what you want? It can be arranged. Show me your driving licence and I.C.'

Alvin's hands shook as he pulled out the documents from his wallet. The officer whipped out a pad, wrote down Alvin's particulars and shoved a ball pen in his face. 'Sign here,' he snarled. Holding the pad in his hands, Alvin squinted in the dim glow of the street lights and scribbled his name.

The cop snatched back the pad from him. Then he looked around him, making sure there was no passing traffic. Before Alvin could realise what was happening, the cop had hooked a gloved fist into his stomach. Alvin doubled over in pain. His mouth flew open as the wind was knocked out of him. While Alvin groaned in pain, the cop tore away the summons and crumpled it into a ball, then shoved it inside Alvin's open mouth. He pressed Alvin's jaw upward to close his mouth.

'I'll see you in court,' he said, sneering.

The cop left Alvin there, still bent over and reeling in pain. He strutted to his motorbike, straddled it and rode away with an ear-splitting roar.

Saturday 8 May

Inspector Chu stood outside Agate Apartments, surveying its surroundings. Matahari Mall loomed across the road. Apart from the shops, the mall also contained a Cantopop nightclub, pubs and restaurants.

He walked further down Changkat Thambi Dollah Road to the building that stood adjacent to Agate Apartments and saw that it housed a bank, a karaoke centre, a coffee shop, a goldsmith store, a unisex hair-dressing salon, two hardware stores and a vegetarian restaurant.

He stood outside the bank and looked up. Two CCTV cameras stared down at him from each corner of its entrance. *People who passed by or entered the bank would be captured by them. Aha, a source for possible leads.* He proceeded ahead and stopped outside the goldsmith shop. He noted that CCTV protruded from the archway of its entrance too.

Chu began to walk around the area, covering a three-block radius around the apartment block. *Assuming the killer came here in his car with the victim, he would surely need a place to park his car.* But not a single car park was available nearby, save for the yellow-lined lots at the road shoulder.

He returned to Agate Apartments, walked across the road to Matahari Mall and entered its parking entrance. A camera was installed at the shopping complex's ticketing machine. He skirted the zebra-striped bar, entered the basement and scrutinised the pillars. A few pillars had CCTVs fixed onto them too. He proceeded to the lift foyer and noticed that a camera was installed there as well.

He took the lift up to the office and introduced himself to the building manager. 'I'm investigating a crime. I need to view all your CCTV recordings, between 11 p.m. on April 5 and 3 a.m. on April 6. Can you save the footage onto CDs for me?' The manager was happy to help.

Chu made the same requests from the bank and the goldsmith store then returned to the police station.

'I'll take care of the recordings from Matahari Mall,' Chu informed Sergeant June. He passed the video CDs from the bank and store to her, along with instructions to look out for anything that could give them any clues.

He then sat at his desk and slid a CD into his computer. He watched as the first vehicle crawled to a stop at the ticket machine; its driver lowered his window, reached out for the ticket and drove on. The driver's face could be clearly seen. It was not the suspect. Six other vehicles successively entered the mall; none of the drivers looked suspicious. When the seventh car appeared, Chu jumped up from his seat and backed up a few frames. He clicked 'Pause'. The car was a Kia Spectra. The driver's face matched the one in the photofit. Chu sat upright, his eyes gleaming, blood rushing to his face. No one was seated in the car's passenger seat. The suspect had probably dropped the hooker outside her flat while he had gone to park his vehicle. Chu shot a glance at his partner seated a few feet away. 'Sergeant, take a look at this. I think we've found our man.'

Sergeant June looked over his shoulder at the video. 'That's the killer's car?' she said excitedly.

'Yes.' Chu clicked on 'Play': the video showed the maroon Kia Spectra moving down the parking lot and reversing into a parking place. Chu jabbed 'Pause' again hurriedly, then 'Zoom'. The number plate of the vehicle became visible.

He flashed June a triumphant smile, and then scribbled down the number on a sheet of paper. He handed it over to her. 'Here, run a check with the Road Transport Department. Find out the owner's particulars.' He ejected the CD and replaced it along with the others. 'We're almost there, Sergeant. We're going to nail this bastard.'

Wednesday 12 May

It was 6:00 a.m. The roads were empty. The residents of Kepong Kukus Garden were seemingly still in bed. Chu and June stopped their police car in front of the subject's house. The dim light coming from a street lamp outside the house revealed a padlocked gate and rows of potted plants lining both sides of the cross-wire fencing. A Yamaha scooter was parked on the front porch, and a tomcat lay curled on the doormat, fast asleep. The house was dark; the living room's glass windows were closed shut. Chu and June, both dressed in their uniforms, got out of the car. They went round the block of houses and entered the back lane, slowly moving towards the backyard of the suspect's house. They climbed over the back gate.

Light shone out from the house's kitchen. They looked through the slanted glass louvered windows and saw a lean man with unkempt hair sitting inside at a table. He was clutching a foot-long bread knife in his left hand and a whetstone in his right. The man ran the blade across the stone and smiled as a shiny edge of steel began to emerge. Chu observed that a row of knives hung from a metal rack on the wall behind him: a peeling knife, a puntilla knife, a carving knife, a cutlet knife, a fillet knife, a Santoku knife, a French knife and a sinister-looking cleaver. *Damn it! The killer is spoilt for choice regarding the weapon he could use to mutilate his victims.* Chu's insides began to turn.

Quietly, he drew his Walther P99. He nodded at June, who nodded back at him. Half-crouched beside Chu, she drew her semi-automatic Beretta Px4 Storm, her finger placed ready on its trigger.

Chu hammered his fist on the grille door and shouted through the window, 'This is the police! I'm Inspector Chu. I'm executing an arrest warrant. Open the door at once.'

The long haired-man was startled. He gazed out the window for a moment then got up, abandoning the knife and whetstone on the table. He moved to a cupboard and took out a set of keys from its drawer. After fumbling with the keys anxiously, he finally opened the kitchen's wooden door. 'Please don't shoot!' His voice trembled as he swung the grille door open.

'Get back against the wall!' As the man retreated several steps, Chu stormed in. 'Put your hands above your head!' The lean man nervously pushed aside his long hair and revealed a pimply face with a big mole on the right cheek, then raised his arms.

The sight of the man's face made Chu's heart shrink with regret. *Shit! It's the wrong man!*

'What're you doing with that knife?' he asked him.

'I'm preparing for work.' A puzzled frown wrinkled the man's forehead. 'Why're you trespassing? I've not done anything against the law.'

June moved closer and pointed her gun at the man's face. 'Are you Koay Kimsai?'

'No.'

Chu glanced at the bread knife for a moment. 'What kind of work you do?'

'I'm a butcher at Tat Seong Abattoir in Balakong.' He jerked his chin in the direction of a cell phone that lay on the kitchen table. 'If you want me to, I can call my employer. You can verify with him.' Sweat glistened on his forehead.

'Who else stays here?'

'My wife and I. She's sleeping. We just moved in six months ago.'

Chu lowered his gun. So did June. They let out a sigh of exasperation.

Back at the police station, Chu reported to Superintendent Sofian about what had happened.

'What? A screwed-up raid?' Sofian's hairy fist pounded on the desk. The framed photograph of his mother that stood on it wobbled but did not fall.

'The suspect's address with the Road Transport Department was not current,' Chu explained. 'Assuming he owns a Kia Spectra and assuming the car has insurance and road tax, we can still track him down. We just need to run a check on the vehicle with the motor insurance company. Koay Kimsai's latest address should turn up.'

'Of course.' Sofian scoffed at him. 'Why did you miss out that crucial step?'

A few hours later, Chu received an email from Wiraberani Insurance. They provided him with the current address of the suspect as per their policy records.

* * *

Chu and June strode into an apartment complex in Rawang, a small town ten kilometres north of Kuala Lumpur. The inspector carried a bag that contained a hydraulic jamb spreader. As they went past the guardhouse, a small wooden shed covered in peeling paint, they noticed a white-haired security guard slumped forward on a desk inside. An empty beer bottle lay on its side beside him.

The apartment's compound was filthy: it was covered with overgrown weeds and strewn with plastic bottles, rusty cans and old newspapers. Spray-paint graffiti covered the walls at the lift foyer. 'Out of Order' signs hung from the closed doors of both the lifts.

They rushed up the staircase to Koay Kimsai's flat on the second floor. The adjacent apartments were also locked; their residents had probably left for work. Chu took out the hydraulic jamb spreader from his bag and placed its bar onto the door frame, just above the knob. He started to pump the handle of the equipment, and within a few moments, the latch bolt was released from its mortise.

With weapons drawn, they entered the living room. They saw no one there, so they split up. June sneaked into the bedroom while Chu took the study. As he walked in, he saw three glass jars placed on the mantelshelf, a pair of severed breasts floating in each of them.

'All clear,' June shouted from the adjoining room. 'Kimsai is not home, Inspector.'

'Yes, all clear,' Chu said back.

He pulled his eyes away from the jars and looked around the room. A wooden writing desk stood at one side of the room: a fax machine, a computer, a conical party hat and a red-rubber lapel flower sat on it. He walked over to the desk and yanked open its drawers. Inside one he found a hardcover A4-sized exercise book.

Chu turned to its first page: the words 'First Victim' were

scrawled across the top in red felt-pen. Below the heading were four colour printouts of a long-haired girl dressed in a miniskirt and standing beside a banyan tree with a small red shrine. Chu recognised the background: it was the One Stop Food Centre on Gelang Road. He flipped through the next few pages of the book. Several colour printouts were pasted on them, showing the same girl. But now, she was dead, her breasts cut out, her torso carved open in a horrific manner. Obscenities were written below the images.

As he flipped through more pages, he saw more such pictures, of Kimsai's second and third victims.

He finally came to the page entitled 'Fourth Victim'. Below the heading was the printout of a pretty and very voluptuous China doll. Chu realised he knew this girl. *But from where?* He closed his eyes for a moment, trying to remember. *Who is she? Where have I seen this girl before?* He raked through his memory.

I got it! She works at New Peng Hwa. I've seen her there. The last time he had seen the girl, she had come to the food court to meet an art painter client of hers. A drunk who had gotten into a fight for her.

Holy shit. She's going to be the serial killer's next victim! Chu ripped out the page.

'Sergeant, could you come in here, please?' he yelled out.

'What is it, Inspector? Did you find something?' June said breathlessly as she rushed into the study.

'Yes, Sergeant. Call HQ and get backup to set up an ambush tonight when the killer returns.' He showed the book to her, and then opened to the page that had the fourth victim's pictures stuck to it. 'This prostitute might be his next victim. I'm going undercover in New Peng Hwa tonight. Make a copy of this. I want you to cover

One Stop Food Centre and Pudu Food Court. We must stop Kimsai when he tries to pick her up.'

* * *

Thunder rumbled in the sky. Silver arrows of rain lanced at the room's glass casement windows. With his head slumped against a pillow, Alvin took a swig from a bottle of whisky. He shuddered as his insides burned. His heart pounded against his chest in irregular beats. He knew that he was in a dangerous condition. Sometimes, his heart missed a beat, and sometimes it thumped loudly like a bass drum, and sometimes it fluttered quickly like a hi-hat cymbal. The upper right area of his abdomen, just under the rib cage, throbbed with a dull ache. He knew it was his liver protesting against the merciless onslaught of alcohol, and it was possibly bleeding.

But this is exactly what I wanted – to waste away like this, to die drinking. He hadn't eaten for days, nor showered or taken out the garbage. *Why bother? There is nothing for me out there anymore.* He had simply lain in bed, drinking bottle after bottle of liquor: rum, gin, vodka, whisky and brandy, whatever he laid his hands on.

Eight 1.5 litre empty bottles of liquor were strewn on the bedroom floor now. And the count was increasing.

His eyes felt heavy, were beginning to close. The blurry images of his parents suddenly appeared before him. *They need to know. I can't leave without telling them.* He rolled over to his side, dragged himself to the small table on the side of the bed and yanked open its drawer. From within, he pulled out a letter pad and pen.

He placed the pad on the table and wrote with weak, trembling fingers: 'Dear Papa and Mama. When one is not useful anymore, one must leave this world. To die now is the happiest thing that can happen to me. To live is an agony. Thank you for loving me and for all the years of care you have given me. I love you both.'

He tore the paper off the pad, folded it in half and put the suicide note into the half-open drawer.

A fit of violent coughs wracked his chest, making him clench his fists. Then he drew a deep breath and forced his mind to focus on the task at hand. He wrote another note: 'Karen. I don't hold any grudges against you. My only regret in life is not having made you happy. Have a good life.'

Alvin ripped the note away from the pad, folded it then slipped it into the drawer. His thoughts now turned to Meisu, and to the last note he had to write. *What should I tell her?* She had given him great happiness yet she had inflicted him so much pain. *No, a suicide note would not do justice to their relationship.*

Alvin crawled on his belly to his former spot on the bed and reached for his cell phone. His heart pounded as he heard the phone ring. There was no reply, only a prompt asking him to leave a message.

'Meisu, this … This is Alvin.' His voice faltered. 'Can you come see me? Please. For one last time?' A pause. 'I'm about to … I'm going to die soon.' He gave Meisu his address, and then hung up.

Outside, the storm continued to push at the trees. Peals of thunder rang through the dark sky, while the pounding of rain against the glass window created a hypnotic drone. His cell phone rang. Was it Meisu? He looked at his phone eagerly. Bah! It was Inspector Daniel Chu. *Who is he? Where have I met him? Do I even know him?* Alvin couldn't remember, and he didn't care to recall.

He put the bottle to his mouth and guzzled down the whisky until he was out of breath. The bottle was empty. He needed another one. With wobbly knees, he rose to his feet, staggered out of the bedroom and into the kitchen. He opened the fridge, grabbed a bottle of vodka and walked back shakily towards the room.

He tripped. The bottle dropped to the floor, shattering to pieces. Alvin lay face down in a puddle of alcohol, motionless, surrounded by pieces of broken glass. A big shard had pierced his arm when he had fallen. Blood trickled out of the wound. He plucked out the shard, wincing, and threw it across the room.

Will I be able to open the door for Meisu when she arrives? He tried to lift himself up, but couldn't. He didn't have the strength. He remembered that he had left the door unlocked. *She can just open the door and come in on her own.* His throat was parched and burning, as if it were on fire. He put his head back on the floor and just lay there, his eyes drooping shut.

He was awoken by the sound of the doorbell. *Is it Meisu?* He tried to pull himself off the floor, but his head spun like a withered leaf blown about by the wind, and he fell down again. He saw that his arm was still bleeding, that it hurt to even move it.

'The door's not locked,' he yelled. 'Meisu, come on in.' The door bell rang again. He yelled louder, 'Come in.'

He heard her turn the doorknob. She walked in and closed the door behind her. In the kitchen, she blanched on seeing Alvin lying on the floor, soaked in alcohol and his blood, surrounded by broken glass. 'Alvin, what've you been doing?' She rushed over to him. 'And what is all this talk about dying?'

'I want you to comfort me in my final moments. With you, I

was born again. Now, there's nothing left for me to live for. We were not meant to be together. We're from two very different worlds. I had loved you very much, Meisu, but it just wasn't meant to be.' He sobbed. 'I'm sorry that I brought that escort into your room.' A fit of coughs racked his body, and he stopped to take a breath. 'I didn't mean to humiliate you. I just wanted to make you jealous.'

Pain shot through his body. He felt as if he were being stabbed all over by needles. 'You should know that I once loved you, Meisu,' he repeated, breaking into coughs again.

'Yes, I know,' she said blandly. 'Why don't I call an ambulance? You're dying, Alvin. Let's get you to hospital. We can still save you.'

'No, please, let me die. Don't force me to stay alive, Meisu. I know what's best for me.'

Alvin heard his cell phone ring again, the sudden sound jangling his nerves. It was probably that annoying Inspector Daniel Chu again. *What the hell does he want? Can't he let a man die in peace?*

* * *

Meisu stared out the glass doors of the balcony. The rain had stopped, and the wet skyscrapers glittered like sequins against the night sky.

She had helped Alvin get to his feet from the kitchen floor, given him a shower and then taken him to bed. She had then picked up the scattered shards of glass and thrown them away, had mopped the floor clean of alcohol and blood. She had then made Alvin a cup of hot coffee and let him get some rest.

Oh god, please help Alvin. Help us. She prayed, holding the locket that lay on her neck. She couldn't bear to witness him inflicting so much pain on himself. *How did I lose his love? How did it all go wrong?* Everything was so confusing to Meisu. Yet she knew one thing for sure: it was over. Their relationship was done for good.

'Meisu! Help me!'

She rushed into the bedroom. Her former lover was twisting on the bed, his body shuddering, his hip jerking.

'Shit, my bowels ... They feel like hot acid!'

The smell of faeces wafted from him. Meisu undid his belt, unzipped his pants and slipped them off his legs. She saw that a patch of crimson stained the bed sheet under and around his butt. *Oh heavens, he has purged blood.* Pity and revulsion coursed through her veins.

'Let me just die ...' he moaned. He burst into sobs. Meisu didn't know what to say. She had never been around a dying person before.

Meisu rolled his pants into a bundle and threw them in a corner. She went to the bathroom and returned with a wet face towel. She turned Alvin onto his stomach, removed his boxer shorts and gently wiped him clean with the towel. Then she set him on his back again and covered him with a blanket.

She sat down on the edge of the bed, gazing down at his face. His bloodshot eyes were sunk deep in their sockets, his skin jaundiced.

'I'm sorry I didn't finish your portrait,' Alvin was dragging the words out. Sweat beaded his forehead.

'It doesn't matter.' She leaned forward, lifted his chin with her hand and traced the outline of his mouth with her fingertip. Tears started to trickle down her cheeks. Alvin reached to wipe away her tears with his thumb.

His body racked with coughs. He gasped for breath, blinking his eyes rapidly. Meisu gasped when she saw blood dribbling out from his nose.

'I ... I can't breathe,' he gasped. 'My God, I can't breathe ... I ... I ...' His body convulsed one last time. Then, his eyes closed.

Meisu was weeping. *There is nothing more I can do for him. It's too late.* She got up and went into the bathroom. She splashed cold water on her face until she had stopped crying. Then, she left Alvin's condominium.

Outside, she hailed herself a taxi. 'Take me to Opal Condominium, Cheras,' she said to the driver, her voice hoarse and breathless.

* * *

Inspector Daniel Chu headed to New Peng Hwa Food Court a little after 9 p.m. By then, the sky was clear of rain clouds; there was no sign of the storm that had raged during the day. The inspector, wearing a casual denim jacket, occupied a seat at a table only five feet away from the stage. Nobody wanted that table as sitting there meant getting an earful of blasting music during the singing performance.

Thronging about the food stalls and tables were hookers and their johns. A few triad thugs were also part of the steaming sleaze of the food court. Ceaselessly, Chu continued to survey the place. He searched for the pale and lean face of the murderer, for any signs of his long hair tumbling down the forehead, of the prostitute's double-lidded cat-like eyes and high forehead. He kept at it for five hours. He finally called June. 'There's no sign of Kimsai here. Did you see him or the girl?' A pause. 'Let's call it a night then. I'm deadbeat. Let's continue tomorrow, shall we?'

Thursday 13 May

The pale man stood outside the front entrance of New Peng Hwa. It was 8:15 p.m. He had just reached Kuala Lumpur an hour ago, after having spent a night in Malacca, one-fifty kilometres south, where he had performed at a company's annual dinner. He had come well-prepared for the night: he was wearing a baseball hat to conceal his hair and forehead, and a pair of tinted aviator sunglasses to hide his eyes.

He watched the crowds of men and women flowing in and out of the food court. He was waiting for the big-breasted whore. The first hour of watching and waiting passed without spotting her, and he found that he was getting impatient. *What if she doesn't turn up? My plan will fail again*, he thought angrily.

Suddenly, he saw her. He snapped back to attention. Adrenalin welled up in his gut as he watched her walk into the food court from the back, treading past tables and towards the entrance. She was wearing a spandex tank top and miniskirt. Behind her trailed a paunchy middle-aged man with rodent-like teeth. He wore a ratty t-shirt and baggy pants. They walked past the archway of the entrance, down the perron and into the street.

The pale man swallowed thickly. *That cheap, buxom whore – so sexy, yet so evil ... Just like the one who stole Papa. It's only right that the pot-bellied prick dies too.* The man was like his Papa, so weak, without any morals or dignity. But then, he wouldn't have gone astray if that whore hadn't tempted him, hadn't lured him away. *Yes, it is the whore who is to be blamed. Soon, very soon, she'd be burning in hell.* His Mama would be proud of him. Another evil woman would be wiped off the face of the earth.

The pale man stepped outside, lingered for a few seconds, watching the whore and the pot-bellied man walking down the road. He unzipped the bag he was carrying. It contained a four-inch folding stainless steel knife, two plastic bags, an Olympus camera, a pair of surgical gloves and a coiled length of cord. These items were hidden beneath a folded t-shirt, a towel, a sports-drink bottle and a ping pong bat.

He treaded down the concrete pavement, following the hooker from a distance of about twenty feet, his face hot with anticipation.

* * *

Inspector Chu stood outside the food court, his Walther P99 concealed under his faded denim jacket. His eyes focused on the motley groups of men and women walking across the front access road. Several of them entered the food court; the others headed to Ace Electronics Building. He watched them all carefully, especially the women: ample breasts, slim thighs, deep cleavages, big bums, pretty faces, they all went past him. His gut feel told him that a static surveillance would not achieve anything. *What are my other options?* Chu was getting desperate.

As he stood there wracking his brain, he noticed a car zooming into a parking space on the access road. A scruffy dark-skinned man emerged from the shadows and walked towards the vehicle. The driver of the car stepped out immediately; the scruffy guy handed him a parking ticket in return for money. *This guy is here all the time. He might know something about the hooker. Or he might have even noticed the killer.* It was a long shot but there was nothing to lose. Leaving his spot, Chu approached the scruffy man and produced his police card.

'Come here, please. I only want to ask you a few questions.' He led the man to the archway entrance of Ace, where there was some light and they could see each other. 'Have you seen this woman?' he asked, showing him the hooker's picture. 'There's a reward for you if you help me find her.' He pulled out a ten-ringgit note from his wallet and handed it over to the man. 'Here's a little something for you to buy a few smokes.'

The scruffy man looked at the paper, then at Chu. 'I have seen her,' he said. 'She is a hooker. A regular at this food court.'

'When did you last see her?'

'Tonight. Just a short while ago. She left with a customer.'

'Where to?'

'I don't know. Usually, if a hooker doesn't use a room in the Ace building, she takes her customers to one of the nearby motels. Either Loveboat Motel or Springtime Inn.'

Chu started in a half-run towards Pasar Road. He pulled out his mobile phone: 'Sergeant June, get here quick. The girl's in this area. I'm on my way to Springtime Inn now. I want you to go to Loveboat and keep a lookout for her.'

Fifteen minutes later, Chu barged into the cramped lobby of the hotel. The receptionist, who looked like someone's grandma, was crocheting a doily at her desk. She looked up as Chu approached her. 'Can I help you?' Her voice sounded like the honk of a goose.

The policeman showed her the China doll's photo. 'I'm Inspector Daniel Chu. Did this girl come in here tonight with a customer?'

The woman shook her head. 'No, she didn't come here. Sorry.' She turned back to her crocheting, and Chu hurried out the hotel.

I hope the killer doesn't get to the girl before I do, Chu thought, panting, his legs pounding against the asphalt, as he rushed to Loveboat.

* * *

The pot-bellied man stared into the dresser mirror. 'Any stains on my face?' he asked Meisu. She was sitting on the edge of the bed, re-applying her lipstick.

Oh, Lord Buddha, what a generous client! He had given her a fifty-ringgit tip for French-kissing.

She dropped the lipstick into her handbag, got up and moved to scrutinise her client's face. 'Your ear, darling. You didn't get it off your ear.'

'Oops!' he smiled.

Meisu pulled out a Kleenex tissue from her handbag and wiped at the man's ear. Then, together, they walked out of the hotel room.

The sky was overcast with dark and heavy clouds. *Damn. It's going to rain again.* Meisu sighed in exasperation.

'Bye!' the pot-bellied man said, putting a hand to his lips and blowing a kiss to her. He started to walk down the main drag. Meisu fluttered her hand and called out to him, 'Come see me again when you've time.'

She had walked about twenty paces and was about to turn into an alley, a shortcut to New Peng Hwa, when a man emerged from the shadows.

'Miss, you want some business?' he said to her. He was in early thirties, and was lean and quite pale. His long hair hung over his forehead untidily. A bag was slung over his shoulder. The man smiled broadly at her. 'I saw you come out of Loveboat, and I would like to book you for tonight. So, how much for a quick session?'

'You've been following me?' Meisu did not like the looks of him. *There is something odd about the man.*

'Of course not. I usually wait around Loveboat to pick up working ladies. That's because I prefer to use a room here. It's safe. No police raids.'

Meisu eyed him cautiously. 'What's in your bag?'

He laughed. 'Only my t-shirt, a towel, a sports-drink bottle and a table tennis racket. Also my cap and sunglasses. I just played ping-pong with some friends.' He stepped forward. 'Wait, let me show you.'

The man opened his bag and shone the light from his mobile phone into it; Meisu saw that the bag did contain the items the man had just mentioned.

She was satisfied that he was harmless. 'OK, then. One hundred and eighty for a session, room included.'

* * *

A ten-minute sprint through a grid of garbage-strewn back alleys brought Chu to Loveboat Motel. He threw open the front door and rushed to the reception counter, where a forty-something man with a short, wiry moustache was seated, busy playing solitaire on his computer.

He flashed his police ID at the man. 'I'm Inspector Chu. Give me the number of the room booked by this woman.' He slapped the colour printout of the China doll on the counter. 'She most probably came in a while ago with a customer.'

The moustached man dropped his gaze on the paper. 'Yes, she did. Room 130, first floor.'

'What did her customer look like?'

'The first customer? Or the present one?'

'Present one.'

'A pale guy. Thin. With stringy hair hanging down his forehead. Sort of fish-eyed.'

Chu's blood went cold. His heart pulsed with terror. 'Key! Give me the spare room key!'

The hotel-keeper opened a closet behind him to reveal dozens of keys hanging there from hooks. With trembling hands, he pulled out the key that had '130' painted on its wooden holder then gave it to Chu.

Chu reached into his jacket to pull out his Walther P99. He bounded up the stairs two steps at a time then sprinted down the corridor towards the room. He pounded on the door. 'Koay Kimsai! This is the police! I know you're in there. Give yourself up!'

He unlocked the door then kicked it open. He entered, his finger placed firmly on the gun's trigger, ready to shoot. The metallic smell of blood flooded his nostrils, making him retch. The room was dark, except for a yellow glow spilling out from the bathroom.

Chu could make out a dark shape lying on the room's bed, motionless. As he moved closer, he saw that the girl had been left mutilated like the other victims, her breasts cut off, her blood pooling around her.

Chu noticed that the room's casement window was open, and the curtains fluttered in the wind. He ran to the window and stuck out his head. Beneath the window was a ledge, measuring about two-by-eight-feet; on it sat a large air-con compressor, humming like a motorboat engine. Beside the ledge was a drainpipe. It ran down the building to the ground. *Shit, the killer probably climbed down the drainpipe and made his escape.*

Placing the revolver in his holster, Chu climbed out the window, jumping onto the ledge. He glanced to the left and to the right, to make sure the killer wasn't hiding himself there. As he looked up, his breath caught in his throat. Outlined against the sky, Chu could see the dark silhouette of a man's head and shoulders. The killer was still here. He was crouched on the ledge above his, only a few feet from Chu's head.

Before he could act, a noose dropped down and settled around Chu's neck, and was pulled tightly at his throat. Chu felt the noose tightening—tightening—tightening. He began to choke. With both hands, he grasped the cord and yanked it downward with all the strength he could muster. Both Chu and the killer lost their balance and fell off their respective ledges. They landed in a dumpster filled with bulging black bags of garbage. Chu hit the bags with his back, and the force knocked the breath out of him. The killer landed beside him, but safely, on his hands and knees.

The killer got up and pulled out a folding knife from his pocket, then pinned down Chu with both knees so he couldn't get up.

The killer pressed the handle and a shiny blade clicked open. Chu watched helplessly. 'Die! You can't stop me, you bloody cop!' The killer raised the knife, ready to plunge it into Chu.

It's all over, Chu thought, his arms flailing about helplessly. *This psycho bastard's going to kill me in this garbage dump.*

Then, a shot rang out. The killer let out a guttural scream and dropped down limply beside Chu.

Chu clambered to his feet and looked out the dumpster. He saw Sergeant June Qwong standing thirty paces away, holding a semiautomatic, the gun still smoking in her hand.

Also by Ewe Paik Leong

Kuala Lumpur Undercover

[NON-FICTION]

From the crumbling backstreets of Chow Kit to the gleaming highrises of Sultan Ismail Road, ladies of all ages and ethnicities patrol the dark alleys, fancy clubs and dingy massage parlours of Malaysia's capital city of Kuala Lumpur, cruising for customers and surviving on their wits, born in some cases out of true desperation but in other cases out of lifestyle choice. Veteran writer and author Ewe Paik Leong uncovers a hidden world of KTV lounges within hair salons, massage parlours that offer services beyond the therapeutic and food courts that transform at night into whirlpools of vice, drawing both young and old, the curious and the regulars. In a series of fascinating encounters and interviews with high-end nightclub hostesses and their mamasans, freelance escorts, surreptitious streetwalkers, *urut batin* 'therapists' and more, the author confronts head-on important issues of trafficking, poverty, heart-wrenching misery, wayward morals and even black magic. This is *Kuala Lumpur Undercover*.